[handwritten: John]

[handwritten: Enjoy]

[handwritten: John E McDonald]

W9-AWD-436

When John McDonald writes about the weight of a rucksack, the exhilaration of a firefight, and the actions of young infantrymen, he gets its right. He has "been there, done that" and has the medals to prove it. As a result, his fiction is some of the finest produced about the Vietnam War and the men who fought it. McDonald is a grunt who writes for grunts—or for anyone wanting a better understanding of what went on in America's longest conflict.

Michael Lee Lanning
Author of The Only War We Had, Inside the
LRRPs, and Vietnam at the Movies.

[handwritten: My CO Bravo 2/3 199th Light Inf Brigade]

A Salt

Dead Accurate at 800 yards

A Novel

John E. McDonald

ISBN 13: 978-0-9728715-2-5

Printed in the United States of America
Bloomington, Indiana
This book is printed on acid-free paper.

To learn more about novels by John E. Me Donald visit sgtmajorbooks.com
Editor - Charles W. Sanford, Jr. c.sanford@mchsi.com

Cover design and layout by
Selfpublishing.com

1

Made from empty wooden mortar boxes, the doghouse was a work of art. The flat design of the roof doubled as a bench to sit on. Fitting perfectly in the space between two of Viper team's bunks and nailed to the wall at the end of the aisle, Rags now had a permanent home. She had taken it upon herself to guard anything left on top of her house. The "ugliest dog" had two old canteen cups hung on each side of the door, one for water and the other for food. She even had a wool blanket for a mattress. Now all the partying Rangers had to do was figure out a way to get the dog to use it. Rags was glued to Mac's side, as she had been since the Ranger rescued her from the stew pot down in the gook village.

Staff Sergeant "Flash" Gordon could see three dogs lying on Mac's bunk. "I now have a plan. Listen up, you bunch of drunks." The party had started that afternoon and was continuing in the Ranger barracks after chow. "Mac, you grab that dog, shove her in the doghouse and the rest of us will nail the door closed," and the sergeant popped another brew.

Specialist Fourth Class Ronnie "Bones" Washington started to laugh. "Ain't no motherfuckin' door, Sarge."

Two stereos blasted out two kinds of music. Neither was being listened to. Rattler, the second Ranger team, had gotten in before chow. Just having two teams together was

enough reason to have a party. As more beer was con-
sumed, the green was temporarily forgotten.

Flash Gordon had taken his team down to the headquarters building to pick up Mac. Sergeant Major Bill Mateau
had called the team into the map room and briefed them on
what was supposed to happen the next day. He'd given
Flash a copy of the newspaper story about the mercenary
in the American Army who had quit. That made the team
laugh, especially when they found out it was about Mac.
The sergeant major had taken them back to his office and
Flash had to wake up the Ranger who was sleeping on the
sergeant major's rug with that ugly dog. Now everywhere
the skinny grunt went the dog wanted to go too. When the
whole team had to take their khaki uniforms to the gook
tailor shop on post and have them pressed, Rags had nearly caused a riot. She ran through the shop, snapping and
trying to bite the gooks who were working there. Mac had
finally tackled the dog and waited outside, holding the dog
while the rest of the team took care of their dry cleaning.
Mama San had their uniforms done pronto. Every time she
looked out of the shop Rags would start growling. If this
kept up, he'd have to take the dog to the whorehouse downtown.

The team had to be on the chopper pad at 0900. The
general and the sergeant major were taking the team down
to MAC-V headquarters to meet the MAN, four star
General Creighton Abrams himself.

The beer drinking had started as soon as the four
Rangers had returned from the tailor shop. They'd made
two trips to the PX for more beer so they could build the
doghouse. When the second team of Rangers hit the
hooch, it was cause for a third trip to the PX and really
stock up.

The ambush that Viper team had gone through was discussed with Rattler team and the lessons learned were passed on. The mistakes the team made were written on the board and ways to avoid them on upcoming missions were discussed. The fallacy that the gooks didn't have radios was put to rest. They talked about the cave and how the team would never have found it except for Mac falling in it. Details of the escape of the team by climbing up into a tree and waiting for the tracker to pass by was added to. Hollywood Stevens thought that an added bonus for the team to use up in the tree would be for the escaping team to have a claymore mine or two at the bottom of the tree.

The claymore mine—700 steel ball bearings backed up with a pound and a half of C-4 explosive—was deadly. As drunk as they were, everyone agreed that a claymore left on the ground was a very good idea. Their thoughts on the trackers and their infantry guards were a little different. Both teams did agree that the gooks were hunting them and that they might have to find another way to get into the areas they had to recon.

Mac was a very mellow camper, not so much from the beer—he just felt that surrounded by his teammates he was at home. The near escape from the jungle firelight, the B-52 strike, and finding his lady-gook-fantasy dead, had started to settle down the young Ranger. Lying on his bunk and having his say right along with the rest of the team made him feel he was making a contribution. His team leader, Staff Sergeant Gordon, had said something that afternoon that he couldn't stop thinking about: "Once a grunt sees the elephant, Vietnam is in him forever."

His thoughts were smashed when Hollywood parked his ass next to Mac on his bunk and handed him another beer. "Bro, you shot two of them motherfuckers. Maybe three. Thanks for saving my ass." Burping, Hollywood asked the embarrassed grunt, "How'd you ever see that little motherfucker, anyway?"

Mac took another sip of beer. "I bent down to catch my breath from that hump, and that's when I noticed that my boot lace was untied." He looked around at all the Rangers. Everyone wanted to hear this. "I knelt down to retie my boot and that's when I saw that gook squatted down behind the palm frond. He had the fuckin' thing tied down with fishing line. If I wouldn't have bent over to tie my boot I'd have never seen that little shit. He was camouflaged good."

Flash jumped into the silence. "Man, you did good. I saw Leon go down and pieces flying off of him. I thought that you shot the guy. That's when all hell broke loose."

Staff Sergeant McCleod asked Mac, "You really goin' to Hawaii?"

Mac looked at the Rattler team leader. "Yeah, I gotta go over there and get my citizenship and then I can come back."

"That's fucked up," McCleod went on. "If that reporter hadn't made that shit up in the newspapers, nobody would have cared whether you was a citizen or not. You're a dumb fuck though. Most people are going to Canada, not coming over here." Both teams of men started laughing over that remark.

"Just for that, fuck you guys. I ain't never comin' back here." Mac kept it going. "I'm gonna find me about four or five bitches and shack up, and every six months I'll send you guys a postcard." Too much beer hit right then and he just made it out of the barracks before it all came up. When Flash came out behind him to use the piss tube, Mac was puking his guts out.

Flash slapped him on the back. "You feel something round and furry coming up—that's your asshole. Save that," and he walked off laughing.

Mac felt better after losing all that beer. He went back

into the barracks, kicked Rags off the bunk, stretched out and was asleep. By nine o'clock the all-night party was over and the Rangers were asleep. Rags carried one of Mac's dirty socks into her new doghouse. She scratched her new blanket-mattress into shape, laid the sock in the corner and went to sleep, her nose pointed at the man she'd picked to be her friend.

Brigadier General Walt Davis had his sergeant major in his office going over the day's plan for what he hoped would happen at the MAC-V head shed down at Tan Son Nhut. The bullshit story about the "mercenary" grunt from the 199th Light Infantry Brigade—that the U.S. Army was hiring soldiers—had caused a real shit storm. It started in the States and by the time it got back to Vietnam it was a full-blown hurricane. This McDonald grunt, who was from Canada, was nothing but a volunteer, and now, thanks to that reporter, he would be going back to the States—or at least as far as Hawaii—where he would get his citizenship. After ten days in Hawaii, Mac had the choice of going any-where in the States or returning to the Rangers in Nam. The general and the sergeant major had a running bet on whether Mac would or wouldn't come back to Nam.

"It'll be all right, sir," the sergeant major said. "Everything will go smooth as silk. Have him on the air-plane and General Abrams will be off your ass. Come on, sir, I'll let you buy me a steak dinner."

2

___

The man woke up slowly in the darkened room.
Grinning, he got out of bed without disturbing the two
women. Thomas "Tex" Payne was staying at the Carravelle
Hotel—finally in the big time. The *Dallas Star* was now his
new boss. The story Tex had done about the mutiny in the
bush between the officer and the grunt had gotten all twisted and changed to the Army hiring mercenaries. Tex didn't
give a flying fuck about the distortion, but the *Star* wanted
a follow-up story and Tex had been racking his brain trying
to figure an angle. The party with the two women had
relaxed his mind. The grin he woke up with was still plastered all over his face out on the balcony. All Tex had to do
was track down the skinny grunt and find out if he still
wanted to frag the lieutenant who'd kicked his ass out in the
bush. He hoped the lieutenant was already dead and buried
back in the States. *Then I can write whatever the fuck I want.*

Now that the Amarillo native was playing in the big
leagues,he had begun to put his team together. Packer
would continue doing the film developing and Andre
LaRue was going to be his cameraman. He had also hired
two gooks to do all the grunt work. The interviews he'd
done, one with Dan Rather and the other with that little rat-
faced fuck from API, had put him on the map. Tex had
rented a villa for himself and while it was being painted
he'd decided to stay at the Carravelle Hotel. First class all

the way.

Tex had come in off an operation with the 25th Infantry to find that the story he'd sent off had been published in all the large papers back in the world. Instead of having to head back to Amarillo to write about high school football, he could now stay in Vietnam as long as he wanted. The General—all four stars—Creighton Abrams had tried to railroad Tex all the way back to the States, but now that Tex had the fast track with the story about the grunt, the general could do nothing but rant and rave. Tex's friend who worked in MAC-V had told him that the general had damn near had a heart attack trying to get rid of "that commie-dope-smokin'-pinko-fag-reporter." After the interview with Dan Rather, the general had singled Tex out following one of the five o'clock follies and had been rather nice, but Tex had looked into the general's eyes and thought, *I damn sure wouldn't want to be riding on the same chopper.* The general might throw the reporter right out the door and not even say he was sorry. Tex knew he'd have to do some kind of halfway complimentary story on the general. He had enough to worry about without a four star general for an enemy.

Going back to bed, Tex slid in between the two Vietnamese women and thought, *I'll get up early and get my ass over to Redcatcher and find the end of the story.*

It was 9AM before Tex even headed out of the hotel and got in his jeep. His old jeep had gone the way of his old life—passed on to some other third-string reporter. Now he had a fairly new jeep, complete with canvas top and driver. He had even gotten rid of his old .45 and now had a chrome .38 Special which he planned to carry in a shoulder holster. He hadn't worn the holster yet, still carrying the piece stuck in his waistband. Tex made one stop on the way out to the Redcatcher main base camp. Just before the Y bridge he stopped at old mama san's hooch and bought a carton of primo grass. Bargaining and haggling with the old woman, his gook driver had gotten a cheaper price for the grass. Lighting up one of the jays, Tex thought, *I hope this war never ends.*

Waving at the grunts guarding the bridge, Tex hoped like hell that Mac had not gone back to the jungle. When he showed his press pass to the MP guarding the main gate at Redcatcher the jeep was not even stopped. At Bravo Company headquarters, Tex grabbed a fresh pack of dew and went in to talk to the company clerk. The reporter came away from Bravo Company pissed. He'd wasted a whole pack of grass just to find out that Mac had gone to the Rangers and the lieutenant was gone also, but all the clerk knew was that the el tee was transferred somewhere down south. Tex had the gook driver head over to the Ranger Company. After some searching and finally having to ask directions, his jeep pulled up in front of M Company, 75th Rangers. The reporter didn't bother to stop at the orderly room. He headed straight for the barracks.

Tex hadn't even gotten in the door to the barracks before he was attacked by the ugliest dog he'd ever seen.

Rags had him by the pant leg, snapping and growling. Kicking the dog loose, the reporter went inside where he found the team getting ready to go to lunch. Tex talked to them, trying to find out where Mac was. Staff Sergeant McCleod finally told Tex that Mac was on his way to Hawaii to take out his citizenship. The Rangers were hoping Mac was coming back but they wouldn't know anything more until Staff Sergeant Gordon got back from escorting his Ranger down to Tan Son Nhut.

As Tex turned to leave the barracks, one of the Rangers made the comment that Mac was probably going to get the Medal of Honor and everybody started to laugh. Walking back to his jeep Tex thought, *Man, that would make a great story or at least a fitting end to the mutiny story. Shit,* he thought as he got in the jeep, *people wanna know about officers getting their shit blown away by their own men—not getting medals.* The Rangers had said they'd never even heard about the lieutenant.   Frustrated, Tex told his driver to head back to Saigon. Taking out his ever-present notebook, he started reading over his notes. *How do I get that man the Medal of Honor for fragging that lieutenant?*

3

Staff Sergeant Flash Gordon had his team up at 0500. By
the time he was done with his inspections, the troops were
standing tall. All four of the team had the new jungle
boots bloused just right and spit-shined so they could see
their faces in them. All except Mac had pistol belts with
.45 caliber pistols attached. The team had flown down to
the sprawling airbase in the general's chopper. The sergeant major and the general were in standard work uniforms for the Nam: jungle fatigues and side arms. While
the team waited on the chopper pad after landing, the sergeant major gave all four men a quick brief about what to
say to General Abrams if he even talked to them.

Mac was pissed. The splendor of the MAC-V compound
and the short ceremony in the conference room had lasted
only fifteen minutes. Staff Sergeant Gordon got pinned
with a silver star. Hollywood and Stevens got bronze stars
and Mac got a promotion to acting sergeant because
General Abrams said he was not having Mac go to Hawaii
without a set of stripes.

Reporters had taken pictures of the whole team and at
least one asked Mac if he was a mercenary. Mac had
answered "No" and everybody just laughed. The team,
along with General Davis and the sergeant major, had left
Mac right there in the map room. They had to head back to
Redcatcher and Mac was left with a captain—one of those

REMFs (rear echelon motherfuckers) who had taken Mac to another part of the building and started his handful of speech about how the Army wanted him to conduct himself in Hawaii and what to say to reporters. He was still pissed that he didn't get a medal. *After all, I was the guy that fell in the hole that led to the team finding the gook headquarters in the first place.* The captain told Mac that he was picked from the general's staff for this mission because he was going on R&R to Hawaii anyway and they were going to be flying military all the way to the island. Mac would be staying in the Sheraton Hotel, compliments of Uncle Sam, and all Mac had to do was what the captain told him to do. After the citizenship ceremony he was free to do whatever he wanted for the rest of the ten days in Hawaii. Mac ignored the captain and put on a new khaki shirt with the sergeant chevrons already sewn on. He wondered if Rags was missing him and staying close to her new doghouse. Mac knew the team was betting he wouldn't come back to Nam, but he couldn't think of any place back in the world where he wanted to be stationed. Also, he had friends over here and he liked being able to use some of the skills the Army had taught him.

The captain had left, then came back in and told Mac that the plane was going to start loading passengers and to get his shit and they'd be on their way. After a short ride to a gate marked "Airlift," Mac and his captain escort joined ten other passengers waiting to board. He noticed that everybody was in civilian clothes and some of the civilians had briefcases chained to their wrists. *From the bulges under their shirts they're armed too,* he thought. The canvas-covered seats weren't very comfortable but they had plenty of leg room. All they had to do was check off their names with the Air Force guy and have a seat. Mac heard one of the other passengers say that it was eight thousand miles to Hawaii. He wondered how many times they'd have to stop. As soon as they got seated the captain handed Mac a stack of orders and other mimeographed stuff to read.

Mac asked the captain, "Sir, do we have to go through customs or anything?" He had the .38 the nurse had given him from the wounded pilot in his duffle bag and he didn't want to give it up.

"Naw," the captain replied. "They check the R&R flights, but not the military aircraft."

Mac slept most of the way, even through the fuel stops. When they arrived in Hawaii at 0430, he felt like he'd been flying forever. The captain and the sergeant were the only ones to get out at the hotel where the Army van took them.

The captain came right into the hotel room with Mac and began reading off the mimeographed sheet. "OK, they want us at the immigration building at 1000 hours, so get squared away and cleaned up. Says here," and the captain looked at the sheet, "it should take you a couple of hours and then they'll take all you brand new citizens to lunch and that will be it. Remember," the captain went on, "be real careful what you say to the press."

Mac was still in shock. It had been only seven weeks since he'd left the states but everything he looked at seemed different. He couldn't wait to get rid of the captain, who was supposed to meet his wife over at Fort De Russy, the R&R center for the GIs coming from Nam. The officer was cramping his style and Mac just wanted the citizen bull-shit over so he could hit the beach and score with the ladies.

The Ranger was disappointed. The raising of his hand, the small American flag given to all the new citizens, and lunch afterward didn't make him feel any different than a few hours before. The Army had a reporter and photographer there. A reporter from the local paper had asked, "Like, are you going back to Nam?" *Stupid question,* Mac thought. *Where else am I gonna go?* The other ten people in his citizenship group were all excited and waving their flags. He was still scratching his head over all the fuss. He'd been the only one in the Army and English was his native language. The queer doing the paperwork had even asked if he spoke English and who was the first president of the United States. *Dumb fuck.*

The lunch over, Mac took the elevator down to the first floor with the rest of the new citizens. The van that drove him over was gone and so was the captain. It had only been a five minute drive to the immigration and naturalization building so he decided to walk back to the hotel. Walking along in downtown Honolulu, the sunshine and fresh air felt great. He parked his ass on a bench and lit a cigarette, just to watch all the girls. Looking sharp in his uniform, he didn't think he'd get his cigarette finished before the girls were all over him. Two cigarettes later and not one girl had sat down beside him. *Fuckit,* he thought. *I'll head back to the hotel—get out of my uniform and hit the beach.*

Walking through the hotel lobby, he saw the most beautiful woman sitting on the couch next to the lobby door. Blonde hair cut kind of shaggy, the shortest miniskirt he'd ever seen, and *What a set of tits.* When he sat down on the couch she looked up over her magazine and gave him a little half smile. *Oh man, I've got it made.* "Ahhhh, Miss, you come here often? I'm in the Army." *So cool. Ranger all the way.*

The angel looked at Mac. "Would you do me a favor?" she asked in the softest voice.

"Sure," Mac answered. *She wants to go up to my room.*

"Fuck off. I'm working," and she went back to reading her magazine.

Mac turned stop sign red. He'd never heard a girl talk like that before. "Ahhh, catch you later," and he headed for the elevator.

In his room on the fifth floor Mac still felt his face burning. *I wonder what kinda job she's got. Must be a real bitch to get her to talk like that.* He dumped his old brown canvas duffle bag on the bed. He needed to get into his civilian clothes. Money. He needed money. He knew his wallet had only thirty-seven dollars in green money and sixty-three bucks in MPC. The crumpled envelope the sergeant major had handed to him back at BMB sat right on top of his clothes. Ripping the envelope open, Mac counted four hundred and eighty dollars in MPC and one twenty dollar bill in green money. He read the note the sergeant major had put in with the money: "Cash this in before you leave Nam and have a good time. See you when you get back." The note was signed "Redcatcher all the way. Sergeant Major B. Mateau."

Fuck. Why didn't I look in the envelope before I left Nam? Maybe the bank will cash it in for me. Thirty-seven dollars won't last long in Honolulu. He unwrapped his .38, then pulled the box of ammo out of a pair of socks he'd folded around it. Laying the pistol and ammo aside, he started looking through his clothes. Mostly what he had were uniforms, or parts of them. One pair of semi-clean jeans, one Hawaiian shirt and one pair of flip-flops. *Man, I need to cash that money in so I can get some new shit. Fuckit.* He took an extra pair of khaki pants and, using a razor blade, made them into a pair of cutoff shorts. He hung his uniform in the small closet. Everything else went back into the duffle bag and he put it in the closet beneath his uniform. He was now ready to party on the beach.

Waiting for the elevator, he was really surprised when the door opened and the blonde got off holding onto an older guy's arm. *Shit, she didn't even smile. That fucker she's with—old guy about forty—wearing a suit. Fuck 'im.* And Mac was off to have a good time.

Leaving the hotel, he thought he'd spend some money at

the liquor store, grab a jug, and head for the beach. Walking down the street, he was still amazed that he was here. The first liquor store he went into threw him out. Had to be twenty-one. He told the guy he was in the Army, stationed in Nam.

Guy told him, "I don't give a flyin' fuck. You're not old enough."

Mac hollered back at the Hawaiian from the door, "Fuck you, asshole," then hauled ass down the street.

Mac just started wandering, passing numerous bars. He didn't want to take a chance on getting thrown out so he didn't even bother going in.

He looked up at the street sign. "Highway 61." He knew all the streets ended up at the ocean. He was thinking of turning around when a taxi pulled up next to him. The big Hawaiian driver hollered, "You wanna ride, brah?"

Mac leaned in the open window. "Naw man, I ain't got any money. Don't even know where I'm goin'."

The driver laughed. "Brah, I'm goin' home. No charge. Live over on the other side of the island, brah."

Mac hopped in the front of the bright yellow cab. "Any beaches over there? Any women? I'm in the Army," and the grunt started to laugh.

The big Hawaiian driver thought Mac would have a better time on the other side of the island. "Too many tourists over on this side, brah. Where I drop you, brah, surfing beach right there, brah. Lotta girls, brah. Plenty of shit to get into. Have a lotta fun." Mac thought the driver must know what he was talking about. He really enjoyed the short ride across the island—the road even went through a tunnel. There was a beach across the highway from where the cab driver dropped him off. The Seven Eleven clerk didn't even ask for ID when he bought his beer and other stuff.

He tried to run across the highway but halfway across he lost a flip-flop. Stopping to grab it, he was nearly hit by a car. Once on the other side, he put the flip-flop back on. He needed it—the beach was some kind of black rocky sand.

There weren't many people around. The table and the benches were all made of one piece of concrete and they had roofs made out of palm fronds. *Cool deal,* he thought. Sitting at the table he could see that his knobby knees were already turning red from the sun, but the jungle sores were dry and scabbing over nicely. Digging into his brown paper sack he pulled out a cold beer, his loaf of bread, and package of baloney. Two beers later he'd eaten the pound of baloney and half the loaf of bread. He burped and thought, *Man, that was good. Bring on the girls.*

He'd parked his ass on the first table he'd come to, right next to the parking lot. As he sipped his beer, he watched the surfers. *I could try that,* he thought. The sound of Hollywood mufflers from the parking lot made him turn. Four cars had pulled in. The Mustang sounded the best to Mac's ears. *And a convertible to boot.*

Watching as the parking lot filled with people his own age, all he could think of was *That old taxi driver knew what he was talkin' about.* The girls all wore brightly colored bikinis and the guys were wearing baggies. There seemed to be more surfboards than people. The orange Chevy pickup that pulled in last had even more boards. The driver had a whitewall haircut and to Mac it seemed kind of funny to see a Hawaiian with a whitewall.

Transistor radios all on the same station added to the party atmosphere. Railroad ties laid end to end divided the parking lot and the beach. When the large group of kids crossed the divider and headed in his direction, Mac thought he'd better get some more beer. Sipping his beer and eyeballing the skinny girl with the big tits, Mac never even heard the big Hawaiian with the surfboard. "Hey, brah, get the fuck off our table and get the fuck outa here, howly." Everyone started laughing. The Hawaiian stopped two feet in front of Mac, leaned on his brightly painted board and reached right in and took a beer out of Mac's paper bag. "You hear me, brah? Get the fuck outa here," and he popped the beer open which made the group of young people laugh even more.

Blam-Blam! Two shots from the smoking .38 went right through the surfboard.

"Whatthefuckbrah?" The brightly painted surfboard was on the ground and the young people were backing up toward the parking lot. The murmur of the ocean breeze was all that could be heard.

Mac heard the skinny girl with the beautiful tits say, "I told you not to fuck with him, Brian."

Mac continued to sit there with the pistol in his hand. Whitewall haircut walked up to the Ranger. "Come on, brah, we gotta get out of here before the cops get here."

"OK," and Mac stuck the pistol in his belt and followed him over to the Chevy pickup. The truck fired up and headed for the highway.

Shit. Mac had forgotten to pick up the bag with the beer in it. He lit a cigarette.

Whitewall had the pickup floored and he was laughing like crazy. "How long you been outa Nam?" Before Mac could answer the young man stuck his hand out and introduced himself. "Jimmy Matamura."

"John McDonald," and he shook the driver's hand.

"Did you see the look on Brian's face when you shot his surfboard?"

Watching the man laugh, Mac lost it and started to grin. He couldn't hold back his laughter. Every time they looked

at one another as the truck raced down the road they started to laugh even harder. The sight of the police car with its
lights going sobered them both. "Them cops are lookin' for
you, brah," and Jimmy looked in his rear view mirror to
watch the police car disappear.

"Shit, man. That guy didn't have to be fuckin' with me."
Mac turned to watch out the back window.

Jimmy leaned over to Mac. "We can't take you back
downtown. That's the first place the cops will look. I'll take
you out to the fort. They won't look there."

"What fort? How you gonna get there?" Mac asked.

"Shit, man, I'm in the Army, too. I work out at the fort.
Be no sweat hidin' you out there, brah."

Fort Shatter was not an open post but the sticker on
Jimmy's bumper got the troopers right in. The MPs guarding the gate just waved at the orange Chevy.

Now driving at the speed limit, Jimmy told Mac, "You
can stay over at my unit until the heat's off." Passing the airfield, the pickup took the first left down a dirt road. After
half a mile Jimmy pulled the pickup in-between two dilapi-
dated olive drab Quonset huts. The small sign read 9th
Special Forces Group.

Mac got out of the truck and asked Jimmy, "You a green
beanie?"

Jimmy laughed. "Yeah, brah. This is it. There's only six of
us here, and we fix all kinda shit for the guys in Nam. We
steal anything we can. Send that over there, too. Let me give
you a quick tour. The hooch with the most windows, that's
our barracks. Even got a small kitchen and TV room. The
other one, with the porch, that's where we do all our work."

Mac looked around. "Fuck. Looks like World War Two
shit."

"You got that right, brah. They don't want us on main
post, but it's close to the airfield, so nobody sees us comin'

and goin'. Come on, I'll introduce you to the boss." Jimmy headed for the Quonset hut with the porch. Just inside the door on the right was a well-lighted office. All Mac could see through the doorway was that it was neat and clean. The room on the left was dark and the office door was closed. "Come on." Jimmy took a left and disappeared down the hallway. The back end of the old building had an open rollup door. A man sitting at a picnic table was working on what looked like a rifle part.

"Hey Sarge," Jimmy hollered.

The dark figure put the part down and stood up. The voice that answered back sounded like an exploding mortar round. "Where the fuck you been you nonworking little pineapple cocksucker? Fuckin' off with the rest of your fuckin' hippie friends? Who's this asshole?"

Holy shit. The man who stood up was at least six-two and so ugly Mac thought that Halloween was real.

Jimmy just laughed. "This here's Sergeant John McDonald. Ranger outa Nam."

The big sergeant was not impressed. "Looks like another one of your hippie friends. Where in the fuck you get that outfit, white boy? The Salvation Army?" and the laugh that came out of the man shook the walls.

"Don't be fuckin' with him, Sarge. He's got the fastest draw on the island. He shot the shit outa Brian's surfboard. Scared the shit outa that pineapple." Grinning, Jimmy sat down at the table.

The big sergeant was not only black, he moved like a cat. Mac never saw him budge, but all of a sudden he was right in front of the Ranger. "If you pull that gun on me, boy, I'll shove it so far up your ass there be shit on the grips. You understand me?"

Mac stood there, nodding. Only now—up close to the sergeant—could he tell that the green beret on top of his head was not his haircut.

Sticking his hand out, the big sergeant introduced himself. "Master Sergeant J.L. Taylor." Mac's hand was lost in the big black mitt. "Have a seat. Let's hear what kinda shit you been into." The big sergeant turned and went back to the table.

Mac sat down at the table with the two Green Berets. Sarge leaned over and quietly told Mac, "Lay your shit on the table."

Mac knew an order when he heard one and he laid his .38 on the table. Sergeant Taylor reached in a cooler and pulled out three beers. Setting them on the table, he asked Mac, "Are you a kluker?"

Mac didn't even know what that was. "Ahhhhh... I don't like chickens, Sarge," and he popped the brew that was handed to him.

Jimmy looked at the big sergeant, then sprayed beer everywhere and fell to the floor laughing. Even the big man was chuckling.

Jimmy was holding onto the table and looked at the black man. "He don't even 'like chickens'," and off he went again.

The master sergeant asked Mac, "Where in the fuck you from anyway?"

"Ahhhh, I'm from Canada," and Mac took a sip of brew.

"Shit, too cold for them klukers up there anyway," and the sergeant rested his arms on the table.

"Ahhhh, no Sarge. We got chickens in Canada," the Ranger said.

At that the big sergeant lost it. Tears were flowing down his cheeks and he was laughing so hard he had to hold onto his sides. Mac just sat there wondering what the two were laughing about. Jimmy finally quit laughing enough to tell Mac that what Sergeant Taylor was talking about was the Ku Klux Klan. Then Mac got it and had a chuckle too.

Master Sergeant Taylor wanted to hear all about what happened at the beach and when he did he told Mac, "You better learn to control that temper of yours. This ain't the Nam."

Mac got a little hot under the collar. "Well them people shouldn't a been fuckin' with me," and he finished his beer.

Master Sergeant Taylor asked Mac how much longer he had to go on R&R. Mac told him about getting his citizenship and that he was on a ten-day leave and not R&R.

"Well fuck, brah, you can stay in my room out here and I'll take you to a luau tomorrow night," said Jimmy. "A big party at the beach, brah."

"Fuck, Jimmy, I ain't got any money. The sergeant major gave me a whole bunch, but I gotta get to a bank and cash it in."

Sergeant Taylor leaned in. The questions came fast. "What sergeant major's that? What fuckin' outfit you with? What kinda money you got?"

"Ah, Sergeant Major Mateau, 199th Light Infantry Brigade." Mac pulled out the envelope full of military payment certificates and laid it on the table.

"Shit, didn't anyone tell you to cash that shit in before you left Nam? That shit ain't any good over here," the sergeant let Mac know. "You can't even cash it in at a bank. They don't want the gooks gettin' regular American money. That's how they try and control things over there. Pay everybody in MPC."

"Shit," Mac said. "I guess I won't be able to take that girl out after all."

"What girl you wanna take out, brah? That one with the big tits? She's married to a big MP, brah," and Jimmy laughed.

Master Sergeant Taylor asked, "Your sergeant major a skinny little Cajun fuck? Black hair?"

"Ah, yeah. That's the guy, Sarge."

Taylor laughed. "I've known that fucker since Italy. 1948 or '49. Wait till I see him."

Picking up the rifle barrel from the table, Mac asked, "Where'd you get these old 1903 A3 barrels at?"

"What the fuck you know about these old weapons?" the master sergeant asked, taking the barrel from Mac's hands. "We got a bunch of these old fuckers from Nam. They want me to fix them and send them back for sniper rifles." Looking over at Jimmy, the sergeant went on. "This lazy little cocksucker is supposed to be an armorer and all he do is run around the island fuckin' everything in sight."

Jimmy just laughed. "That's OK, Sarge. My shit comes through, I'm off to a team in Nam and you can do this shit your own self. Hey, Mac," Jimmy continued, "where you stayin' at downtown? I'll go get your stuff and I got an extra bunk in my room. Come on, I'll show ya. You can come help old Sarge here while I'm gone," and the two young men got up.

Taylor looked up. "Give that motherfucker a clean pair of coveralls," then he went back to checking the rifle barrel.

Mac expected the Hawaiian to have a shit pit for a room but to his surprise it was neat and clean. Jimmy pointed to the extra bunk. "Take that one," and he handed Mac a key for the door. "Gimme your hotel key where you're stayin' at down there, brah."

Mac handed him the key. "Fifth floor at the Sheraton. You know where it's at?"

"Shit yeah, brah. Make yourself at home. See you later. Oh, yeah—extra coveralls in that locker there," and Jimmy left.

Mac put on a pair of coveralls, then, on the way back to the weapons repair hooch, he took a look around at the barracks. *Shit, might be a dump from the outside but the green bean-*

ies have everything squared away on the inside. The kitchen and TV room were one and the TV was a 25" color set. Right next to that was a big, full bookshelf. *Man, this is even better than downtown,* and he headed over to help the old sergeant.

"You're cleanin' that from the wrong end, Sarge," Mac said, sitting down.

The sergeant looked at him. "That's OK, you little smart ass cocksucker. Ain't none of these rifles worth a shit. They're all in pieces and they'll more than likely blow your fuckin' head off if you could find a whole rifle in the pile of shit they sent me," and the sergeant handed Mac a beer. "That little pineapple cocksucker ain't comin' back till tomorrow. You know that don't you?" The master sergeant leaned back in his chair. "Tell me about yourself, boy."

Mac saw red. "That's enough of this shit," and he reached for the pistol on the table. He was fast, but the old sergeant was a lot faster and had Mac's .38 between his eyes before Mac's hand got halfway to where the pistol had been on the table.

"Now, boy, I told you about that temper of yours," and Taylor pulled the trigger. Mac turned white as a sheet. The sergeant pulled the gun away and flipped open the cylinder. "Now, you stupid cocksucker, the first rule of a grunt: 'Do not separate thyself from thy shit,'" and he laughed.

Mac learned just that quick not to be fuckin' with the old master sergeant. "What do you mean?" Mac asked after his heart stopped racing. "What do you mean, Jimmy's not comin' back?"

"That little pineapple gonna party down there in your hotel. Maybe he'll be back tomorrow," and the sergeant handed Mac his pistol. "You need to get some hollow points for this. Fuck that military ball ammo. Fuckin' shit won't stop nothin'. Now tell me about yourself."

Mac told him about growing up in Canada, his stint in

the Canadian Army, what he had done in Nam, and what he was doing in Hawaii.

"You that motherfucker they said was a mercenary?" asked Taylor.

"Yes. That old Tex Payne—he's that crazy reporter— the cat that picked me up comin' out of the jungle. He made the whole thing up." Mac went on, "I'll bet they hung that fuck for writing shit like that."

Master Sergeant Taylor looked at the young grunt. "Don't you believe that shit, boy. This fuckin' war is the most fucked up. Got more fuckin' reporters runnin' around than VC," and the black man laughed, picking up the rifle barrel.

"You're cleanin' that barrel from the wrong end," Mac again told the sergeant. "Gotta use the other end. Pull the cleaning rod through from muzzle to the chamber."

The black man dropped the barrel on the table. "What the fuck you know about these old rifles? Show me."

Mac picked up the barrel and inserted the cleaning rod and bore brush soaked in solvent. Standing, he rapidly ran the rod up and down the barrel. Then, holding the barrel, he pulled the cleaning rod out and held it up to the light. He looked through to see if he'd gotten it clean. "Just needs oil down there, Sarge," and he started to do that. "I learned about these old rifles from my dad and uncle. My uncle had one of these '03s and my dad had a .303 Lee Enfield. It was my job to clean them after their hunting trips. My uncle even had an old World War Two manual on the '03s."

Taylor told Mac that the Special Forces camps wanted sniper rifles—two per camp—and they had sent twenty-one of the old 1903 A3s. So far, he could only get one to work.

4

The Smith Corona serial #4751637f first came together in early 1942. The rifle was test fired on the range right outside the factory. Two clicks on the windage knob and the factory rifle shot a half-inch group at two hundred yards. Eddy, the test shooter, wanted to steal the weapon for himself. Laying the rifle on his workbench while he wrote up the paperwork to go with the target full of holes, Eddy laid his lit cigarette across the stock. When the bell rang, all the test firers left their weapons and headed for the lunchroom. Thus, a cigarette burn across the stock marked the weapon—its first battle scar. After lunch, with his supervisor there, Eddy had to put the rifle into the weapons rack quickly before the supervisor saw the scar. The paperwork went into the supervisor's file.

Betty was the first woman to hold the rifle. Twenty-six years old, a short dumpy blonde, mother of two. Her job was the final wipe-down with linseed oil and warm cosmoline, then packing the rifles in cases of five. Her husband had been drafted and was off in the Army Air Corps. She was having a ball and enjoyed working outside the home. World War II had women working in all kinds of factory jobs that weren't available before the war. She just wasn't too sure about whether she loved her husband, and working with so many men had certainly given her the chance to pick and choose. Paying no attention at all to the rifle that finished the crate she was packing, all she could think of was the cute truck driver who would be picking up the crates of rifles. Hammering the case closed, she paid no mind to the USMC logo on top of the case, burnt right into it. Busy hammering nails, Betty didn't hear the door to the shipping room close. She lost all thought of nails when her ass was grabbed from behind and her foreman had his other hand grabbing her tits. All he wanted was for her to give head. Sitting on the rifle case, Betty sucked his cock, thinking she had to hurry. She didn't want to miss the truck driver, who had also promised to take her out after work.

Wallace Wallace, USMC, from Crockett Mills, Tennessee, had made private first class right out of boot camp. He'd missed two shots on the rifle range. The range instructors were always hollering at him for not using the windage and elevation knobs on his rifle sights. *Fuck 'em.* Growing up, he'd never had all that fancy shit and he'd always put meat on the table for his mom and brothers and sisters. The extra ten dollars a month from his promotion went home with his pay allotment.

India Company spent their time running around Parris Island, training to fight the Japs. The company kept getting new equipment all the time. Shovels; canteens; even new shelter halves, brand new, with not a patch on them. Marching down to Supply once again, the company was already bitching about what they'd get this time to weigh them down.

The bitching stopped as soon as the company stopped in front of the supply room. Freights and crates of brand new rifles. Pfc Wallace was the last man to get a rifle, the Marine Corps way—last on the troop roster—last alphabetically: last to get anything, but this time he got the best. The last rifle in the case was handed over after the supply sergeant copied down the serial number.

When the supply sergeant saw the scar on the stock, he asked, "You want this motherfuckin' piece?"

It was too late. Wallace already had his hands on the greasy rifle. "Yup, I'll take it, Sergeant."

Next came a new cartridge belt, a bayonet still in the grease, and an oil bottle and bore brush. With his arms full of stuff, Wallace could still point out the burn scar to his platoon sergeant.

"Fuckin' shit! Fuckin' civilians treatin' a rifle that way! You want that rifle? We can send it back." The platoon daddy wanted to know "What ya wanna do?"

Wallace had already given the rifle a name. "Fuck no, Gunny. Brand new—I'll keep it. Probably the best shooter in the company anyway."

"OK. Get over there with the rest of the platoon. Get all that shit cleaned up. Next we'll get on the range and find out if these things will even fire," and the gunney chuckled.

Fuck Smith Corona—I'm gonna call you Shirley. And so, as Wallace stripped and cleaned his new rifle, he could tell that the .30-.06 was going to be a fine shooter. The caliber .30-.06 rifle, with 150 grain ball ammo, held five rounds in the magazine—six altogether if he cheated and had one up the spout.

The rifles India Company received were a mix of Remingtons and Smith Coronas, some of the last of the model 1903 A3. The M-1 Garand was taking its place as the new service rifle. On the rifle range the next day, Shirley fit better in Wallace's arms than his cousin—who the rifle was named after. The first three rounds out of the rifle were right in the bull's-eye at one hundred yards. Thirty rounds later Wallace had not missed a target. The farthest targets at six hundred yards fell just as fast as the targets close in. By the middle of the afternoon the company had zeroed all their new rifles and with a lot of spare ammo the first sergeant gathered the company and told Wallace to start shooting. At the six hundred yard targets he missed on the twentieth shot and that's when he got found out. Lying down beside him, the first sergeant saw he had the peep sight set on two hundred yards. Instead of chewing Wallace's ass he moved the peep sight up to six hundred yards and said, "Now you won't miss at all."

Behind the six-hundred-yard targets was a twenty-foot-high dirt berm for stopping fired bullets after they went through their targets. The first sergeant got up, told Wallace to rest, and went to talk to the captain. Coming back with more ammo, the first sergeant lay down beside Wallace and said, "You see that black rock about the center of the berm out there behind the targets?"

Squinting down range Wallace said, "It don't look too big from here, Top."

"Well right here's twenty rounds. Five at a time, put them all in the rock."

With the company looking on, Wallace fired twenty rounds and never missed. The adjustments on the peep sights convinced the mountaineer to start using them. The first sergeant won the twenty dollar bet with the captain. Both men agreed that if there weren't a war on that man and his rifle would be on the Marine Corps rifle team and would win a championship at the shooting matches held every year at Camp Perry. The first sergeant and the captain knew that India Company was going to an island in the Pacific—Guadalcanal. That's why they'd gotten the new rifles. Once back in the company area, all the grunts had cleaned their rifles, stripping them all the way down. Wooden parts were cleaned with soft cloths, hand rubbing the linseed oil into the grain. Wallace used steel wool on the burned stock. It blurred the edges but didn't remove it. Using the linseed oil and hand-rubbing, the scar faded to a shiny character mark.

Wallace and two other shooters from India Company were joined by the best shooters from the rest of the regiment. The Marines were ahead of other services by recognizing that snipers were going to be needed. They put the first group through extra training. The shooters practiced camouflage and stealth. During the last week they shot their weapons on the long distance rifle range, where they had to creep and crawl into different positions before firing. When they had finished the two week course, the Marines were called scout snipers.

The Smith Corona 1903 A3 looked better now than when it came from the factory. Wallace had polished the hardwood stock and foregrip till it glowed. The rifle slept in its own rack built right into the sniper's wall locker. The last time he was assigned to Supply, Wallace had the shit detail of unloading trucks and whatever else the supply sergeant wanted done. Even when he was doing the detail work, Wallace's rifle leaned against the wall. After all the work was done, the supply sergeant surprised the Pfc by giving him a canvas rifle case. "Here. You're gonna need this." The rifle fit the case perfectly. Wallace stenciled on his name and stock number with black paint. The rifle was now on its way to war in the far off Pacific. The fortunes of war would mold the rifle and its operator into an awesome team.

5

___

When Tex Payne left the Redcatcher base, he wondered how he was going to catch up to the grunt he'd done the story about. The only smart thing he'd done with the story was make it into two parts—and kept all the copies. Sometimes when writing a story, he'd get so drunk he'd forget to make copies before sending it off.

This time he had the stories but not the man. *Fuck.* He couldn't even find the lieutenant that Mac wanted fragged—at least in the story.

Shit, fame, and fortune were now his and he was finding out that staying on top in the news business was a lot harder than getting there.

His driver had to stop for the traffic jam at the Y bridge on the way back to Saigon. Watching the grunts check ID cards and just generally fuck with the gooks had Tex thinking of another story. Surfacing from his daydream, Tex finally paid attention to the patch on the grunt's jungle shirt. The Redcatcher patch registered and Tex hopped out of the jeep and asked the ID-checking grunt what company he was from.

"Bravo Company two-thirds," the man answered.

"Where's your platoon leader?" Tex asked.

"Ain't got an el tee, but the platoon sergeant is over there," and the grunt pointed. The sergeant was sitting on the edge of the bridge drinking coffee from a canteen cup as the reporter walked up and introduced himself.

Tex could hardly get a word out of the man. Then, when he mentioned the name McDonald, the reaction he got was not what he had expected. The platoon sergeant's black eyes all of a sudden looked exactly like the barrel of the M-16 that the reporter was looking down.

Eddy set his canteen cup down. "You the fuckin' cock-sucker that wrote that fucked up story about him being a mercenary?"

Tex was thinking on his feet. *This man is pissed.* The way he was pointing his rifle let Tex know the platoon sergeant would use it.

"Ahhhhh, Sarge, that whole story was not what I wrote. I wrote about that lieutenant kicking his ass and almost causing a mutiny."

Staff Sergeant "Fast Eddy" Felter believed the reporter—at least enough to move the rifle's muzzle away from the reporter's belly button. *I should shoot this cocksucker and throw him in the river,* he thought.

As soon as the sergeant moved the rifle barrel, Tex start-ed talking again. "Look, I just wanna set the story straight here. Find out where Mac's gone. Talk to him. Get the straight skinny, you know?"

The platoon sergeant picked up his cooling coffee. "Little motherfucker went to the Rangers and by now he should be in Hawaii."

With the platoon sergeant talking, Tex didn't stop ques-tioning him. "What happened to the El tee?" "Did he go to Hawaii too?" "Did he make it out alive?"

Eddy just laughed. "No. The fuckin' lieutenant went down south before he got killed. He's workin' with nothin' but VC and NVA prisoners—and good riddance."

Tex kept on. "Was that the real story...about the ass kickin' and Mac falling in the river?"

When Eddy stood up he towered over the reporter. "Hey, this is a fucked up place and shit happens over here, like people falling off of bridges," and he looked down at the water.

Tex figured he had all the answers he was going to get. "Hey, thanks Sarge. I appreciate the help," and he hopped into his jeep.

I wonder if the paper wants a follow-up bad enough to send me to Hawaii? Sure as shit that grunt isn't comin' back to Nam. I'll do the story and lie about the officer getting fragged. That should hold 'em till I find out for sure about the skinny fuckin 'grunt.

6

___

Shirley's first shot fired in anger was not at a Jap at all. India Company went in on the second wave, landing on the island of Guadalcanal in August of 1942. The landings were unopposed and Shirley—carried by Corporal Wallace Wallace—took up a position inland along a slow-moving green river. Providing security for the Marines digging, Wallace and Shirley were in front of the line of foxholes. So far the Japs hadn't been sighted at all. The rumor had it that the Japs had bugged out.

Wallace was looking across the river into the jungle. The V-wave coming across the lagoon caught his eye. Something was in the water and coming fast. The corporal, his stripes only two weeks old, backed up, facing the moving ripples. On his first swift lunge the crocodile came out of the water and halfway up the bank. Wallace's first shot hit the croc just above the eyes and didn't faze it at all. The second shot went right through the open mouth and the .30-.06 bullet took out the back of the crocodile's head. Wallace ran like hell for the foxhole line. In his death throes, the huge croc whipped his tail from side to side. It could have broken the strongest man in half.

The second scar Shirley got was when Wallace used her barrel to pry the crocodile's jaws open. Its reflexes clamped and the croc's jaws closed just behind the stacking swivel making three tooth marks on each side of the hardwood foregrips. All of India Company came to see the huge dead crocodile. Nobody had told them about the crocs on the island. It was gone the next morning, eaten by fellow inhabitants of the river.

The second day also brought the Japs. They came in broad daylight. Mortars and artillery, then the first human wave. With Wallace on the trigger, Shirley piled up twenty-three Japs in the day-long attack. Little did Wallace know that together they would account for many more before the war's end.

Shirley's longest shot was on Iwo Jima—six hundred yards across volcanic ash. Waving his sword and rallying his troops, the Jap officer fell, shot through the heart. Walking up to the dead officer, Sergeant Wallace Wallace paced off six-hundred and two paces. The sword that lay beside the dead officer went home to Tennessee.

Okinawa was the last island the pair visited and it was where Sergeant Wallace Wallace picked up his second purple heart. A piece of shrapnel tore open his right cheek—not bad enough to be evacuated, but it did have him off the line—and that's how their war ended.

India Company boarded a ship for the long trip home. The last thing Sergeant Wallace did before picking up his discharge at Camp Pendleton was to clean and oil Shirley before he turned it in at the supply shed. He did get to keep the leather sling. Cracked and torn from being packed all over the Pacific, the supply sergeant told him to keep it, that the rifle was going in for an overhaul and would come out with a new sling.

The rifle never made it to the arsenal for an overhaul. It got as far as Barstow, California, where it got a new firing pin and a leather sling. The inspector deemed it was still in fine condition. The crated rifle headed for the 40th Infantry, California National Guard. Packed ten to a case the rifle sat in a warehouse for five years. It next saw daylight on a ship taking the Guard to a place called Korea. The used car salesman who was issued the rifle hated it. Too heavy to carry. He wanted a Tommy gun or an M-l carbine. Ten rounds off the fantail of the ship was the only time the salesman fired the rifle. He hated the heavy rifle even more after that because it kicked like a mule and left his shoulder bruised and sore.

Once in Korea, the Guard took their place on the line. The company the salesman was in got the order to pull back. He left the 1903 A3 with a complete cartridge belt in a foxhole full of muddy water. As he went by the aid station, he found stacks of weapons laying around from all the wounded. He finally got his carbine. Sleeping on guard, he was killed in action two days later. He never did fire his carbine.

Marine recon went through the Guard lines on patrol. Six-hundred yards was as far as they got when the North Koreans opened up with machine gun fire and mortars. Forced back, the Marines took over the abandoned foxholes. A Marine recon private jumped into the water-filled hole and not until the next day did he bother to reach down and find out what he was standing on.

The private leaned the rifle—still draped in its muddy bandolier of ammo—on the side of the foxhole. That night the position was hit with wave after wave of North Koreans. Nearly out of ammo, the private's rifle jammed. Not even having the time to think about it, he grabbed the .30-.06 and started killing the soldiers who were trying to kill him. The first thing he did the next day was clean the muddy rifle and give his M-l Garand to a replacement. He called his new-old rifle his lucky piece. Every time the Marines came off the line he was offered a new rifle and for two years he kept the rifle by his side.

Marines from the recon unit were being sent to Japan and from there back to the States. At the embarkation point the private—now a corporal—had his rifle taken away and he was given a brand new M-1 Garand for his trip home. With the rest of the Marine weapons, the rifle was taken to a warehouse right on the docks where inspection and crating were done in a hurry. Oiled and in a crate three days later, the rifle was in the hold of a ship, going to a place called Hanoi.

Three days after that, the ship was unloaded and the French garrison had the weapons uncrated and issued to their soldiers. The rifle and one hundred rounds of ammunition were issued to a truck driver who never fired the weapon. A slow ride ended in a place called Dien Bien Phu. It was the truck's last journey. After it was unloaded, the truck was hit with artillery fire. Still on the floor when the truck exploded, the rifle was flung clear and landed near an underground bunker used as the operations center. A lieutenant picked up the rifle, dragged it into the radio bunker, leaned it against the wall, and forgot all about it.

The French garrison surrendered and the officer whose Tommy gun had taken a direct hit from an artillery shell while he was in the shithouse needed a weapon to surrender to the Vietnamese. The French officers were stripped of not only their weapons but all their personal possessions. The skinny Vietminh officer grabbed the dirty old .06 and the lieutenant had to hide a grin—the Vietnamese could hardly lift the rifle. The Viet officer took the lieutenant's Rolex watch and Zippo lighter. The rifle followed the prisoners to Hanoi, riding in the back of a truck. The prisoners walked all the way to their prison and many died. Never cleaned, the Smith Corona 1903 A3 was sprayed with hot used motor oil and stored in a moldy warehouse.

7

Mac liked working with the old master sergeant. The more beer Sergeant Taylor drank, the more he talked. Picking up the barrel of the .03 that Mac had just finished cleaning, the sergeant declared, "Well, this motherfucker's shot. It won't even match up to the stock."

"Hey, Sarge, these old motherfuckers got to be matched up. Probably not a rifle in the lot that's all together. Let me work on these fuckers, see what I can do," and Mac took a sip of beer.

"Okey-dokey. I'm goin' home. Maybe see you in the mornin'" and the sergeant got up.

"What d'you mean? You live here on the island?" Mac asked, disappointed that the sergeant wasn't staying.

The big sergeant laughed. "Fuck. My wife wants me home for dinner. She an island gal. Hell, been married almost twenty years." Walking out of the Quonset hut, the sergeant yelled back, "See you tomorrow."

Putting his feet up, Mac grabbed a rifle from the stack on the floor. It was another Remington. He removed the wooden hand guards and stock, tagged the bolt and laid it aside. The front stacking swivel had its screw missing. Trying to look down the barrel, all he could see was dirt. No shine at all from any of the metal in the barrel. He went outside and cut a branch from a small tree. It was time for the trick he'd learned while cleaning his dad's and uncle's guns. He whittled the branch to fit and jammed it tight into the bullet chamber. Leaning the stripped rifle barrel against the work bench, he carefully poured Coca-Cola down the barrel until it was full. He did the same for two more barrels and left them there. He cleaned the work table, then closed the overhead door and went back to the barracks.

Mac flipped on the big color TV, then pulled out a box of fried chicken. The freezer was full of steaks, pork chops, all kinds of chicken, frozen potatoes, and three or four frozen pies. The whole box with frozen chicken and a tray of frozen French fries went into the oven. Grabbing a Coke, he headed for the shower. *Fuckit.* He turned around and stuck a frozen cherry pie in the oven.

The closet in Jimmy's room had extra towels and bedding, so after his shower and while waiting for his food to cook he made up his bunk. Mac was one happy grunt, being there in the barracks, eating all he wanted— three different channels on the television. He didn't give a shit if he saw downtown at all.

After his meal he fell asleep in front of the TV and the clock on the wall read midnight when his nightmare woke him up. Mac went right outside and pissed on the grass. The night breeze cooled the sweat on his body. The cave and body parts from the B-52 strike just went on and on in his dream. *Must be the cherry pie that caused the nightmare,* he thought as he went back into the barracks. He made a pot of coffee and took it with him to the workshop. After Mac dumped the Coke out of them, all three rifle barrels were shiny and clean. All he had to do was run an oil-soaked patch through them. Holding the barrels up to light, he could tell that all three were good to go if he could find parts to fit each rifle. Noticing the beat up wall locker for the first time, he walked over and opened the door.

He found everything he needed. Gallon cans of linseed

oil, steel wool, cans of bore cleaner, boxes with all sizes of patches. Neat notches in the door held bore brushes and cleaning rods. Screwdrivers, punches, and tools for working on weapons were rolled in tidy pouches. Sheets of fine sandpaper were what he needed most and sure enough, he discovered whole boxes of it in the bottom of the locker. Drinking coffee, he sat at the table and, using the fine grit sandpaper and steel wool, he redid the three stocks. One thing he could tell from sanding down the stocks—none of the rifle barrels went with the stocks. The first rifle barrel he cleaned fit like a glove on the last stock he'd sanded. With all the metal removed from the stock for cleaning, it was a simple matter to set the barrel in and see how the screw holes matched. He tagged rifle barrel and stock, then lay the cleaned wooden stock in a tank and dumped in two gallons of linseed oil and a half quart of turpentine to speed the soaking process. While the stock soaked, and before he even tried to match bolts to barrels,

he cleaned the bolt assemblies in gas and dried them. The first bolt didn't fit the clean barrel so he tried another bolt. This one slipped into the receiver without clicking or hanging up. The third bolt he tried fit with a slight touch and clicked into place. Removing the bolt he took it all the way down, even using a pipe cleaner to clean the firing pin hole. He used steel wool on the firing pin itself and after a light coat of oil the bolt went together smoothly. After matching components were set aside on a clean rag, he pulled the stock out of the tank where it had been soaking. Letting the excess linseed oil and turpentine run back into the tank, he began to rub the wood finish with his warm hands. Setting the stock back in the tank to soak, he finished cleaning all the other metal parts. He switched stocks in the tank and with a soft clean cloth started polishing the stock. Fifteen minutes of brisk polishing and the wood glowed. He used steel wool and the pipe cleaners to clean the peep sight so that all the adjustment lines became visible once again. The first rifle went back together easily. The top wooden hand guards took a little more work and the metal parts needed to be reblued in some spots but there was nothing Mac could do about that. Standing in the open rollup door, he dry-fired the rifle across the airstrip. Everything worked, but the only true test was to fire it on the range. The last thing Mac did to the rifle was rub a light coat of oil all over the weapon and tie a tag to the trigger.

He was putting the second rifle together when he lost the screw to the stacking swivel. Looking for it on his hands and knees, he got tangled up in a homemade rifle sling made of braided rope. He pulled on it and found another .30-.06 attached to the other end. When he took the rifle out of the pile, Mac could tell that this rifle was just a little bit different. It was beat to shit like all the others, but as he rubbed his greasy hand over the receiver he brushed off enough dirt to read "Smith Corona." *Huh, not a Remington.* He set the rifle on the table and resumed his search for the fallen screw. Before he had a chance to break down the new-found rifle, Jimmy and Master Sergeant Taylor showed up.

The black master sergeant picked up the first rifle Mac had completed. Working the action, he said to Mac. "Nice job. Smooth action, too." He turned to Jimmy and told him, "Pay attention to what this guy's doin'. Maybe you'll learn something."

"Shit, Sarge, I learned a whole lot last night." Jimmy went on about his stay in Mac's room downtown and had both men laughing. "You're gonna have to buy Brian a can of fiberglass to pack those bullet holes in his surfboard, brah," and Jimmy sat down. "Gimme some coffee."

Mac asked, "We still goin' to the party tonight, Jimmy?"

"Yeah, brah, we're goin'. Gonna be lots of fun." As he handed Mac his room key he said, "I got your stuff. Put it over in the room already." He picked up the second rifle that Mac had done. "We'll have to fire these things before we send them back to Nam. Action is a little tight on this one." Jimmy dry-fired across the airstrip.

Taylor dropped a hundred dollars on the table. "Mac, gimme a hundred dollars in that MPC. We're goin' back to Nam next week and we're gonna need it." Mac was only too happy to comply. He needed extra money for the upcoming beach party.

"Hey, Jimmy, that guy Brian really pissed cause I shot his surfboard?"

Jimmy laughed. "Naw, brah. You scared the shit out of him. He'll be more careful who he fucks with next time. Just leave that gun at home tonight."

Mac finally got a chance to pick up the rifle with the homemade rope sling. The cardboard tag wired to the trigger guard read, "Captured Quang Tri RVN 9/69."

"Hey, Sarge where's Quang Tri, anyway?" Mac asked.

Taylor was checking another rifle. "That's up north of where you guys work. Up towards the highlands. Is that where that came from?"

Mac had the rifle lying across his lap, studying it. "That's what the tag reads. Long way from home. I wonder how it got there?"

Mac first tried to clear the weapon and make sure it was unloaded. He pulled on the bolt three times before he could get it to the rear. The magazine still had four rounds in it. He couldn't get the bolt to the rear because the first round had ruptured in the chamber. Mac took the dirty bullets out of the magazine and handed a round to Sergeant Taylor. "How old is this shit, Sarge?"

The master sergeant looked at the round, then got up

and leaned over Mac. "Look. See that '42 R' on the bottom of the round here?" and he pointed. "That's the year it was made, 1942, and the 'R' means it was made by Remington. No wonder the motherfucker came apart. These motherfuckers used to come with a ruptured cartridge case extractor. Shotgun Charlie down at the gun shop might have one. If I go over there this afternoon I'll check and see."

Mac started paperwork on the now unloaded rifle. "Smith Corona #4751637f and the date, followed by "1903 A3 cal .30-.06, ruptured cartridge case."

All metal parts from the rifle went into a cardboard box. The wood stock and hand guard were almost black from dirt and wear. He had to use three full sheets of sandpaper just to get down to the wood. The burn scar across the stock never did come out and the three tooth marks on the hand guard and front part of the stock came clean, but like the burn, were just too far into the wood to even change color. Mac whittled a smaller branch, plugged the barrel and filled it with Coke. Sergeant Taylor wanted to know where Mac learned that trick. "We were poor folks where I grew up so they did all kinds of shit like that."

"Son, you don't even know what poor is. Why, we was so poor when I was a kid we had to sell the white off the rice," and the sergeant had them laughing.

"Shit, Sarge, we was so poor when I was a kid, if I didn't wake up with a hard-on I had nothin' to play with all day." The laughter and the work on the rifles made for easy times. The three men got along well which made the work more enjoyable.

After Mac stripped and cleaned the bolt, he checked the scarred stock soaking in the linseed oil and turpentine. The tank was full now, and with Sergeant Taylor and Jimmy helping there were bare stocks waiting to soak. The old wooden stocks were soaking up so much linseed oil Mac added another full quart of the smelly liquid.

As he worked on the rifle, out of nowhere Mac began talking mainly to Taylor, telling him about the B-52 strike, about all the body parts he'd come across on his way out of the jungle, and how the nightmare woke him out of a sound sleep the night before. Jimmy was paying attention to the back and forth between the two. The reason Jimmy kept getting turned down for Vietnam was that he was the sole surviving son and the visits he made to Nam were quick. Right in and right out.

Maybe his latest application would be approved so he could spend a tour with an A team out in the jungles of Nam.

8

—

The 199th Light Infantry Brigade was helping the hospitals stay busy—not from contact but booby traps and malaria. Sergeant Major Bill Mateau had been adding figures from the morning reports and every day the gooks were getting more of his people hurt without a solid contact anywhere in the brigade's area of operations. Leaning back in his chair, he thought, *It's been quiet since that B-52 strike and the enemy headquarters were wiped out.* Both he and the general had gone in for a look after the grunts had secured the area. The pictures his Ranger had taken—once developed—were good, but the smell was terrible. Closing his eyes, he could still feel his nose clog up. Intelligence was still working with all the stuff the grunts had collected. *Sure as shit, Charlie will come back,* but when and where had everyone guessing.

One of the stacks of paperwork on his desk was from Intel, asking for Rangers to check this and check that. Most of the requests went into his trash can. *Where do they dream this shit up,* he wondered. Snatch a payroll officer. Carry a five-hundred pound bomb to a trail and booby trap it. On and on. The only two missions that were at all possible for the Rangers were a trail junction to watch and a new area on a river that could be used for sampans.

The stack of paper that brought a smile to his face was the one where the Criminal Investigation Division was conducting an ongoing investigation at the 93rd Evac hospital. Someone in one of the wards had submitted twelve patients for the Medal of Honor. One of the names—Sp/4 Juan "Pepe" Leon—had been a patient in the ward and CID would like to talk to him. The sergeant major laughed out loud. Pepe Leon was the Ranger that Mac had visited down there. *Naw, he wouldn't do that.* He thought a moment, then, *Maybe he would.* Thinking of Mac off in Hawaii, he wondered what else that skinny shit had pulled.

The sergeant major—paper still in hand—headed down the hall for the general's office. One star General Walt Davis, commander of the 199th, looked up when the sergeant major knocked on his door. Both said the same thing at the same time: "You're not gonna believe this."

Laughing, the general said, "You first, Bill."

The sergeant major told the general about someone adding the Medal of Honor to twelve patients' paperwork down at the hospital and the ongoing investigation by CID. That had them both laughing.

The general grabbed a piece of paper off his desk. "You remember that Rolex watch the Ranger picked up after the air strike?" The sergeant major nodded. "Well, I took it to the French Embassy and they not only found out who it belongs to but they sent it to the guy."

The general was also concerned with the casualties the brigade was taking from the booby traps and mines. Most of their discussion was about the traps, maybe having classes on spotting them before they went off. When the general asked if the sergeant major had heard anything on the mercenary, both men chuckled. "Nope, he's still comin' back here. Personnel never got any kinda transfer papers, not even a request." At that both of them started talking about future missions for the Rangers and sending more of them to the recondo school if the brigade could get slots for them.

The logistics of keeping a man with a rifle in the field to kill the enemy were staggering. It took a ratio of nine men in the rear to support one grunt in the field. There was a time warp, going from the field to the rear— especially in Nam. Going from stark terror in the killing fields to a band and a strip show was done in a few hours. No wonder people went a little nuts. That was one of the things the general and the sergeant major had done since taking over the brigade. Units involved in a tough fight usually got a day or two of rest in a secure area—like outside a firebase—so the men got to let off steam and mourn any lost comrades before being brought in to so-called civilization. This had worked out rather well. Killings in the rear were much less frequent now. As he returned to his office, the sergeant major was already starting to plan Ranger missions and who to assign.

9

—

The Recoil Gun Shop was two blocks outside the main gate of Ft. Shaftner. It had been there since the end of World War II and the weapons sold there had traveled all over the world. The Recoil was owned and operated by the same man.

Shotgun Charlie Johnson had opened the shop after taking his medical discharge, having lost his lower right leg in the Pacific. So far the gun shop had put all of his kids through college and provided his wife a new car every two years.

Charlie was working on an order form. The .357 Smith and Wesson was his biggest seller. Next were Colt .45s with matched trigger and sight. It was natural that his biggest customers were right there at the fort. It seemed that every guy going to Nam wanted an extra weapon. 12-gauge shotguns were also hot items. Shotgun Charlie marked his weapons up a modest ten percent. He marked up holsters, fancy gun belts, and belt knives two hundred percent. Charlie spotted the wannabe gunslingers right off and sold them a lot of the fancy shit.

He'd lost his foot and ankle stepping on a mine at Guadalcanal. He'd lost the rest of the leg up to the knee somewhere between the island and the hospital in Hawaii. Infection had set in while he was on the hospital ship taking him stateside. The ship had docked in Hawaii and

Charlie and several other Marines with the same problem had been hospitalized here. Corporal Charles Johnson had been medically discharged and—thanks to his wife Leah, a full-blooded Hawaiian he met in the hospital—he'd never left the island since.

Leah worked in the hospital's kitchen. A take-charge gal, she made sure Charlie saved his discharge money and invested it wisely. Learning to walk with a wooden leg came first, then the gun shop. Babies arrived in there somewhere. They had gotten married and bought a home, which was a lot quieter since the kids had all left.

Part of Charlie's business was word of mouth. Lots of times the fighting men arrived in the middle of the night, passing through Hawaii. They would call Charlie at home and he'd go down to the gun shop and meet his customers. Marines on their way to Korea had made his business. Marked as cookies, boxes and boxes of 12-gauge 00 buckshot were sent from the shop. The mail room staff at the fort hated to see him and his crates of cookies coming in the door. Charlie had never put a price on the ammo, but money orders poured in, many with a cardboard top from a C-ration box saying thanks. His huge safe in the back office had a special box in it full of cash that was for any Marine or doggie who needed a loan. Payback when the GI had it, no interest. His worthless brother-in-law supplied Charlie with a lot of untraceable guns. He gave those away to Marine recon Special Forces troopers. Once—and only once—he gave away a fully automatic 9mm Sten gun to a Navy seal.

The shop itself was full of war trophies, pictures, old weapons, and uniforms. They were all marked with the donor's name and the place where captured.

Mid afternoon was slow in the shop. The soldiers were all working so the bell ringing over the door interrupted his paperwork.

"Shit, the pimp guns are all locked up, you ugly sono-fabitch," Charlie said to the black man.

"Fuck you, you fuckin' jarhead cocksucker," and the two men grinned at one another. Master Sergeant Taylor was Charlie's brother-in-law and they had been best friends ever since Taylor had married Leah's sister.

"Hey, you crippled up old goat, I need an extractor for a .30-.06. Got a ruptured cartridge casing stuck in the chamber." The master sergeant came around behind the counter and sat down.

"Shit, J.L., those are startin' to get a little scarce, but I got some in the back room. Wanna beer?" and Charlie headed into his office.

"Yeah, gimme one," Taylor said to the retreating back. Sitting there waiting for his part and a beer, J.L. looked at the blown up black and white photo on the wall. Two men standing beside a dead crocodile. Taylor knew that one of the men in the photo was his brother-in-law on Guadalcanal before he'd lost his leg. When Charlie handed him the beer he asked, "Who's that other guy in the picture? The one with the .06? We're workin' on some of them old rifles now."

Charlie sat down and began. "Only fucker I ever knew that had two first names. Wallace Wallace was a corporal, like me. He was my buddy since boot camp. From some place in Tennessee. Motherfucker sure could shoot. That picture was the first day on Guadalcanal. Fuckin' croc came right out of the water to get him. Man, we didn't even know they had that kinda shit on the island. I was diggin' a fox-hole and next thing I know he shot that croc. The first shot bounced off the croc's head. The next one from that .06 killed him deader than shit. The next mornin' the croc was gone. We figured his buddies ate him." He paused, then added, "That rifle he's carrying, well, we got 'em brand new. He slept with his. I always wondered if he made it out alive. I lost track of him after I got sent home."

Taylor handed his brother-in-law a list. "We're goin' back over to Nam next week. Hope you got all that shit." Along with the list he handed Charlie a thousand dollars. "Let me know if that's not enough and I'll collect some more."

Charlie looked at the small list. "Three .357 Magnums— got that. Next, .22 Colts. How many of these Colts you want? What the fuck you guys doin' with these .22s, anyway?"

"Ahhh, shit, they use them for shootin' rats out at the camps. Motherfuckers are as big as dogs," and Taylor laughed.

"Looks like I got everything on the list, but send Jimmy over with another 55-gallon drum. Everything should fit right in OK. Leah told me that some GI Joe shot the shit out of Brian's surfboard," and Charlie looked inquiringly at Taylor.

Taylor was already grinning. "Yup, sure as shit did. Mac's workin' on the rifles with me and Jimmy. Motherfucker's eatin' his baloney sandwich," the big master sergeant continued, "and Brian goes to fuckin' with the guy. Bet he don't do that shit anymore. Jimmy's gonna take him a can of that fiberglass shit to fix his board." Finishing his beer and getting ready to leave the sergeant added, "They're havin' a party out there tonight. Hopefully, Mac will get laid and get that temper under control. I'm gonna make sure he leaves that pistol with me tonight." Both men were laughing, thinking back on their own wild days.

Charlie asked, "You com in' over tonight?'" Nope, Leona and I are going to the Sheraton. Mac don't wanna stay there and the Army gave him the room free so we're gonna make good use of it," and the sergeant headed out the door.

Mac and Jimmy were in Jimmy's pickup and their first stop had been the auto parts store. Mac bought a fiberglass repair kit for Brian's surfboard. He saw metal toothbrushes and got all six of them. What he really wanted were cans of spray-on oil. When Mac asked the Hawaiian clerk if he had any, the clerk talked him into buying three cans. The clerk pointed out that this new shit had silicone in it which made everything twice as slick. The clerk told Jimmy, "You could even spray it on your dick. Better than Vaseline, brah." They were still laughing as they paid for their stuff.

In the pickup Jimmy said, "We're goin' to the PX, brah. Get you some beach clothes. You look like shit runnin' around dressed like that."

Mac was learning. "OK, brah."

He got Jimmy laughing and Jimmy said, "Got to hide those chicken legs, brah. Only go out at night."

Having a good time, the men headed for the PX. Twenty dollars and Mac had his Hawaiian outfit. Blue baggies with bright yellow sunflowers all over them. Two loud Hawaiian shirts and two pairs of grass sandals. Jimmy had explained that the sandals lasted a lot longer than flip-flops and everybody would know that he was cool. The last stop was at the commissary.

Seeing Mac's puzzled look, Jimmy told him, "We buy the shit for the beach party here, brah. Everything's cheaper." They bought hamburger meat, beer, and a case of hamburger buns. Everything went in the back of the Chevy pickup. Heading back to the workshop, Jimmy told him, "We get all our shit put away, then clean up our work area, and us, then we're off to have a good time."

Master Sergeant Taylor pulled in behind them as they went into the work area. Mac went over and took the stock he had soaking out of the tank. Wiping off the linseed oil, he rubbed it briskly for five minutes. The stock glowed and the burn scar blended right in.

Taylor handed the two bullet extractors to Mac. "There you go. That should clear the casings out of the weapons. Don't lose them. They're getting scarce."

Mac put the extractors aside. Then he picked up the Smith Corona barrel, went to the door, and dumped the Coke from the barrel onto the ground. Next, he fit the bolt holding the extractor cartridge remover to the receiver and slid the bolt forward. Pulling the bolt to the rear, the ruptured cartridge slid right out. "Works like a champ, Sarge." Using a bore brush soaked in nitro solvent, he cleaned the bullet chamber. He walked outside, held the barrel up, and looked down the bore. Sunlight through the clean bore made his eyes water. *Clean as a whistle.*

Mac went back out to Jimmy's pickup and brought in the bag from the auto parts store. He tried the spray of silicone oil on the first rifle he'd cleaned and put together. Jimmy and the master sergeant watched as Mac sprayed the new oil all over the bolt and receiver. Mac started to grin as he tried the action. Just one click when the bolt seated. He handed the rifle to Taylor. "Try that, Sarge."

Working the action, the sergeant said, "Slicker than snot on a door knob," and he handed the rifle to Jimmy. "Where'd you get this stuff?"

Jimmy told him, "We got it at the auto parts store. Brand new shit. Just came out."

"OK, let's get this shit cleaned up and get ready for Saturday night. I'm gonna borrow Mac's pistol," and the big master sergeant held his hand out.

Mac handed the .38 over. "What's-a-matter, Sarge? You don't trust me?"

The sergeant looked at him. "No, I don't. Hangin' around with this pineapple and your hot temper—no, I don't. Try usin' the gun in your pants tonight and I'll take care of this one."

Jimmy was laughing. "He's right, brah. Supposed to fuck that pussy, not kill it"

Everybody was laughing and the cleanup went fast. Mac took everything that went with the Smith Corona, laid it all out on a blanket on the floor, and covered it all with a piece of torn up bed sheet. After securing the Quonset hut, the three soldiers headed for the "living room" in the barracks. They all grabbed a cold one from the refrigerator and Mac's head was tilted back as he guzzled his beer.

Sergeant Taylor asked him, "What happened to your head?" Mac ran his hand over the rapidly healing cut that his blonde hair hid rather well. "That's the place where I hit the tree and knocked myself out."

The black sergeant peered at the cut. "Yup, healin' up nicely. Probably won't even have a scar."

Holding his hair back as he looked in the mirror, Mac said, "Yeah, I used a tube of first aid cream I found in the hospital. That shit was so hot it damn near burned my hair off."

"What did you use, brah?" Jimmy asked.

"Fuckin' shit in a tube called hemorrhoid ointment."

Mac couldn't believe his eyes. Taylor dropped his beer can on the floor and fell back on the couch and tears flowed down both of his cheeks. Gasping and choking every time he tried to talk, he'd start to laugh again. Jimmy just stood there. Like Mac, he didn't know what the sergeant was laughing about. Finally the sergeant calmed down enough to tell both of them that "Hemorrhoids grow on your asshole and that's what the cream is supposed to be used for."

Mac scratched his healing head and said, "It works," and all three soldiers cracked up with laughter.

10

The hamlet outside Quang Tri didn't even have a name. It was marked on military' maps as Hamlet #4. Le Vinn Suong was the eldest son and had let the NVA officer talk him into volunteering to serve as a private in the VC militia. Five miles was the furthest the young man had been from his farm village and the only Americans the farmer had seen had been the few who had walked through his village. The farm boy had waved at the helicopters flying over and thought he would like to fly in one.

Three of the other farmers from the village had been with the VC for years, but all Le Vinn knew was that they went out in the jungle at night. Le Vinn and his two friends had looked down the business end of the AK-47 that the NVA officer was waving around and agreed that now was the perfect time to join the militia. They would be given uniforms and guns as they became available. Also, they would stay at home and continue to work their rice paddies. The thing that bothered the young farmer the most was that now the NVA would be taking half of LeVinn's rice crop. "For the people," the North Vietnamese officer said. "The people's revolution," and "Down with all capitalist dogs." The officer's speech went on and on, almost putting Le Vinn to sleep, since the farmer didn't understand what he was talking about.

He didn't understand what the war was about and had no

plans of ever leaving his home and farm. *Well, maybe to Quang Tri to buy a wife, but that's a very long time in the future.* His mother, brothers, and sisters concerned him more. With his rice crop half taken away, he'd have to find another way to feed them all. Maybe with the guns they were going to get he could learn how to hunt. His father had been killed in the jungle, logging with other village farmers. He'd died when a teak tree fell on him. The other farmers had dragged the broken body back to the hamlet and he was buried next to his father in the small graveyard. Le Vinn was twelve-years-old and already working in the paddies when his father was killed. He just kept right on and got better at growing rice. The girls and his mother grew a vegetable garden behind the house. Dogs were eaten on special holidays, and fish from the river also added to their diet. Poor diets, along with accidents and malaria cut down most men in the village before they were fifty.

During the monsoon season, all the men gathered on the banks of the river to keep an eye out for game killed in the floods. After bloating and rising to the surface, whatever drowned in the rolling water was pulled from the river, dragged back to the village and divided between all of the families. Even the dogs were given scraps from the drowned carcasses.

Seventeen-year-old Le Vinn hoped that the NVA gave them guns before they took half his rice crop. He also hoped he would get a pair of boots for running around in the jungle. The farmer hated snakes.

Three nights later Le Vinn was awakened, and— sleepy and grumbling about being up in the middle of the night— taken into the jungle. His grumbling stopped when the NVA sergeant punched Le Vinn in the mouth. He and his two friends had to dig punji pits all night long. The sharpened bamboo stakes were dipped in human shit, inserted point up at the bottom of each pit, then carefully covered over just as dawn started to light up the sky. Tired, the three farmers were marched back to the village and the small cadre of NVA wanted to be fed. They slept that day in the farmers' homes, but before they went to sleep the soldiers made sure the farmers went to their fields.

Dragging his tired body back to the village just before sundown, Le Vinn was very thankful that the soldiers were gone. Hoping that the NVA were never coming back, Le Vinn's reprieve lasted only three days. He was awakened once again after dark, this time for a political indoctrination that went on half the night. At the end of his speech the officer had his sergeant hand each new recruit a bright blue shirt, and all three farmers were given a rifle and ten bullets. The rifle Le Vinn received smelled of motor oil and he could hardly lift it. The rifle had no sling and the stock, with its metal plate on the end, was too big for his shoulder. The sergeant made it clear that they were to take their shirts, rifles, and bullets home and hide them. He would return and teach them all how to fire their weapons. After they killed Americans with them they would get weapons just like he had, pointing to the AK-47 at his side.

Finally, the three tired farmers were told to go home. Thinking of his sleeping pallet on his way home, Le Vinn knew there were only a few hours before dawn. He did not like the heavy rifle he was dragging along by the barrel. Too tired to do anything with it, he shoved the old rifle and the bullets beneath his sleeping pallet. His mother's hand shaking him had him awake before dawn. Le Vinn now knew that he didn't like the army life at all and he hoped the NVA would not come back to his village.

Three days and nights later the NVA were back, this time without the officer. The sergeant slapped Le Vinn for not cleaning his rifle, then gave all three farmers pieces of rope to use for slings. Next, he taught the farmers how to load and aim their rifles. They hated their heavy weapons; they were too big for the short, small Vietnamese. Now that all the three farmers had been trained, they would have their rifles with them in the fields. If the sergeant caught them without their rifles he would shoot them. Two days later Le Vinn and his friends were having lunch in the shade of a small nipa palm. Le Vinn was the one who spotted the enemy, coming across the paddies in a column. Their lunch forgotten, the three farmers picked up their weapons and advanced to meet the enemy. They decided to meet the advancing army where the jungle met the paddy dike. Le Vinn was the first to fire. Big as a knife blade, the front sight wavered in the heat. He yanked on the trigger. The heavy weapon fired. Le Vinn was knocked on his ass and the rifle landed three feet away. He crawled away and when he got to his feet he ran into the jungle. His two friends died standing up, trying to aim their rifles. Under the leadership of the two Green Beret sergeants, the Montagnards had riddled the two farmers. None of the VC farmers had a chance to wear their new blue shirts. Terrified, Le Vinn ran as fast as he could through the jungle and died screaming by his own hand. Looking back over his shoulder, he fell forward into one of the punji pits he had been forced to dig. The sharpened shit-dipped bamboo went right through his torso. His screams brought the enemy. The Yards circled the pit and watched the young farmer dying in the grave he had helped dig. The Green Beret sergeant shot Le Vinn in the head, ending his torment. The Yards were disappointed. They had bets on how long the VC would take to die. The Yards picked up the three rifles and handed them to the Green Berets. Both sergeants realized that if they didn't carry the rifles their Yards would just throw them away. Brushing the dirt off the rifle the Yard handed him, the sergeant read "Smith Corona model 1903A3." *Old motherfucker,* the sergeant thought. Continuing their mission, the Yards—led by the Green Berets—focused on winning the hearts and minds of the Vietnamese and burned the farm village to the ground.

The Green Berets celebrated the successful completion of their patrol when they returned to their outpost with the Montagnards. The old rifles were stacked in the communications bunker and eventually sent to the rear. Then the three, along with others from previous missions, were sent to Hawaii. Master Sergeant Taylor was supposed to recondition those rifles he could and return them to Vietnam. Special Forces wanted a longer-range rifle for use from the berms around their camps. The rifles were too heavy and cumbersome to be humped out in the field.

11

___

The reporter's jeep was found in an alley in Cholon, a crowded suburb of Saigon. The driver was dead behind the wheel, shot once in the head and once in the heart. The body and the jeep were stripped of all valuables. Tex Payne was not anywhere to be found. When MAC-V personnel heard that the reporter's jeep had been found with its driver dead and no reporter, they hoped for the worst—until the *Dallas Star* started raising such a stink over its missing reporter and accusing the Army of dragging its feet over finding him. Slow to pick up the investigation, the Army carried Tex as missing in action. Without a body, they had nothing to report.

The roadblock had been simple. Both Tex and his driver were caught completely by surprise. With her bundle of chickens, the old mama san just fell in front of the jeep. Slamming it to a halt, the driver started to holler at the old woman and he died just that suddenly. Coming from the exit wound, his brains were all over the reporter. Tex reached for his pistol. The VC who yanked it out of his hand broke his trigger finger. Slapped above his right ear with his own .38, Tex was unconscious and never saw the rest of the ambush. Before they left the jeep in the alley, four men gagged, blindfolded, tied his hands and feet and had the reporter under a load of straw in an ox cart. The .38—in the hands of the VC who captured Tex—fired one shot into the heart of the already dead driver. The killing and capture went unnoticed in the sea of people. The jeep, guarded by the dead driver, kept the kids from stealing anything from it. Only the stench of the rotting body brought the MPs to the southern edge of Saigon.

Regaining consciousness, Tex was nearly suffocated when he came to under a load of straw. The reporter hurt all over, his broken finger most of all. He'd pissed his pants and in the darkness of his blindfold thought that the gooks had broken his nose. Trying to breath through his bloody snot and straw-filled nose caused him to panic and pass out again. The ox cart had stopped when he came to again. This time he was yanked roughly out of the cart and slapped around until he could stand on his own. The cart was driven away, squeaking and groaning. He was untied and the blindfold was removed. Choking for air, he took the gag out of his mouth. The ambush had happened in mid-morning and here he was in the middle of nowhere facing the setting sun. "I'm a reporter, not a soldier," he gasped at the gook who had Tex's .38 stuck in his belt.

Much to Tex's surprise, the Vietnamese spoke perfect English. "We know who you are, Mr. Payne. My orders are to take you to a meeting, so you will follow or you will be very fuckin' dead here in this ditch," and the VC put his hand on Tex's .38. "No questions, Mr. fuckin' Payne.

Let's go." The VC officer barked out a set of orders. The five men under his command got in line with the reporter in the center and they marched toward the setting sun. The Vietnamese set a brisk pace. The banged-up Tex had a hard time keeping up. Except for the one with the .38, he was sure that these guys were not the ones who had kidnapped him. The area they were in was thin jungle, rice paddies, and what looked like banana plantations. They walked for two hours and never saw a soul. Even in the darkness the enemy soldiers never slowed their pace. The faint outline of the trail they were following seemed to end at the edge of a wood line where two more soldiers appeared. Tex's captors talked quietly for a few moments, then Tex's guards reached down beside a tree where they had stopped and lifted something from the ground. Only after the soldiers stepped back could Tex see what looked like a darker hole in the ground.

The NVA that Tex called "Thirty-eight Special," spoke softly in the reporter's ear. "You will treat the man you are about to meet with much respect. Now follow the man in front of you." Tex was not prepared for the steps that led down into the darkness. Tripping once and bumping against the wall of the tunnel, Tex was amazed when they rounded the first corner. A soldier turned a hidden switch and a string of electric lights came on. The deeper into the tunnel Tex went, the more afraid he became. *Why do they want me here?* he wondered. *I don't want to die down here. I could have been at home already. I'm in the shit now.*

The room Tex stepped into took him by surprise. Straw mats covered the floor. There were tables and chairs, and soft music from a stereo.

Three men sat comfortably in easy chairs. None of them were armed and all wore khaki uniforms. The man in the center chair dominated the room. He looked up when Tex entered the room, then he stood and said, "Ah, welcome Mr. Payne."

No doubt this guy is the boss, Tex thought. *Late forties maybe. . . tall for a Vietnamese. . . not fat. . . short black hair with a touch of gray... lots of gold teeth in his smile.* A gentle touch against Tex's back brought him to a stop in front of the man.

"I am General Duc Vinn Hoa. Please, have a seat." As he sat, the general barked something in Vietnamese and tea appeared instantly.

All Tex could think of was, *I wonder if any of our generals speak Vietnamese?*

"What the matter, Mr. Payne? The cat got your tongue?" The general was handed a cup of tea.

"Ahhhh, General, Sir, I'm a reporter, not a soldier. Why am I here? And where am I, by the way? My newspaper will be looking for me." Tex drained his cup of tea in one swallow. He was thirsty and held out his cup for more. The general nodded and his cup was refilled.

"Now Mr. Payne, let's cut to the chase, as you Americans say, shall we?" The general had a slight British accent.

"'Fuck you,' General, as we say in Texas, and I was brought here against my will." That was as far as Tex got. The rifle butt slammed across his foot and Tex cried out as he fell out of the chair.

"Now, Mr. Tex Payne, 'Remember the Alamo.'" The general gestured and two Vietnamese helped Tex back into the chair.

"What do you want with me, General?" Tex gasped through the waves of pain shooting up his leg. "I won't be a spy against my country, I don't care how fucked up this war is."

"Come, come, Mr. Payne. We don't need any spies. We have plenty of those. We would just like you to continue writing stories for your newspaper. From time to time you will add a story from our side, that's all," and the general leaned forward, sipping his tea. "You need a new driver and you have already met Trann." He gestured to the Vietnamese who still held Tex's .38.

"No General, he won't do for my driver because the first chance that I get I'm going to kill him," and Tex shut up.

"Very well, Mr. Payne. Hire who you like, but..." and the general waved his hand, " .. Swan Blossom is going to be running your household for you. No, Mr. Payne, in this you have no say." The general barked a single Vietnamese word.

Holy shit, Tex thought, looking at the woman who had suddenly appeared next to the general. *She's beautiful!* Tall for a Vietnamese. Big tits even in her baggy shirt. Beautiful heart-shaped face, half French and half Vietnamese. *I want some of that,* Tex thought. He even tried to stand—she was that much woman.

"She's not yours to fuck, Mr. Payne. Swan Blossom will meet you in Saigon at your house."

Shit, the general's reading my thoughts.

"Remember, Mr. Payne, you will be watched and if you come back here it will be in pieces. Just write the stories that Swan Blossom will give you from time to time." Then the general added, "We liked the story about the mercenary."

"Ahhh, General, I made that story up. The grunt isn't even in Vietnam any more. I make up stories, General."

"Exactly, Mr. Payne. That's what we want you to do. Nothing more." The general was turning away and barked commands.

Tex's arms were grabbed and he was led back down the tunnel. With his last glance at Swan Blossom, Tex could see the grin she was trying to hide.

Back outside—after his hands were tied behind his back—Tex had his face slapped. "You made me lose much face, Mr. Payne, and I will not forget this," and Trann turned to lead the way back the way they had come. Tex had no idea where they were and he kept wondering about the gook general and how they knew so much about him. The relief he felt about still being alive was short-lived. Trann would kill him the first chance the Vietnamese got. That much Tex was sure of. It was the last thought Tex had.

The morning sun shinning on his face woke him. He tried to stand and all he could do was roll over in the ditch. His body screamed in pain. *The gooks worked me over pretty good*. His tongue was stuck to the roof of his mouth. His ribs felt that every one was broken. His foot was still giving him fits. The pain came from everywhere. Finally, he managed to get to his knees. In his first look around, all Tex could see was a short stretch of paved road and a small dirt trail. *That must be the trail I was on.* Swaying drunkenly, he got to his feet. The reporter started lurching east. Beat to shit, Tex lurched down the highway, hoping he could find some people, but the stretch of highway was deserted. The more he walked, the more his pain became easier to bear. The general's words about what would happen if Tex went back there kept sending chills down his spine. Tex had no doubt that the general was serious. The ARVN deuce-and-a-half truck that came along and stopped had Tex wondering if his ride had been planned along with his kidnapping.

12

Mac felt cooler than fourteen motherfuckers with his new baggies on and the Hawaiian shirt was so bright you had to wear sunglasses at night just to look at him. Jimmy's clothes were just as bright. The Green Beret sergeant was laughing and telling Mac how to act at the party.

Hauling ass down the highway toward the beach, Jimmy almost ran over the girl hitching a ride, then slammed on the brakes. Mac was out and holding the door open for the girl almost before the pickup stopped. The cute blonde hopped in and asked for a beer almost before the truck got rolling. Her long legs turned into a perfect ass and Jimmy had his arm around her as soon as he got done shifting gears. Candy was her name and she was game for any party they were going to.

Pulling into the parking lot that was already half full, Mac hopped out looking for Brian. He found the big Hawaiian surfer throwing wood on a fire. Mac walked right over and held out the bag with the fiberglass repair kit. Watching Mac warily, Brian stood.

"Got shit to fix your board, brah," and Mac shoved the kit into Brian's hand.

Brian's frown relaxed into a grin. "You ain't got your gun have you, brah?"

"No, man. Left that motherfucker at home," and Mac grinned.

"That's good, brah. We here to party," and Brian looked over the fire at the girl with the big tits. "Hey Karen, here's that gunslinger you was lookin' for," and Brian laughed.

Everybody was having a good time. Mac told Brian, "Jimmy wanted me to just bring you two pieces of glass to patch those holes in your board. Said then you could see where you're goin', brah." Brian thought that was as funny as Mac did and the party was off to a good start.

Mac walked over to Jimmy's pickup and was surprised to see Jimmy still sitting behind the wheel. Grabbing a cooler out of the back, he stopped alongside the door. Jimmy pointed at his lap and Mac looked in the window. Candy was busy, her head in Jimmy's lap. She looked up from her blow job and her eyes grinned at Mac. All Mac could say was, "I'm next."

Carrying the cooler toward the campfire, Karen, with the big tits intercepted him. "Can I help?" she asked. His dick had the front of his baggies bulged out and he moved the cooler to hide it. Karen just grinned. "I do that better than she does." Mac's face was the color of the sunset as he dropped the cooler next to the fire. "Come on, let's go swimming. My name's Karen, by the way," and she held out her small hand.

Mac held his hand out and on impulse shook her small hand with both of his. "I'm John. Ahh, I've never been swimming in the ocean before."

Looking into his eyes she said, "Just hang on to me and I'll do all the work." Her laughter made his blood sizzle. The first time they made love was standing in the ocean with water up to their chests. Handing Mac her bikini bottoms, Karen turned and using her hand, guided him into her. Hanging onto his neck, all she said was, "Oh, my God, I love to fuck." Mac came as soon as she said "fuck." Karen laughed and said, "Let's head into the beach. I don't have to be home until after midnight." Flat on his back in the surf, Mac let Karen do all the work. Both naked in the surf, the two young people enjoyed each other. Mac was surprised that they were ignored. The group around the fire was pairing off and as Mac was putting his shorts back on, he could see Candy getting pumped on Brian's surfboard, and two couples cheering them on.

Walking over to get a couple of beers for Karen and himself, he surprised Jimmy cooking burgers. "Be ready in a minute, brah. Better get Karen over here quick or everybody else will eat it all," and Jimmy flipped another burger.

Mac ran over and grabbed Karen by the hand. "Come on, let's eat. The burgers are ready." Karen ran alongside him yelling, "I'm starved." Mac ate four burgers and while he was still trying to stuff the last one in his mouth Karen was dragging him down the beach. The party Mac glimpsed through Karen's long, dark hair was wild. Couples were making love everywhere. Four girls were hula dancing nude by the fire. After making love again and coming up for air, Karen asked the Ranger, "You're not serious about going back to Vietnam are you?"

Mac tried to explain that he was, and why, but it didn't come out the way he wanted. Nestled against her tits, he ran his hand lightly over her pussy. "Eat me," Karen whispered, and Mac learned how to eat pussy.

Karen sucking on his neck brought him half awake. "I have to go." Mac got dressed and walked her to her car, the little red Mustang. Her goodnight kiss made his bruised lips seem like they were swollen and six inches long.

Mac headed for Jimmy's pickup then crawled in the back and wrapped up in an Army blanket they'd brought. Wiping his hand across his swollen lips, he could smell and faintly taste Karen's pussy. He fell asleep thinking, *I must look like a glazed doughnut after she came all over my face.*

Mac was only vaguely aware of Jimmy driving back to the barracks. When they got there, Jimmy shook him awake and Mac stumbled sleepily inside. Jimmy still had Candy with him. Remembering that Karen had said Candy was only sixteen, Mac bounced once when he hit the bunk and he was out.

Getting up in the morning, Mac hurt good all over. The clock read 10. *Man, it's nice to sleep in,* he thought. He looked over at Jimmy's bunk and saw two heads so he got up quietly. In the shower, Mac found out what the sand had done to him. With Karen on top, the beach had sandpapered his ass and back raw in spots. *Fuckit. War's hell,* and he grinned, thinking of the night before.

He'd finished shaving and was still brushing his teeth when Candy came into the latrine and sat down behind him on a toilet. "Be done in a minute," he said through the toothpaste. In the mirror, he watched the cute girl pissing.

Mac was caught off guard when he turned to leave and she said, "Good morning," and yanked his towel off. Grinning, Candy said, "A promise is a promise," and pumping his dick, she sucked him off while she sat on the throne. She sucked and swallowed every drop. Taking his limp dick out of her mouth, she asked, "Can I borrow your toothbrush?"

His legs felt like jello. Trying to keep his feet, Mac said, "Sure," and went back to his bunk.

Jimmy was up, sitting on the edge of his bunk smoking. The two soldiers looked at one another. Jimmy had tooth marks all over his chest and his eyes were bloodshot. "How you like the party, brah?" Pointing at Mac's chest, Jimmy started laughing.

Looking down, Mac saw hickeys and scratch marks of his own. "Fuckin' great party, man. Ahhhh, Jimmy, that Candy's only sixteen, man. She just sucked my dick in the latrine," and Mac sat on his bunk.

"Yeah, I know, brah. She do give good head. I gotta take her downtown. Her parents are stayin' at a hotel down on the beach. She didn't feel like stayin' around by herself last night, so she found us. After I drop her off," Jimmy continued, "I'm goin' over to my sister's. You wanna come, brah?"

"No, brah. I gotta rest up. Feel like shit. I'm just gonna hang around here today," and Mac got up to get dressed. Candy came in nude, still damp from the shower.

"We got time for one more fuck, Jimmy," and she jumped on the Hawaiian. When Mac headed for the kitchen the couple was hard at it.

Jimmy managed to holler, "Put the coffee on, brah."

Mac put the coffee on and went outside. The intense Hawaiian sunshine warmed him and the soft breeze made the heat bearable. *What a nice place to live,* he thought. Waiting on his coffee, Mac unlocked the Quonset hut door, then went back to the kitchen. With a cup of black coffee in hand, he went back to the Quonset hut, put his coffee on the work table and opened the overhead door. The odor of linseed oil and turpentine filled the room. Mac's ass was feeling the effects of the sandpapering it had taken the night before so he put a bundle of rags on his chair. He picked up the rifle he was already calling his own, laid it across his lap and just sat and enjoyed his coffee.

Jimmy had told Mac that Karen was married to an MP and that she started fucking around after she caught her husband fucking a fourteen-year-old girl in the back seat of a police car. Karen was bringing her husband a lunch that she'd made. Taking a shortcut through the park, she'd walked right up on him. *Man, that's gotta be tough,* Mac thought.

Candy and Jimmy came in carrying their coffee cups. "We gotta go, brah."

Giggling, Candy said, "I'll be here for two weeks and I'll see you, too."

Carrying the rifle, Mac went back to the barracks for more coffee. He looked at the barracks and kitchen area. *Damn sure is a mess.* He laid the rifle on the table and got to work. He even made Jimmy's bunk when he cleaned their room. With lipstick all over it, he placed Jimmy's pillow in the middle of the olive drab green blanket. He had to open the window all the way to get the smell of sex and perfume out of the room. The short clean-up done, Mac grabbed the rifle and headed back to the work area. He gave the rifle another coat of oil, set it against the wall, and went to work on the rest of the so-called junk .03s.

Sometime during the afternoon his hangover went away and he wasn't prepared for the smell of perfume and the arms around his neck. Karen had come up behind him and he hadn't heard a thing. When Mac turned around he was stunned. Her bright blue miniskirt, white blouse, hair falling loose, and her dark glasses made her look like a movie star. "Wow," he said, stepping back. The young people looked at one another and the kiss was long and deep. She was the first to step back.

"I thought I'd find you here. What are you doing, any-way?" She raised her dark glasses and looked all around. Mac explained what he was doing with the rifles and laughed when she picked up his rifle leaning against the wall. "Shit, this is heavy. You have to carry this in Nam?" she asked, dropping the butt back down on the floor.

"Naw," Mac answered. "This is a long gun for real shoot-ing. We use M-16s over there. Lighter, and you carry a lot more bullets." She sat with him while he finished the rifle he was working on. Presently, the eight rifles were nearly done. He had her help him finish. Taking a small white bot-tle from a paper sack, he stuck a rifle between her knees.

"Hold that just like that," he said.

"What is that stuff?" she asked, watching Mac use the small brush attached to the cap. Carefully, he painted the front blade of the rifle.

"The white paint is automotive touch-up. Putting it on here like this lets you pick up a sight pattern better." Seeing her look of confusion, he handed her another rifle to hold. "When you're aiming one of these it makes the target stand out better."

Her lips curled. "You mean when you're trying to kill somebody?"

Mac looked at her. "Sometimes," he said.

"Mac, you ever kill anybody?"

Mac put another rifle between her knees. Rather than answer her question he kept his hand going up her leg. Smiling, Karen gave him and his hand a slight push. "Not now. Let's get in a real bed." She really laughed when Mac told her about his sandblasted sore ass.

The Smith Corona was the last rifle Mac painted. He took care doing it, blowing softly on the quick-drying paint. He gave it another coat, then, sitting back, he looked at Karen holding the rifle between her knees. *Wow*, he thought. *She's beautiful.* He put more stocks and hand guards to soak in the linseed oil mix. With Karen hanging on his arm, they went into the barracks. In the kitchen area Mac realized how hungry he was. He asked Karen if she was hungry and she said, "I'm starved. Do you want to go out and get something to eat?"

Thinking of her husband, Mac said, "I don't think that would be a very smart thing to do around here." They both knew what he was talking about.

"OK, go take a shower and I'll find something in here." She turned to the refrigerator, but not before Mac saw her tears.

Getting the oil off his arms in the shower, he realized how puzzled he was by Karen. He didn't have much time to think about it. Karen was in the shower and her soapy hands were all over him. Mac slammed her against the wall and tried to get inside her, but she was just a little too short. Chasing her down the hallway, dinner was forgotten. Mac's bunk dried them off. On his knees between her legs, Mac asked, "Can I eat some more?"

Grabbing his head, Karen smashed it into her pussy. "There. Right there. Ohmygod! Right there!" She lifted halfway up off the bed. Right after that, Mac learned about sixty-nine. Nestled in his arms and slick with sweat, she murmured, "Dinner should be ready." Wrapped only in towels, they ate dinner and their quiet conversation made both of them realize they really liked one another. Doing the clean-up together, Karen looked at the wall clock. "I have to be home in an hour."

As they dressed in Mac's room, desire overtook them both at the same time. Karen was still getting dressed on her way out the door and all Mac could do was lay there and grin.

Mac got up to piss about midnight. Jimmy still wasn't back, so Mac went outside and smoked a cigarette. Back inside, he turned out all the lights and found his bunk. Smelling Karen all over again, he wondered what it would be like to come home to her every night.

Four more rifles were done when Master Sergeant Taylor came in Monday morning and he was grinning from ear to ear. Sipping his coffee, the big sergeant told Mac that he and his wife had a great time at the Sheraton and that some dumb captain had called, checking to see if Mac was having "a good time."

Mac told the sergeant about the beach party and, using the captain's words, said, "It was a very 'good time.'"

Taylor looked over—all serious—and said to the Ranger, "You wanna stay, right? I'll fix it. Stay here and work with me."

Mac thought seriously before answering. "Naw, Sarge, I gotta get back to my buddies. Ahhh, can I fly back with you when you take this shit over?"

Taylor knew that was the answer Mac was going to give. "Yeah, you can fly with us if there's room."

Grinning, Mac said, "OK, Sarge, but if you got any ammo let's test fire these. Don't wanna drag these back if they don't shoot."

The sergeant understood what Mac was saying about his buddies. "OK, let me check out what kinda ammo we got," and the sergeant stood up.

Mac leaned over and picked up his rifle where Karen had put it against the wall. The butt plate was full of sand, so he took out the two screws holding the plate and cleaned it. Wiping a few stray grains of sand off the wooden stock, he put his finger in the oil bottle hole—drilled for that purpose in all the stocks. His was packed with cosmoline that had turned black with age. Using a screwdriver, he began to pull out the old grease. He was hoping to find a forgotten oil bottle in the hole. No such luck. The old grease came out in chunks. Mac kept dropping the grease on a rag and had to keep using fresh rags to clean the screwdriver. The last chunk of cosmoline came out in the largest piece of all. He got up and went outside with the rifle. In the bright sunshine, he looked down the hole he'd just cleaned. *Good. Got it all.* Screwing the clean butt plate on, he leaned the rifle against the wall, but this time he placed a rag under the plate to keep it clean.

He went back to the barracks to get a Pepsi and his smokes. Returning to work on the last of the weapons, he started wrapping up the rag containing the old grease. The largest chunk of the black, smelly stuff had begun to melt in the sunlight. A small sliver of white in the grease caught his eye. He picked up the warm piece of grease and turned it over and over. He could see some kind of paper in the grease. Laying the chunk back on the rag, he used his pocket knife to carefully separate the grease from the paper. Laying it flat on the work table and using a soft, clean rag, he wiped the small piece of paper. "INSPECTED BY BETTY 1942" *Wow this is an old motherfucker.* He turned the paper over and found more writing. He had to go outside to read it. It looked like it had been written in pencil. Holding it to the light, he could make out, "Sgt Wallace Wallace USMC RR 2 Crockett Mills Tenn.," and what looked like, "shoots good." Disappointed that it wasn't a treasure map, Mac carefully folded the paper and put it in his wallet, wondering if Betty the inspector gave head as good as Karen. *Probably not. They didn't do shit like that way back then.*

Sergeant Taylor came in lugging a wooden crate of ammo and slammed it on the table. "A thousand rounds to get started," and he chuckled. Both men pried the case open and found that the bullets were wrapped in greasy waxed brown paper.

Really old shit, Mac thought.

Reading his thoughts, Sergeant Taylor said, "Korea. So this shit ain't that old." Sitting down, he added, "I got the long distance range for tomorrow."

"Shit, Sarge, we'll be able to do some shootin' for sure. Hey, Sarge, I saw a gun shop outside the gate. If you're goin' by there, how about drop me off? Might as well spend some money."

Taylor looked at the young man. "Sure. He's a friend of mine. Let's go down there for lunch."

The master sergeant drove a black Camaro. Seeing Mac's

admiring glance, the sergeant said, "It's a '68. Got the 327 under the hood. My fuckin' kids always wanna borrow it." Both soldiers were laughing as they got in the car. On the way to the gun shop Sergeant Taylor told Mac more about the car. Then Taylor wanted to know exactly what they did back at the Quonset huts over the weekend.

"Where's Jimmy?" Mac asked.

Taylor explained that Jimmy was picking up radios and spare parts. The trade in "war souvenirs"—which were usually semi-legal weapons the green beanies got in Nam— were sold and the money was used for shit that the teams needed and couldn't get through regular supply channels. The money also went to the family of any Special Forces trooper wounded or killed in action. Pulling up to a red light the big sergeant added, "The Army takes care of its own."

Mac hardly heard him. Karen's Mustang pulled up next to them. Her husband was driving. Karen was in the passenger seat and didn't even look in Mac's direction.

Sergeant Taylor caught Mac looking in the Mustang. "You be careful with that, Mac. That pussy can get you killed quicker than the VC."

"I really like her, Sarge." Mac looked at the black sergeant. Taylor was already pulling into the Recoil Gun Shop's parking lot.

"It's time you go back to Nam before you get it any worse. You don't need that on your mind where you're goin' back to." Both men got out of the Camaro.

As they went in the door Mac said, "You're right about that, Sarge."

Several customers were in the shop so Taylor didn't get his normal greeting. "Hey, J.L., this skinny shit the gunslinger you were telling me about?" Shotgun Charlie introduced himself to the embarrassed soldier.

"Ah, John McDonald," and Mac stuck his hand out. Mac looked around while J.L. and his brother-in-law were talking. When they took a pause, Mac asked if Charlie had any hollow points for his .38.

"How many boxes?" Charlie asked, reaching behind him.

"Two boxes, sir." Charlie laughed at that. Mac was looking at the picture of the two Marines with the dead crocodile. Pointing at the picture and the Marine with the rifle, Mac asked, "You got any hot ammo for those .06s? I'm gonna try out that rifle." Mac was still staring at the picture.

Charlie put two more boxes of ammo on the counter. "Hundred and eighty grain Winchester. Now these will really get out there. Make sure your rifle is in as good a shape as old Wallace's there," and he nodded at the picture.

Mac reached for his wallet and removed the folded piece of paper. Smoothing it out, he handed it to Charlie. Puzzled, Charlie put on his glasses and, holding the paper under a bright light, started to read. "No," Mac said. "Read the other side."

Charlie got a little pale under his tan and handed the notepaper to Taylor. "I don't believe this. Mac, where did you get this?"

Mac told both men how he'd found the note hidden in the grease that he'd pulled out of the Smith Corona's butt stock. "I can't make out that word there," and Mac pointed at the last word.

"Ahhhh hell, that's easy, if you knew Wallace Wallace and that rifle. Says 'Shoots good.'" Charlie picked up the note. "Motherfucker made sergeant. I'm gonna write to this address and see if he's living there, or if they know where he is. If that rifle you got is the one that Wallace had," Charlie continued, "then that's the one he had here and killed that croc with." All three men were now staring at the picture.

Taylor asked Mac, "What're you gonna' do with this high powered shit? Blow yourself up? Those old rifles may not take to firin' this shit," and Sergeant Taylor picked up a box of bullets.

"Shit, Sarge, these ain't those Mattel toys we're usin' in Nam. These motherfuckers were built to last. Usin' this 180-grain hot round will let me get out there. Just wantin' to see what they'll do."

The conversation went from man to man, talking about all the good weapons they had shot. Charlie took the note into his office, copied the address and when he came back out he handed the note back to Mac.

"No, sir. You keep it and send it in the letter."

"Don't call me 'sir,'" Charlie said. Snapping his fingers, he said, "'Shirley,' that's what he called that rifle. Yeah. 'Shirley.'" Charlie charged Mac cost for the ammo and tried to sell him a gunslinger leather belt and holster. Both soldiers were laughing as they went out the door.

Mac wanted to know what kind of soldiers were going to be firing the reconditioned rifles back in Nam. All Sergeant Taylor could tell him was that the rifles would be divided up, two per Special Forces camp, and the Americans would be firing them. The little people didn't like the heavy weapons. They wouldn't be humped in the bush—"Just used at the bases to knock Charlie's dick in the dirt when he comes fuckin' around."

Mac could picture the firebases in Nam. Back at the Quonset hut, he started thinking of a way to improve the shooting. In the dumpster full of trash, he found two pieces of 2x2 pine and immediately began measuring and cutting.

Sergeant Taylor went over all the rifles. He liked the painted sight blades. "What are you making now?" the big sergeant wanted to know.

Finished, Mac set the pieces of pine on the work table.

He laid a rifle on the pine X he'd made. He'd used a piece of string and a couple of small nails to make the shooter's rest adjustable. "These old rifles will reach out there and hit whatever you're shootin' at. Just need to be rock steady."

Really gonna have to be steady with that hot ammo."

Mac grinned. "Where's my pistola, Sergeant? Gotta try that too." Sergeant Taylor pointed to the wall locker. When he took the pistol from the locker, Mac saw that Taylor had already cleaned it. "Thanks, Sarge." Mac and Sergeant Taylor finished the last two rifles as they talked about the oddity of finding the rifle that had been used by the old marine. Of all the rifles they'd reworked, only one was unserviceable. It was the only other Smith Corona in the bunch and the barrel had been shot out.

Taylor was working on it, making it look as good as the others. "What are you gonna do with that one, Sarge?" Mac asked.

Taylor looked over. "I'm gonna give this one to Shotgun Charlie to hang in the gun shop."

All the weapons were done before the afternoon was half over. Spraying the bolts of the rifles to be test-fired the next day, Mac finished the first can of silicone oil. As Taylor prepared to leave, he said, "I'll lay on a truck for us to use tomorrow, and I'll drop this rifle off at Charlie's. Then I'm gonna help Jimmy get those radios together." Heading out the door, Taylor added, "See you tomorrow."

Mac found a can of olive drab spray paint and coated the rifle rest. It took him another hour to clean up and put all the stuff away. Then, next to the weapons, he put earplugs and various screw drivers and other items he needed for the range the next day. He added both of the extractors, in case shells got caught in any of the rifles. He picked up his rifle from against the wall and locked the Quonset hut. *I need something to eat,* he thought, and went into the kitchen part of the barracks. He laid the old rifle on the table and looked at it. *Shirley, if you could talk, what a story you could tell.* He liked that name. As he rummaged for food, he thought, *I wonder why he called you that.*

When Sergeant Taylor dropped the rifle off at the gun shop, he helped Charlie hang it. Charlie said that he'd typed a letter and sent it off to the address on the note. Taylor saw that the note itself was already stuck in plastic and pinned next to the picture on the wall.

Mac was pleasantly surprised when Karen appeared. She entered the kitchen, kissed him and immediately asked, "Why's that gun on the table?"

Mac told her the story of the rifle and that he was going to keep this one and take it back with him to the Rangers in Nam.

"You're not a Green Beret?" she asked. "What do Rangers do?"

Seeing her worried look, Mac said, "We mostly drive trucks all over Nam. That's why they call us Rangers."

Her relief was evident. She put her arms around his neck. "I'm so glad. It's not dangerous is it?"

Mac had his hand up her skirt feeling around and continuing his fooling around added, "You're more dangerous than the enemy," and he laughed.

She broke away. "Wait a minute," and she ran out the door. She returned and handed him a bag of shrimp.

Mac looked in the bag. "These are huge. Wow!"

"You wash up," Karen said, taking the shrimp, "and I'll cook these."

Remembering the day before, Mac was in the shower as fast as he could get there. And, like the day before, dinner was late but still enjoyable. When Mac fell asleep that night he was still in Karen's arms. When Mac awoke he found that she had left a note stuck to his pillow—a smiley face and kisses and hugs.

Mac saw that Jimmy was asleep, alone in his bunk. After he was done in the latrine, Mac woke him up. As they ate stale doughnuts and drank coffee, Mac asked Jimmy if he was going to come to the range and shoot. Jimmy said, "Hell yeah, brah."

As Sergeant Taylor drove the deuce-and-a-half out Highway 93 to a military post that had rifle ranges, Mac was once again surprised by the sheer size of the island of Hawaii.

The range they got to use only had targets out to six hundred yards. Mac liked the idea that Taylor had brought along a spotting scope to check bullet strikes on the targets. Mac used military ball ammo for the first three shots he fired through Shirley. He only had to move the sight one click and the next three shots were in a half-inch group at one hundred yards. He loaded five rounds of hot ammo. Four targets fell at six hundred yards. He missed his last shot; his right shoulder felt like it had been kicked by a mule. Before he loaded any more of the hot rounds, he took a pair of wool Army socks from a pocket in his coveralls and slipped one over the metal butt plate. Five more shots knocked down five targets. Next, he tried again with the military ammo and got three out of five. He cleared his rifle and got to his feet. "See what I mean, Sarge? That military shit ain't as good as the hot stuff."

The three soldiers got into good firing positions. They fired every rifle and got them all zeroed. All of the rifles did better with the hot ammo and not one blew up. When they were finished, each weapon had a new tag through the trigger housing, the date it was zeroed, and name of the firer. They policed up all their spent brass and Sergeant Taylor asked Mac if he had any more hot ammo. "Got ten rounds left, Sarge."

"See that cinder block out beyond six hundred?" Taylor asked. "The red one on the dirt berm?"

"Yup, I see it. You want me to hit it, Sarge?" and Mac grabbed his rifle.

"Yeah," the sergeant said, sitting down at a cleaning table. "Let's see what it'll do."

Mac used the X-shaped rest this time. Getting into a prone position behind the rifle, he set his sights for eight hundred yards. "Call the shots, Sarge." Taylor didn't have to call anything. Eight of Mac's bullets destroyed the cinder block and the other two shots were so close that if he had been aiming at man-sized objects it would have been a kill. As they cleaned the rifles before heading back in, Taylor asked Mac to make up a shooting rest for each rifle. The three made short work of cleaning the rifles—they'd get the full treatment back at the workshop. Sergeant Taylor stopped the truck alongside the highway on the way back in and they all went swimming.

Back at the Quonset hut, the sergeant left Mac and Jimmy to finish cleaning the rifles and he took off. Jimmy asked Mac where he'd learned to shoot like that. Mac told him how he'd grown up with guns and hunting, about how he got lots of time on the shooting range during his time in the Canadian Army.

When Sergeant Taylor returned, he had one hundred boxes of the hot 180-grain bullets, both Remington and Winchester. "Give me a hand. I got all Charlie had."

"Holy shit, Sarge, this shit musta cost a fortune," Mac said.

"No. I traded for three cases of the military shit. Charlie will double his money."

Mac put a box of each next to his clean rifle. "I'll try 'em both," he said.

The Ranger made shooting rests for each of the rifles and used up all the OD spray, painting the sticks green.

When Sergeant Taylor came back from his office, he said, "The plane gets in at 0400 and leaves at noon. That will give us plenty of time to get our shit loaded. Mac, you make sure you get all the weapons. Jimmy, you get all the radio shit. As for uniforms—everybody in tiger stripes." Anticipating his question before Mac could ask, Taylor held up his hand, "Jimmy will show you where they're kept. And Mac, if you're not comin' back, make sure you got all your shit, OK? Now, anything else that you guys can think of?" There was silence so Sergeant Taylor said, "OK, that's it. Let's get out of here. We'll have plenty of time for clean-up tomorrow."

The three men were sitting at the table—drinking beer and bullshitting—they had the shit scared out of them when Karen came in screaming, "You fuckin' lying little cocksucker!" Crying, then pausing for a breath she continued. "Rangers aren't truck drivers you lying piece of shit!"

Jimmy and Taylor started laughing. "We'll leave you two lovebirds alone." As the two headed out the door, Sergeant Taylor looked back. "Truck driver—huh!"

Mac turned to face Karen and got a slap right across the face. "I already have to live with one liar. Why didn't you tell me the truth?" and her whole body sagged as she sat down at the table.

"Ahhh, honey." Mac knelt beside her and put his arms around her. "You got enough to worry about. I didn't want you to worry about me, too." Mac kissed her cheek. "I'm sorry, honey." The couple went out and sat on the grass, watching the empty airstrip and talking until dark. Not until Mac promised to write and Karen gave him her girlfriend's address did she finally calm down.

When Mac told her they were leaving the next day, she

grabbed his hand and pulled him toward her car. Dinner—already made—was in containers in a box on the front seat. Handing the box to Mac she said, "Here, you carry that. I'll bring the salad." The intensity of their lovemaking that night had both of them weeping. Mac was so sore he had to sit down to piss. He couldn't even hold his sore dick. When Karen left, she was walking like a duck. Her last kiss was as sweet and soft as the first. As she drove away, Mac thought he heard her say, "I love you," but he wasn't sure. Mac found her panties under his pillow and as he fell asleep he had one thought: *I hope I get back here again.*

Jimmy woke him in the morning. He'd been with Candy all night on the beach. "Looks like my orders are gonna be coming through any day now for a full tour in Nam."

"Hot damn, brah," Mac said. "You can come fuck around on the Ranger team with me and we'll get you out there in Indian country."

Most of the morning was spent loading the cargo plane. *Shit,* Mac thought, *might even be the same one I flew over here on.* The last thing they did was shower, shave and get into brand new tiger-striped jungle fatigues. The camoed fatigues were hard as hell to get in Vietnam. Since the whole room was full of brand new sets, Mac turned and asked Sergeant Taylor if he could have enough for his Ranger team.

"Sure," the big sergeant said.

Mac's duffle bag was stuffed when he got all the jungle suits in it. He wore his black Canadian Army beret when Jimmy and Sergeant Taylor put on their green berets.

"Where did you get that?" Jimmy asked.

"In the Canadian army," and Mac fixed his at the same jaunty angle as theirs.

As the old plane was hauling ass down the runway and getting ready to fly, Sergeant Taylor nudged Mac and point-

ed out the porthole window. Mac caught a glimpse of
Karen and her red Mustang. She was standing up in the
convertible, waving. Mac waved back but the plane was airborne and he wondered if she even saw him.

The three soldiers slept through most of the flight and
when the plane opened its door at Tan Son Nhut Air Base
the stink of Vietnam was the only welcome they got.
Sergeant Taylor told them to unload their shit, to double
check to make sure they got it all and he'd go round up their
transport.

Once Mac and Jimmy had all their stuff piled on the
ground, their plane was towed away. Resting on their duffle
bags in the morning sun, Mac felt glad to be back. "Shit,
Jimmy, I've still got four days leave left," and he laughed.

Sergeant Taylor arrived with a three-quarter-ton truck
and a deuce-and-a-half, both with their canvas tops off and
windshields folded down. The two Special Forces sergeants
who were driving helped stack and pile the materiel in both
trucks. Taylor had already told Mac where they were going
so the last thing the troopers did was load their personal
weapons. Mac had his .38 on in its shoulder holster and he
loaded Shirley with six hot rounds—five in the magazine
and one up the spout. One of the Green Beret drivers
asked Mac, "Where'd you get that old fucker? Now that's a
rifle."

Mac told him they had a bunch more in the truck and if
he kissed Sergeant Taylor just right maybe the sergeant
could get one. The laughter over that had everybody in a
lighthearted mood. The youngest driver walked up to the
front truck and asked Sergeant Taylor if those rifles were
any good.

"Well, let's put it this way—I wouldn't want that fucker
shootin' at me," and they both got in the lead truck.

Up in the back of the deuce-and-a-half and breathing

deep, Mac thought, *Hot damn, it's good to be back here.* It was too bad Karen had found out what the Rangers did. *Probably her husband told her.*

Long Khann Special Forces camp had a little bit of everything. The part of the camp that the trucks pulled up to was well away from the recondo school, which was there. Sergeant Taylor took them to a compound all their own—it even had a Yard to guard the concertina wire gate. All the people coming and going were SF troopers. The trucks pulled up between two connex containers, metal boxes used for storage. The trucks were unloaded, then everybody carried their gear, following Sergeant Taylor into the barracks. They all had a choice of bunks and Taylor was the first to bitch about how his feet always hung off the end.

"Shit, Sarge, I'm just glad they're not bunk beds with you on top," Mac said. "Mortar attack and the bunk would fall right on top of my skinny ass." Everybody from out in the camp was coming in to talk to the big sergeant.

After awhile, the master sergeant came over to Mac who was helping Jimmy get his radio gear packed in different boxes. "Mac, I want you to run the range for me tomorrow. Four guys at a time. The longest we got is three hundred meters. Let them zero both rifles that they'll be taking back to their camps."

"OK, Sarge, I'll let them zero with the cheap ammo and then let them fire a couple of rounds of the hot shit," and Mac bent to help Jimmy move a box. Mac quickly made his bunk, then wrapped the mattress with a poncho liner and laid his rifle on top of a special piece of wool blanket he'd cut just for that. Everyone who walked by wanted to pick up the rifle and check it out. *At least they ask first,* Mac thought. Sergeant Taylor came back in and told them they were having steaks and potato salad for chow that night. They all laughed when Jimmy said, "Ain't war grand?"

13

The mansion sat on a quiet street surrounded by a vine-covered, whitewashed block wail. The gate was guarded by the South Vietnamese Army and the ARVN commander made money renting his troops out just for that purpose. Tex had his buddy Andre living in his own suite of rooms. Swan Blossom, who had a room somewhere in the huge house, ran the place better than any sergeant major could. Tex had almost completely recovered from his beating at the hands of the VC or NVA—Tex didn't know for sure who they were. Swan Blossom had come into Tex's bedroom one morning and informed the reporter it was time to get off his ass and back to work and she stood there and made sure that he got up.

The MPs had been to visit Tex once and informed the reporter that the kidnapping was a case of mistaken identity, but that they'd keep checking to make sure. *Fuck you,* thought the beaten up reporter. *It's not your life on the line.* Hoping he could wake up from the nightmare, he knew *I'm in the shit now. If I don't write what the gook general wants, I am most definitely dead meat.*

Limping from his sore foot, Tex left his bedroom. Swan Blossom appeared from nowhere and handed him a type-written list. His day's schedule. "Fuck you," he said out loud to the pretty woman's retreating back,

The list read: "MAC-V headquarters for lunch." There

was a circle around "Find out about any new army opera-tions." The whole day was laid out like that. Tex threw the paper on the floor. *Fuck, I'm really not ready for this.* He head-ed out the door and when he found out the ARVN gate guard spoke English he placed his order.

Andre came to the table where Tex was eating breakfast. Tex's cameraman buddy was still half drunk. "What's up, boss?" and he slumped into a chair at the table.

Tex laid out the day, just like the instructions. Swan Blossom came in with a clean set of chino pants and a bright, short-sleeved shirt. She even had a pair of black Oxfords. "You will wear this."

"And what the fuck's wrong with my fatigues? I'll look like I'm in the CIA," Tex complained. It did no good. She just dropped the clothes on the floor.

Andre said, "She likes you," and laughed.

Tex felt strange wearing the clothes. The ARVN was waiting for him when he left the house. Tex armed himself from the box of weapons the man had brought for him to look over. One military Colt .45 with a pistol belt for out-side and a snub-nosed .38 for his pants pocket. As he paid the ARVN, Tex wondered if he had any grenades. *Shit.* Looking around his compound on the way out, Tex spot-ted four gooks doing gardening work.

Fuck, I'm surrounded. The driver he had hired himself was a suspect too. *All these fuckers are probably VC, just to keep an eye on me.*

The only thing Tex learned at MAC-V was that the ambassador was having a dinner party and Tex was invited. He also received a new ID card. Now he could fly anywhere in the country, at any time. Reporters who wouldn't give him the time of day a week ago were now high-fiving him and stopping him to bullshit. Tex talked to an MP Major who told him, "Too bad about the kidnapping. Fuckin' mistaken identity," and he said they would follow up any leads.

Fuck you very much, Tex thought, and left for his next appointment. *Shit, this is just like a regular job. I can't even stop and drink where I want.*

Back at the house that evening, Tex typed out a bullshit story about how stressful it was for the guys working in the morgue. The strain of preparing bodies for the trip back to the world had them all on drugs. *I'll file this tomorrow,* and he pulled it out of the typewriter. He'd been drinking most of the day just to keep the fear away. Swan Blossom came in and read the story, then she questioned him about what he'd done that day. Tex got really pissed and grabbed the Vietnamese girl. When he got a little carried away and started to pull her pants down, she very quickly bounced him all over the room. *My nuts will never work again,* was all he could think of as he hopped to his bedroom.

He slept nude except he was wearing his .45. The snub-nosed .38 went under his pillow. It seemed like he was up every hour— all night long—looking out the window. Tex went downhill fast. Drinking all the time, not even able to fuck any of the girls that Swan Blossom brought to the house for him to "look over."

The night of the party at the ambassador's residence, Tex was sure one of the gook waiters was the general. He tried going to the field with the grunts and was preparing to leave when his driver disappeared and his jeep wouldn't start.

When he cranked out two stories for the *Dallas Star,* his editor wired back that they were shit. Half shit-faced all the time, he kept trying to find a way out of the mess he was in. Andre got pissed off and moved back into the reporters' barracks. On a day off from the airline, Jeannie had come for dinner and walked out, calling him an asshole. Tex had a small black ball of opium in his bedroom and he was thinking of trying it. Maybe it would make the dragon called fear go away.

14

The headquarters building of the 199th Light Infantry Brigade was a very quiet place, even with everybody working. Charlie Company of the 4th Battalion, 12th Infantry, had hit the shit the day before. In an all-day fight, the company had six killed and fifteen wounded. The gooks had homemade claymores hanging in the trees protecting their bunkers. Nothing more than large metal cans, filled with glass, nails, nuts and bolts backed up with gunpowder and set off by an electrical charge. The grunts had been right underneath the claymores when Sir Charles set them off. Four GIs were killed instantly; two more died that afternoon before the medevac choppers could get in. Wounds were severe. One platoon sergeant, whose el tee was one of the first killed, lost his arm. Late that afternoon, with the bunker complex in American hands, the grunts had found twenty-seven dead gooks and fifteen automatic weapons. There was no telling what the actual count was. Blood trails led everywhere. The gooks had dragged away most of the dead and wounded.

Charlie Company was just outside a firebase, licking its wounds. Hot chow and fresh uniforms were first on the list of resupply. The replacements would be on the second lift coming in that afternoon. They had one extra day to get back up to strength, then a short company-sized patrol and they'd be brought in for a three-day rest. Sergeant Major

Bill Mateau sat behind his desk, just staring at the pile of paperwork on his desk. He and the general had walked into the bunker complex after Charlie Company had secured it. Blood and body parts had been everywhere. Even in the shade of the jungle the heat hammered the men. Water was just as critical as more ammo and it had to be brought in. The sergeant major walked the gear-laden path the grunts had fought on. Except for black patches in the trees where the gooks had blown the claymores he thought, *I'd have walked right up on the hanging mines too.* The bunkers were invisible foot-long gun ports and they were impossible to see unless a soldier was right on top of them. The platoon sergeant who had his arm blown off was on his second tour and the rest of the platoon had an average of three months in country. *What a fuckin' way to fight a war.* The more experience the unit had, the more they kicked the VC's ass and the casualties were low. The area where Charlie Company ran into the gooks was on a list that small teams of Rangers were scheduled to check out, but the brigade didn't have enough teams to get all the tasks done. Morale was high in Charlie Company after their major ass-kick. Hopefully it would stay that way.

With the general at the hospital visiting the wounded, the sergeant major was doing all he could, even signing the letters going out to the families of the killed and maimed. When his phone rang he was glad for the distraction. The sergeant major running the recondo school down at Long Khan was returning his call. After fifteen minutes of shooting the shit, Bill still couldn't get him to give him more training slots so his Rangers could get more training. The sergeant major at the school would see what he could do, but that was as firm a commitment as Bill could get. The 199th had a one-week school for all replacements, taught by "Kit Carson scouts" and guys right out of the bush. Gooks who had surrendered and who now worked for the Americans also taught classes. So far, it was helping. The rotation process still sucked; the men who finally got experience in the bush went home and all the lessons they had learned went with them. *Fuck it. Starting today I'm going to take volunteers right out of the Redcatcher school—anybody that wants to go into the Rangers.* Men in the bush weren't volunteering and the sergeant major could understand that. Guys wanted to stay with their outfits and more than that, with their friends.

The other call he made was to the head Mess Daddy, and he got four cases of steaks to take down to the recondo school. Whatever it took to give the men a chance to stay alive, the sergeant major was going to do it. His driver was on R&R and all the brigade choppers were in use. Even the general's bird was out flying resupply, so the sergeant major ended up driving himself down to Long Khann. The recondo school was in a pretty safe area down by Vung Tau. The sergeant major had heard that even the gooks used it for R&R. The four cases of steaks took up the whole back of his jeep. The Americans he passed on the road would have hijacked him had they known what he was carrying. His trip to the school and the steaks paid off big time. It turned out that the two sergeants major had served in the same unit, way back when.

Sergeant Major Mateau ended up getting two slots per class for his brigade—more than that if some other unit dropped the ball and didn't fill their slots. The recondo school taught rappelling, tracking, trail hiding, shooting, and a variety of other skills. Each student coming out of the school was sent back to his unit with added proficiencies and they were also up to date on Charlie's latest tactics. His business done at the school, the sergeant major headed across the base for the main gate. He was not prepared for what he saw as he drove by the Special Forces compound.

It looked like Sergeant Taylor leaning against the hood of his three-quarter-ton truck, going over paperwork. Bill slammed on the brakes, already hollering: "You ugly queer cocksucker. You are still the ugliest motherfucker I've ever seen!"

Master Sergeant J.L. Taylor looked up and through the fence at the Sergeant Major Mateau. "Come on in, you fuckin' queer Cajun," and he motioned at the sergeant major to drive in the gate. He yelled at the gook gate guard to let the sergeant major in. Taylor was waiting for Mateau as he parked his jeep. The affection that the men felt was evident. They had served together all over the world. J.L. towered over the Cajun sergeant major and they both talked at the same time, trying to get caught up on all the news. The noise from the firing range made it hard to talk, so J.L. dragged Mateau inside the barracks. The men sat, slamming down beers and the latest gossip.

Taylor wanted Mateau to stay in the compound and party for the night, and Bill kept telling him he had to get back to the brigade. J.L. had served three tours in Nam beginning in '62, so the news was all about who got promoted and where their friends were serving now. One more beer and Bill was out the door and headed for his jeep, both men still talking. As Bill was about to start his jeep, he looked over at the firing range.

"J.L.," Mateau asked, "Who's that guy there?"

J.L. looked where the sergeant major was pointing. "Shit, Bill, that's one of your guys. Been workin' with Jimmy and me over in Hawaii."

"You grunt-stealin' motherfucker. He's supposed to be in Hawaii on leave." Bill looked at his friend. "What's he doin' with you?" and he started to get out of his jeep.

Master Sergeant Taylor held him to his seat. "Now don't you go off half-cocked. Just watch." The sergeant major had no choice—Taylor held him to his seat. By the time J.L. told him the story of what happened in Hawaii and how Jimmy had dragged Mac off the beach after Mac had shot up a kid's surfboard, Bill was laughing right along with J.L. "You remember the picture of the dead crocodile that hangs in the Recoil Gun Shop over Charlie's cash register?" J.L. asked.

"Yeah, I remember Charlie before he lost his leg. And I remember the picture," Bill replied.

"Well, the rifle that fucker got up there with him— that's the one from the picture," and J.L. went on and told his friend how Mac had found out who the first guy was who used it.

"I'm glad he's down here," Bill said. "Now I'll put the fucker right over there in school and he can learn something."

J.L. just shook his head. "Waste of time. The fucker's been in the Canadian Army already. Had good trainin'. Besides, you need the slots for guys who need trainin'."

Both men watched Mac giving the Special Forces soldiers instruction on the old rifles. The Special Forces sergeants already knew how to shoot; all Mac did was refine it a little. One sergeant's rifle kept shooting to the right. Mac got down beside the man and, pulling out a pipe cleaner, recleaned the peep sight. After that the rifle was right on. One of the other sergeants needed something to cushion recoil. After Mac helped him put a sock over the butt, the sergeant zeroed both of his rifles without a problem.

The engineers had built the U-shaped range just for the green beanies, but it only had targets out to two hundred meters. Most of the weapons fired on it were pistols and suppressed specialty weapons, like 9mm Uzis. The older sergeant watched as Mac walked downrange and placed a silver #10 can on the berm behind the targets, about halfway up the dirt mound. Both sergeants could see the young man counting his steps on his way back to the firing line. The four sergeants he was teaching gathered around as Mac talked, then he got down behind his rifle, loaded it, and laid it across the X shooter's rest that he'd made.

Baloom... Click... Baloom.. . Click. . . Baloom. .. Click. . . and Mac opened the bolt, laid the rifle on the rest and went downrange to get the can.

"What the fuck is he usin', J.L.?" Bill wanted to know.

"He's usin' 180-grain real hot shit. Zips right out there," Taylor said.

"Yeah, well it don't look like he did very fuckin' good. Seems like there's only one hole in the can," the sergeant major said.

Mac was back on the firing line showing the can to the sergeants. Mac handed out boxes of the hot ammo and the sergeants were down behind their rifle. Mateau waited until the Special Forces sergeants were done shooting before he made his move. Following the sergeant major, Taylor was surprised at the mild greeting between the sergeant major and the Ranger. Mateau picked up the can Mac had shot at. There was only one hole and he could tell all three shots had been close together—almost all in the same hole. The sergeant major was impressed, especially when the other four sergeants held up their targets. Even though their targets were close at only two hundred meters, they'd all shot very tight groups with the hot ammo.

Once everyone cleared the firing range, Sergeant Major Mateau went to town on Mac. "You fuckin' cocksucker. You had ten days leave. What in the fuck you think you're doin' back over here hangin' around with these green wienies?" and the sergeant major went on and on, covering everything Mac should have been doing and wasn't. He almost went too far when he said Mac could stay with the

Special Forces guys for all he cared. Mac would have stayed except the sergeant major added that his Ranger team was getting ready for another mission.

At that, Mac said, "Let me get my stuff, Sergeant Major, and give my rifle a quick clean and I'll be right with you."

The sergeant major wasn't stupid. He needed every trooper he could get. When Mac went into the barracks, Taylor told Mateau, "You're a fuckin' prick, Bill. If you wouldn't have mentioned his team, he'd a stayed right here."

"That's right, and that's why I'm a sergeant major and you're just a green beanie," and laughing, Bill went on to tell how he thought Mac had not only eaten all the patients' breakfasts over at the 93rd Evac hospital, "but they think he put twelve unconscious wounded men in for the Medal of Honor."

"Sounds just like him," Taylor added, laughing.

"And wait, this'll blow your socks off," and Taylor told Mateau about Mac putting hemorrhoid ointment on his cut head, thinking it was first-aid cream. Their laughter continued to build as the sergeant major told Taylor about the MPs who drove Mac back to the brigade. "They weren't only fucked up—they wanted to join the infantry." The laughter was interrupted when Mac came out with all his stuff, ready to get in the jeep.

"Mac," and Taylor stopped him. "If Bill here," and he pointed to the sergeant major, "don't need you any more, you come on back here and work for me," and the black sergeant stuck out his hand to shake. "Thanks for a good job—and take care of that rifle, hear?"

Mac lit up like a Christmas tree. "Ahhh, damn. I had a good time, Sarge. Tell Charlie I'm gonna get an elephant with this rifle." Then he handed the big sergeant a letter. "Would you give this to Karen for me, Sarge?"

"Sure, Mac. See you next trip," and Taylor watched them

drive out the gate.

Sergeant Major Mateau looked over at Mac. "You really get that black beret in the army up in Canada?"

Mac finished loading his bolt gun and set the safety. "Yup, sure did, Sergeant Major," and he pointed the rifle out the right side of the jeep. The sergeant major had served with Canadians in Germany and Korea, so the two had a lot to talk about.

As they rode along, Mateau kept coming back to the same thing—the extra training Mac had gotten. *No wonder the fucker knows what he's doin'.* "What kinda drill sergeants you have up there in the Canadian Army?" he asked.

Mac looked over and laughed. "Only saw a drill sergeant once a week for an inspection. The rest of the time it was two corporals. They lived right with us. They were responsible for the day-to-day shit."

"Well, they did a good job. It sounds like the old army to me. You're gonna have to hold off wearin' those tiger stripe fatigues. Can't have you wearin' that shit and the rest of your team goin' without."

Mac looked over and said, "I got a set for the whole team," and he pointed to his old brown duffle bag.

Little fucker's one ahead of me, the sergeant major thought. "What're you gonna do with that old fuckin' bolt gun?"

"Seriously, I'm gonna shoot an elephant, Sergeant Major."

As Bill looked over at his young Ranger, he could tell that Mac would shoot an elephant if he could. "Taylor's been over here three tours and I've been here for two and neither one of us have seen an elephant." Chuckling, the sergeant major added, "You gonna eat it or what?" Thinking along those lines, the sergeant major thought, *A couple of more missions under his belt and I'll make Mac a team leader.*

As the jeep sped along, Mac pointed to three hooches

alongside the road. "Ahhhh, can you pull in there, Sergeant Major?"

"You need to piss?" Bill asked.

"Naw, I need some chow, Sergeant Major. Fast Eddy showed us this place when we was guardin' that bridge back there. You know my old platoon sergeant?"

Bill answered as he pulled up next to the hooch made of flattened beer and soda cans. "Oh yeah, me and Eddy go way back. I was Eddy's drill sergeant when he took basic training."

Mac looked at the sergeant major. "You don't look like a prick, Sergeant Major," and he hopped out of the jeep.

All Bill could do was laugh and holler, "You're not gonna eat gook food, are ya?"

"Shit yeah. Come on, Sergeant Major" and Mac waved to the sergeant. Mateau had never eaten any Vietnamese food. All the rumors about glass and rat poison in the chow had scared him so badly he'd never even been anywhere they served it. Mac came over to the jeep with a steaming bowl of soupy noodles and a bottle of Tiger 33. Setting both on the hood of the jeep and whipping out a loaf of fresh bread, he said "Try that Sergeant Major. Shit, there's no glass in it. Eddy says the gooks eat it, so it can't be all bad, and it beats the shit out of C-rations." Mac went back to old mama san and returned carrying the same thing. Mac ate gook style. Holding the bowl up to his chin, he used chopsticks and hungrily sucked the noodles. Watching the Ranger eat, Bill tried his bowl of soup and noodles. He was done before Mac.

The fresh bread was French style. Small loaves— three bites and it was gone. Both men had seconds. The sergeant major bought two packets of soup mix from mama san and four loaves of bread. Bill really liked the Tiger-piss beer. Gook kids rolled the brown bottles on a chunk of ice and handed it to the soldiers, chilled. Mac knew there was something wrong when the sergeant major tried to give mama san a five dollar tip. "Man, I really like this shit, Mac," and the sergeant major waved his beer bottle around.

"You're gettin' fucked up there, Sergeant Major. That shit will kick your ass," and Mac laughed.

As he continued to wave his beer bottle, the sergeant major said, "Just call me Bill, Mac."

Mac chuckled and helped the sergeant major into the passenger seat. Mama san hobbled over, wanting the empty beer bottle. "Hey Mac, get us a couple of those to go. I gotta let the general try this shit."

"OK, Bill," and Mac got two more bottles of the potent beer. As fucked up as Bill was, he got to see Mac in action. Mac paid for the beer and was heading back to the jeep. Mama san started to yell and carry on, trying to run alongside Mac. She wanted the bottles back. The gooks refilled the empties. Mac was fine until the old lady grabbed his arm. That old bolt gun came off his shoulder and was aimed right between the mama san's eyes. "Get the fuck outa here mama san," and the old lady had a change of heart right then and there.

Driving away, the last they heard was mama san calling out, "GI number huckin' ten."

The sergeant major thought it was hilarious. Still a little shaky when they got to the brigade main base, the sergeant major couldn't remember when he'd had such a good time. Mac climbed out of the jeep in front of the Ranger company. "You ok to drive, Sergeant Major?"

Bill was already walking around the jeep to get behind the wheel. "Yup, I'm better now. That was a good trip. See you in the green."

Before Mac could get his stuff out of the jeep, Rags had the grunt rolling in the dirt. The ugly dog had come roar-

ing out of the barracks and her tail was wagging so hard
Mac thought her ass was going to fall off. The sergeant
major was driving away as the rest of the Rangers came out
of the barracks. Flash Gordon—the staff sergeant in
charge of the team—came over to the ditch where Mac and
Rags were wrestling. "What the fuck you doin' back here
already?"

Hollywood wanted to know where Mac got the tiger
stripes. Washington was asking if Mac got any pussy. Mac
felt he was home. The questioning continued all the way
into the barracks. After setting his rifle on his empty bunk,
Mac met Larry Alchesay, a full-blooded Apache from the
White Mountains in Arizona. He was the Ranger who had
been in Recondo School when Mac went on his first mission with the team. Shaking hands, Larry said, "Call me
Chief. Everybody else does. Don't know why." Everyone
laughed over that.

Mac opened his duffle bag and pulled out the extra sets
of tiger stripes. "I got these from the green beanies..." That
was as far as he got. The swarm of Rangers were grabbing
at the fatigues. Eventually everyone got the size that fit the
best. Mac reached back down in the bag and pulled out a
bottle of Canadian Club whiskey and handed it to Flash.
"Have to share it out, Sarge."

The Rangers had begun rolling in the aisles with laughter. Mac had given Rags a huge rawhide bone and Rags
couldn't get it through the door of her doghouse. Snapping
and growling, she would back up and take another run at
the door. Laughing as hard as everyone else, Mac took the
bone from the dog and set it inside the door. When the
laughter died down Flash asked him, "Where'd you get that
old rifle at, and what're you gonna do with it?"

Mac took a page right out of his team leader's book.
"Ain't it time for chow, Sarge?" On the way to the mess hall

the Rangers all agreed that now they really looked bad in their new tiger stripes. Flash told Mac that they were going on a mission the day after tomorrow and they'd talk about it after chow.

When the sergeant major saw General Davis going toward his office, he had one of the clerks help him prepare the noodle soup. Carrying the soup, beer, and bread into the general's office, the sergeant major wouldn't take no for an answer. The general was convinced to try the soup after he got a whiff of it. Two slurps later, "Shit, this is good, Bill. Where'd you get this?" and he tore off another chunk of fresh bread.

As he sat and watched the general eat, Bill said, "This is my second tour over here and I never ate gook food until today or drank their beer," and he burped. "I know neither have you. No wonder we have such a hard time. We don't know half the shit we should about these people."

Drinking more of his beer, the general said, "I know I like this stuff," and he waved the half empty beer around.

"You're not going to believe this," they both said at the same time. The general went first. "This is a letter from the owner of the Rolex watch. It seems that he was a lieutenant at Dien Bien Phu and was there when the garrison surrendered. Some gook took the watch away and he never saw the gook again. When the gooks sent the Frenchmen home—after a couple of years in their prison—he retired a captain." Looking at the letter, the general went on. "His wife gave him the watch in England during World War Two. Here, he sent a picture of him and his family."

The sergeant major looked at the picture while the general continued. "Seems he wants to send Mac a personal thank you. Whatta you think, Bill?"

"Well sir, that brings me to the next point," and the sergeant major took a sip of his tiger piss beer. "You owe me some money. Mac's back. I just dropped him off at the Ranger company." Bill told the general all he'd learned about Mac's trip to Hawaii and even told him how Mac had shot the Hawaiian's surfboard. Both men laughed over that. "But that fucker would not admit that he changed the tags on the patients' beds and submitted every one of them for the Medal of Honor. He did admit to eating all of their breakfasts, though."

"That's bullshit, Bill. You owe me the money on the bet. Do you think he could have been the one who drugged up those patients while he was down there at that hospital?"

"I really don't know, sir. The kid leads with his heart sometimes, and if those guys were hurtin', yeah, it's somethin' he'd do. Let me tell you, he's gettin' to be one salty sonofabitch," and Bill told the general about Mac sticking his rifle in old mama san's face. Then he told how Mac had acquired the .30-.06 rifle, "and believe it or not the rifle killed a crocodile on the island of Guadalcanal in 1942, so Mac is goin' to at least try and kill an elephant with it here in Nam."

Listening and talking, both men agreed they'd missed out by not drinking the tiger piss beer before. "Bill, find out if Mac's got a brother. We need all that we can get like him over here."

After chow, the Rangers were back in the barracks and bugging Flash to open the bottle of Canadian whiskey. Flash held his hand up for quiet. Pointing at Mac lying on his bunk with Rags at his feet, Flash said, "Tell us the story of the rifle, then I'll go over the mission. After that we'll get some drinkin' done."

Mac had the rifle hanging by its sling on a four-inch nail he had driven into the wall. He grabbed the rifle, opened the bolt, checked to make sure it was empty, then he handed it to Hollywood. "Pass it around. That is a 1903A3 Smith

Corona .30-.06. Believe it or not, that's a Marine Corps issue rifle," and for the next half hour he told the story of the rifle. He even passed around some of the hot ammo rounds. Hanging the rifle back up, he said, "Your turn, Sarge."

Flash was already at the blackboard and started the pre-mission briefing.

"Mac, you plannin' on humpin' that heavy motherfucker out there?" Flash asked.

"Fuckin' a, Sarge."

Staff Sergeant Gordon wrote ".30-.06" in the weapons column on the board. Every weapon—personal or issue—was accounted for before a mission, even the pistols that some of the Rangers carried. Flash went on and outlined the mission. It would be a combined trail watching—and if they got a chance—a prisoner snatch. Also a move down to the river to check a certain area to see if gooks were unloading sampans there. "Now I don't know if we'll do the river first or the trail, so let's go over the maps." When the maps had been studied, Flash said, "Here's how the team is going to stack up. Chief, you're on point. Hollywood next. Me in the middle. Bones, you're humpin' the radio until Mac gets broke in at slack." The bitching broke out right away. Everybody except Chief wanted to change jobs. Flash ignored them all. "NOW," and everyone paid attention, "we'll zero all our weapons in the morning. Mac, let Hollywood fire that rifle, too, in case you're hit. Then we'll get over to the tailor shop and have all our shit put on these new—thanks to Mac—tiger stripes. Now," grabbing the bottle of Canadian Club, "the bar is open."

Mac passed on the Canadian Club, but he held his own at beer drinking. He caught them all up on Hawaii and that Master Sergeant Taylor would trade them tiger stripe fatigues for all the weapons they captured in the field.

Nobody believed him about Karen, but Hollywood pissed his new pants when Mac told them about the sergeant major getting shit-faced on the tiger piss beer. The all-night party lasted until 9:30. Glad to be where he felt so much at home, Mac fell asleep. He woke up and on the way to the shithouse he remembered his dream about shooting an elephant. *What was I gonna do with the tusks?* he wondered. His morning dump taken care of, he started putting his gear together. He decided not to take his .38 pistol out to the field. *I'm already humpin' an ass-kickin' load.* Two rifles and a hundred rounds for the .06, his M-16 and ammo for that, his grenades, a claymore mine, eight quarts of water, rucksack with enough meals for five days. Still smelling faintly of her, he tucked Karen's panties in the bottom of his ruck, but first he took a smell and wrapped them in plastic. *Fuck 'em, if the guys don't believe me.* Sorting his shit, he kept stuffing extra items. In his old brown Canadian Army issue duffle bag, he found the new collar he'd gotten for Rags. Bright pink, it fit perfectly. The dog was so proud of her neckwear she finished waking the rest of the team with her barking. With everything laid out on his bunk, Mac realized he had too much shit. He was only too glad to go to breakfast and put off the decisions about what to hump and what to leave behind.

Sitting at the table in the mess hall, Bones asked Mac, "Seriously, bro, you eat that pussy?"

"Fuckin' a, bro. All she'd give me," and Mac told them about fucking in the ocean and how he'd ended up with a sandpapered-ass from the beach.

The team cracked up and Hollywood asked Mac, "If you get zapped, Mac, can I have her phone number?"

That ended the laughter. You're a fuckin' asshole," Flash told Hollywood. "Don't be puttin' a jinx on us."

Quietly the team finished their breakfast and headed

back to the barracks to finish putting their gear together. Staff Sergeant Gordon got the team back to earth when he told Mac, "If you fall in another hole out there, fuck you, we're leavin' your ass," and he handed Mac his camera and a brown manila envelope held closed with a string.

"What's this, Sarge?" Mac slid a stack of color pictures out of the envelope.

"That's the pictures you took of the B-52 strike," Flash answered. Mac flipped through the photos quickly, then slowly. *Man, what a mess,* he thought. Holding up the picture of the dead girl he'd buried, he said, "This is that girl I ran into gettin' out of the green." He held up another picture. "This looks like that gook platoon sergeant that was training them. Hard to tell from just pieces that were left."

Looking at the dead girl with her tits exposed, Bones told Mac, "I'da felt her tits, bro," and laughed. Blushing at the memory, Mac stuck the pictures in the envelope and handed it back to his team leader.

"Those are yours if you want them," Flash told him.

"I don't want 'em, Sarge," and Mac concentrated on packing his gear. He didn't want to think about the shit he'd seen, or the smell. Looking at the pictures brought it right back. Flash walked out with the envelope and dropped it in the trash.

The Intel people had kept the negatives and prints had gone everywhere. The B-52 base in Guam had received several sets. The air crews were all excited to get a chance to finally see the results of their work, but when they saw the pictures their excitement vanished. The crews took one look and that was all they wanted. The pictures went into a filing cabinet and nobody mentioned them again. The set of prints that Flash threw in the trash were picked out of the brigade garbage dump and six weeks later they were in Hanoi. The envelope was packed in another envelope and it was marked "Top Secret" and only the highest ranking officers got to see them. One officer in particular had the job of going over each picture with a large magnifying glass. The name of every officer whose face could be identified crossed off a list. This officer's work was checked by his commander and the next decision was how to notify the next of kin. Only ten families per week were to be notified. The bureaucrats didn't want the people to know how many of their countrymen and women were dying in the war.

15

Crockett Mills, Tennessee was still a small town. It hadn't changed much in fifty years. The cafe, the laundromat, and the Chevy dealership were all owned by the same person, a local man who still lived on the 160- acre family homestead. Wallace Wallace had come home from the big war and made good. He'd married Shirley and, as a result of listening to his wife, had slowly gotten away from farming and into business in town. The only farming he did now was helping Shirley in the garden out behind the house. Sitting on the porch railing, watching the dawn break, Wallace sipped his hot coffee. He'd never been able to sleep past dawn; the Marines and the Japs had made sure of that. The tiniest movements along the wood line caught his eye. In the coming sunrise he could just make out a four-point buck warily chewing on the grass. Automatically, Wallace noted the range: *Four hundred twenty yards, no wind, good shooting.* Wallace did this all the time. Old lessons from shooting at human targets all through the war made the man unconsciously prepare for a shot. It was light now. Just the movement of picking up his coffee cup and the deer saw it and was gone.

No one knew about Wallace's shooting in the war—not his kids, not his friends. And even though his rifle had been named after his wife, she knew less than anybody. The Jap sword hanging over the fireplace next to the enlarged picture of the dead crocodile had her always bitching. "Put that stuff in your den." Recently, it had been put in the basement.

Fuck. Women don't understand shit like that. That rifle saved my ass. Finishing his coffee, he thought, *I still miss that rifle.* Entering the house, he still moved like he had a pack on his back. His kids always made fun of his walk. Wallace never explained it—just grinned at the kids. He'd watched the news last night. Vietnam. Always Vietnam. They'd shown some grunts. They walked the same way he and his buddies did. *Tired, all the fuckin' time.*

Shirley had his breakfast waiting at his place when he sat down. Refilling his coffee cup and her own, she began bitching. The new girl he'd hired at the dealership was a slut and he needed to get rid of her. It did Wallace no good to tell Shirley that Patsy was their daughter's friend and that they'd grown up together. *Fuckin' women have an answer for everything.* Shirley shut right up when Wallace dropped three hundred dollars on the table. "You need a new dress, honey," was all he said, hoping she wouldn't spend it all on her dipshit wannabe musician boyfriend down in Jackson.

Wallace kept eating and was just finishing when he was joined by his son. Ruffling Winston's hair, the father and son greeted each other with affection. Wallace had named his son after Winston Churchill. He admired that tough sonofabitch. His son's friends nicknamed him "Winner" and from what the sheriff told Wallace, the sixteen-year-old was definitely doing that with the girls. Shirley already had the money off the table before Winona grumpily sat down. His daughter worked at the dealership after school and between her college semesters.

She drove every man with a dick crazy. From nine to ninety, the blonde twenty-two-year-old would flirt with them all. Still in her pink baby-doll pajamas, Winona got up to pour herself a glass of milk. Watching her bend over, father and son grinned at one another. Winona did have a heart-stopping ass, and it didn't help that her pussy hair was sticking out. Winston always wondered if his dad knew Winona fucked anything with a dick. Wild and beautiful, his older sister drove him nuts sometimes.

His dad was a great guy. Winston just wished he paid more attention to what was going on around town. The only time his dad had ever whipped him had been when he and his friends had taken the old Jap sword from its place over the fireplace and tried to slice and dice one of his hound dogs. His dad had come home for lunch and caught all four of them chasing the hound. He had caught all of the eight-year-old boys and he whacked each of them with the flat of the sword. That night he'd come to Winston's room and explained what it felt like to be hunted like the boys were hunting the hound dog. Winston had listened to his dad and never bothered another animal. He did use the sword again, but that was in the house chasing Winona.

Watching his dad go out the door to work, Winston wondered what his dad had done in the war. He asked his mom but all she knew was that Wallace had been a Marine in the Pacific.

Wallace had to move his new Chevy pickup in and out around Winona's convertible. She'd left the top down and Wallace hoped she got a wet ass driving in to work. Wallace often wondered about his family but that was as far as he got. After what he'd gone through in the Pacific with the Japs, nothing his family did bothered him very much. As long as Winston didn't have to go to war—that was all Wallace cared about. Winona would settle down sometime and probably end up nagging some poor bastard. That brought a smile to his face.

Wallace stopped in at the sheriff's office for another cup

of coffee. Sheriff Smiley had served in the Pacific, too. Wallace always checked the wanted board as he entered the police station. He expected his picture to be right up there in the Top Ten Most Wanted. After mustering out in San Diego, he'd killed two men. He'd kept his issue .45, and the first man he killed had been a Mexican who had tried to steal the Jap sword. The other was a trucker between Yuma and Gila Bend, in Arizona. Wallace had been hitchhiking home along Interstate 8 when the trucker picked him up. The trucker made a pass at Wallace and he'd shot him and left him there at the rest area. He drove the big rig into Phoenix and sold the load and truck for five thousand dollars cash, no questions asked. He finished his journey by rail and dumped the .45 piece by piece from the rolling train.

The five grand had made the down payment on the Chevy dealership. The cafe had come along next and the laundromat was last. They all made money and Wallace had stuck ten thousand cash in a metal box buried out at the farm. The way Wallace looked at it was, if the FBI came looking he had running money.

After his coffee with the sheriff, he spent the rest of the day at the dealership. At five-fifteen he walked into his house. No one else was home and the note Shirley had left said dinner was in the oven. Grabbing a beer he thought, *Fuck dinner. Might go out to the Roadhouse and eat.* Beer in hand, he started into his den when the stack of mail piled on the hall table caught his eye. Going through the stack, one letter addressed to him made him ponder who it was from. He didn't know anybody at the Recoil Gun Shop in Honolulu. Carrying the envelope into the den, he sat down behind his desk. *Must be a gun ad,* he thought.

After reading the contents, Wallace Wallace sat absolutely still for the next hour. Memory after memory came flooding back. He had completely forgotten packing the note in cosmoline and sticking it in the butt stock of his rifle. *After all these years. My fuckin' rifle found, and still in use, going back into war. Fuck that.* He wanted that rifle more than anything. Winona and her friend Patsy came into the house, laughing and carrying on. Winona met a man that she did- n't know. She had no idea her dad could move that fast. Wallace reached out, grabbed his daughter, and dragged her into the den. Sitting her at his desk he demanded, "Type me a letter."

"Geez, Dad," she complained, rubbing her arm.

Patsy stood there with her mouth open. Winona had met the Marine from the war. "You sit here and type me a let- ter. Now, you little shit." Wallace's face was two inches from his daughter's.

"OK, Dad, OK," and she started rolling a clean sheet of paper into the typewriter. Wallace stood right by her side while she typed. Winona had never seen her dad so excited and the letter she typed made no sense at all. It was about a rifle, but she had learned during the last few minutes that her dad really scared her when he was fired up and excited. When Patsy asked what "that" was all about, Winona told her, "Something about a stupid rifle."

Wallace's routine went out the window that night. After he stamped the envelope, he jumped in his pickup, drove straight to the post office, and dropped the letter in the lobby box for outgoing mail. Wallace drove back to his farm and, ignoring the house, went straight to the barn. He went down into the old cyclone shelter under the barn and removed the padlock. Using another key he unlocked the old footlocker he'd bought at a surplus store. As he lifted the lid of the footlocker, a musty odor tickled his nose. Jap battle flags, now moth-eaten, covered the pile of yellowing pictures he was looking for. Under the bare hanging light bulb, he went through the stack of black and white photos.

Certain ones he set aside. He set an old canvas rifle case next to the pictures, along with a broken sling. The last thing he put on the pile was a five-round stripper clip with five moldy green bullets still in it. He shut the lid to the footlocker and sat on the dirt floor, tenderly going through the small pile and looking at each article separately. All the pictures showed him and his rifle. The last picture was taken just after he'd shot the Jap officer on Iwo Jima. The rifle sling cemented his desire. Broken now, the brass grommets green with mold, he continued rubbing his hands over the cracked leather. In the corner of the cellar he checked the loose brick his money was hidden behind. *I'll spend every fuckin' dollar in there,* he thought, *to get that rifle back.*

16

Mac was the only Ranger who couldn't dance. He was too heavy with all his equipment on, but he worked up a real sweat trying. The Rangers danced in the dusty street and taped and tied down all their loose gear. On their march to the rifle range to zero their weapons, they passed the sergeant major getting out of his jeep. The sergeant major called Flash out of line. Mac also walked out of line, handed the sergeant major a crumpled envelope, and said, "Didn't need all that, Sergeant Major. Thanks a lot," and he rejoined the march while the sergeant major continued to talk to the Ranger leader.

At the range the men were already getting ready to fire before Flash joined his team. "What's up, Sarge?" Hollywood asked.

The sergeant clued them in. "We gotta check out the river first, then the trail."

"That figures," Hollywood said. "Now we gotta walk uphill from the river." Their work at the firing range was over quickly. The men zeroed their rifles and Hollywood got to fire the .06. "Kicks like a fuckin' mule, Mac."

"Yeah," Mac said, "but you hit what you aim at, and whatever you hit stays down."

After cleaning their weapons the team went to the tailor shop and had all their patches and name tags sewn on their new shirts. The team agreed the new tiger stripe fatigues were going to work fine in the bush. "What's the weather gonna be, Sarge?" Bones asked the team leader.

"Hot and wet, tomorrow wet and hot. What else we gonna get?" and Flash laughed.

At the tailor shop Flash pulled Mac away from the rest of the team. "Mac, you're pretty uptight. You worried about the mission?"

Mac squinted in the bright sunlight and thought a moment before answering. "I still see that mess after the air strike and that girl blown to shit. That's all, Sarge."

"You'll see that shit forever, Mac, but get ready to put your shit all in one bag. We need you out there," and Flash nodded out toward the jungle.

"You ever seen a commie, Sarge?" Mac asked.

Flash looked at the Ranger in wonder. "What the fuck you think were killin' here? Russians?"

Mac looked at his team leader. "They sure as shit don't look like commies to me. Just look dead is all." Now Flash was really worried about Mac. "It's not the killin', Sarge. It's just that we're killin' more than we can eat," and Mac started laughing.

"You motherfucker." Flash knew he'd been had.

The rest of the day the Rangers prepped for the mission. Everybody shopped at the PX. Hot sauce and chewing tobacco topped their lists. Flash also explained that he bought the gook cigarettes from the tailor shop, so everybody except Chief got gook smokes. Chief chewed tobacco all the time. He said Redman was his favorite. The mess hall served the Rangers steak for lunch and Rags had a busy time dragging all the T-bone leftovers into her doghouse.

Mac's biggest problem was how to carry the .30-.06. Finally, he draped the sling around his neck and the rifle hung down the front of his body. Ammo pouches kept it from hitting him in the nuts when he walked. As they waited on the chopper pad, the Rangers camoed each others' faces. Just before the chopper came in, all the kibitzing stopped and the Ranger team got ready for work.

The insert went as planned and five minutes after they hit the ground the rain came down in buckets. The team felt good. Rain had covered the insert and Flash released the choppers early. The jungle had open gaps and the team got a good start on their hump to the river. The broken clumps of jungle allowed the Rangers to spread out then move slightly downhill. With the rain slowing, the team still had good visibility in the coming dusk. Mac had a hard time trying to cover their back trail. He didn't worry about the boot prints that filled with water, but the wet grass stayed bent over, pointing like an arrow at the team.

Flash picked a tangled web of bamboo for the team to lay up and watch the river. The only way to get into the grove was to crawl. The bamboo grew every which way and it was almost impossible to get through without making noise. The center of the fifteen-foot-wide grove had a small depression in the middle.

Chief made a small hole in the edge of the grove to allow one man to watch the river. The river was huge and flowing fast. Nothing was moving in its swift current. Mac was the last man to crawl in and Hollywood had to drag him into the center. The team couldn't stand upright and it was already pitch dark in the bamboo. Flash had dropped his ruck, crawled back out of the grove and tried to cover their trail in. He set two claymores just inside the entrance. Crawling backward, he ran the wire to set the mines off into the center and tied the wire to the PRC-25 radio. Then he called in their negative sitrep and position.

Each Ranger took a quick peek through the peephole and Flash set watches. Two awake at all times, one looking and one on the radio. Next, the team tried to stretch out and find a place to lie. Their rucks were used as pillows. The five men had their feet touching in the center of the small perimeter. Mac drew the first watch at the window. Looking out at the river, he couldn't see anything except for an occasional flash of white from a breaking wave. The team ate right out of their pockets. Mac had some jerky and he munched on that while he watched.

Lying next to him, Bones nudged Mac who handed over a piece of jerky. Bones found his hand in the dark and stuck half a candy bar in it. Mac munched on that between bites of jerky. The canteen of water came around and Mac drank. *So much for supper,* he thought. Mac was fast asleep when Hollywood put a hand over his mouth and whispered in his ear: "Gooks."

Mac just nodded his head and Hollywood took his hand away. Chief was at the window. Mac quietly slid his M-16 out from between his legs and checked the safety. It felt warm to his touch. The night sounds were drowned out by the gooks. Their talking and odor came into the grove. The enemy carried on like they were the only ones around, then the first set of gooks was joined by another bunch. This group never put in to shore. They made grunting noises and in the darkness it sounded like the first group got into their sampan and shoved off to follow the other one. No one on the team got any more sleep.

Two sets of lights were seen later that night, bobbing their way upstream. Flash had to move the radio in the morning. He was the first to get the shits and the only place to go was in the center of their small perimeter. The team leader barely got the hole scraped out and his pants down before the runs hit. That seemed to set everybody off. Even covering up the shit piles had the bamboo grove smelling terrible. The gooks would smell them for sure. Flash crawled out and peered up and down. As far as he could see in the dawn's light there was not a better place to hide. The possible places he could see were smaller and full of water. There wasn't a trace of where the sampan had landed during the night. Maybe a few footprints full of water, that was it.

After crawling back into the bamboo Flash called in the spot report of the night's activity. He was hoping that higher would tell him to move, but they told him to hold and Charlie Mike, continue the mission. During the daylight hours the river was a busy place with sampans going up and down. The team watched while two Navy patrol boats stopped sampans and checked ID cards. One patrol boat came so close to the hidden Rangers that Chief could see the sweat rolling off their beer cans. The team never moved and only a few whispers were spoken, and then only when absolutely necessary. Each man cleaned and re-oiled his weapon, then lay back on his ruck and waited his turn at the small opening.

The river was about four hundred meters across and Flash was glad they weren't on the other side. He could see through his binoculars that all the activity was there. Once, he saw two NVA come down to the riverbank and look up and down, trying to spot the Navy boats. The second night was a repeat of the first, only they didn't have a sampan stop. The team was ready to move when they got the word that morning. The team was glad to be getting out of their hide. Flash was the last man out and in his final check he was pleased—not a trace of the team was left except five shallow depressions in the ground where each man had been. Crawling out, he stood and Chief helped him get into his rucksack. As they moved away from the river, each team member stretched and made adjustments to their gear. This time progress was slow. No one moved quickly. The small team went from jungle patch to jungle patch only crossing a clearing one at a time and only when there was no other way. With the sun shining, the team dried immediately. The area they moved into after leaving the river was devoid of trails. In a small rocky spot the Rangers ate their first hot meal in two days. With good fields of fire, Flash had three men cook chow while he and Mac watched for any sign of activity. That afternoon Flash called a halt, brought the team together and whispered, "We're taking a break here, and since we're making such good time we'll move into our hide just before dark."

The Rangers were at the edge of a small clearing that was perfect, Mac realized. Everybody was in the shadows and it would be almost impossible for anyone to approach the team without making noise and being spotted. The patch of dirt that Mac lay on was soft and partly in the sunlight. He caught sight of Flash who made a slashing sign across his throat. Mac eased out of his ruck and the sun beating down on his shoulders put him to sleep. The team ate another hot meal cooking over small chunks of C-4. While the team ate, Flash and the Indian did a recon. When they returned, Flash went from man to man and told each one that they were only five hundred meters from where they could set in and watch over the area containing the trail junction. In the gathering twilight the men repainted their faces, got their gear together, and they all checked to make sure they left no trash or any other sign they'd been there.

Each Ranger tried to step in the tracks of the man in front of him as they went to their new hide. Mac had an easy time straightening their back trail. The spot Flash had picked for the team to set in was another small patch of jungle and every team member had a good view of the trail. This time each man set out his own claymore and Flash also set out trip flares in two open areas that the gooks might use in approaching.

The team stayed in the same spot for three days. During daylight the trails weren't used at all, but by night the trails were like a highway. The gooks had bicycles they had loaded and once an ox cart squeaked by. Flash wrote down every sighting and each and every one of the team also had the information written in their notebooks. If anybody was lost the info would get back to the Intel folks. A completely boring mission. The enemy never knew that the team was in the area. Not once did Flash see an opportunity to snatch a prisoner. The smallest group of gooks they saw was four and he was not going to start a firefight and give away his position for a chance at a prisoner. *Too fuckin' iffy,* he thought. On the fifth day, Flash called for and got an extract time and a coded location. Their mission was complete. Now it was time to get out. Bringing the team in close, Flash gave them a rally point in case they got hit on the way out. He also made sure each Ranger knew not to let their guard down on their way to the landing zone. The team made good time after leaving their hide; they were glad to be moving again.

Flash found an overgrown bunker complex when he stepped through the rotten roof of one of the abandoned bunkers. The team halted in thick cover and took time to eat. Chief was the first one who thought the team was being followed. Flash cut back across their trail but didn't hear or see anything. He thought it could have been monkeys. Nevertheless, he warned the team to be careful of making noise. He dropped Mac back even further to cover their trail once the team started moving again. Mac held in place, then carefully covered over all signs that the Rangers had been there.

Moving quickly, Mac ducked under branches and moving backward to watch the back trail, caught up to the rest of the team faster than he expected. In the shadows the team was almost invisible. Bones whispered in Mac's ear. "Chief thinks he heard a dog on our trail." Crouched in the undergrowth, the team faced out and strained to pick up any strange sound. Except for the slight breeze in the trees, all the Rangers could hear were normal sounds of the woods. When Bones snapped his fingers, Mac stood. The rest of the team was already on their feet, getting ready to move. This time the whole team heard the baying of the hound dog tracking them.

Flash made his way back to Mac and shoved a small green can in Mac's hand. "It's CS gas crystals. Find a spot to sprinkle this over our back trail. That tear gas will fuck 'im up. Be careful you don't get any on you," he whispered, and Flash stood and signaled to move out.

Mac followed, looking for a place to dump the gas. The team was heading uphill and he needed a spot that the dog wouldn't miss. Walking backward, Mac kept looking for the dog. He could tell from the small yip sounds at the end of each baying sound the dog made that the hound was young. His dad had two redbone coon hounds and Mac was used to those kinds of dogs. Hounds could track, but he'd never seen one attack anything until men pushed them to a place where the cornered animal went on the offensive. The slight rise between two trees looked like a perfect spot to ambush the dog.

Squatting and peering through the undergrowth at their back trail, Mac got a small quick glimpse of the dog. *Shit, looks like some kinda beagle, but it's all alone. The gook runnin' the hound let him slip the lead.* Mac grinned and continued opening the small can. He never caught sight of the gook. *That fucker don't know what he's doin', lettin' that dog get so far ahead of him.* Mac took the green can, sprinkled it between the trees and turned to catch up to the team. He covered any signs he made, holding branches to stop their movement as he brushed through. All sounds from the dog ceased about three minutes after he'd left. Mac found another good spot, opened the can again and sprinkled it over the ground. Moving on, trying to catch up to the team, he heard no more baying from his back trail. From the slight breeze blowing directly in his face, Mac knew that the dog would have no trouble keeping to the Rangers' trail.

Straight ahead he saw branches move so he knew he'd almost caught up to the rest of the team. He squatted down in the middle of a clump of ferns, with only his bush hat and eyeballs showing. The snorting and snuffing noises came right along the back trail. The dog had its nose to the ground going back and forth across the trail. Occasionally the dog would lick the ground. What an ugly mutt. *Short, stump legs. Looks like a cross between a basset hound and a beagle, and who knows what else.* The mutt halted at the edge of the ferns just as Mac stood up. The dog watched the Ranger warily. Mac kept the small green can in his left hand, moving it slowly back and forth. *Gotya.* The dog's nose was twitching like a rabbit. Mac stepped out of the ferns and just its bloodshot eyes moved.

Mac could see that the dog was covered with open sores and he was so skinny his ribs stood out like piano keys. Mac knelt next to the dog with the green can in his hand. No sooner had he set the can down and the dog was on it. The dog had the can of spiced beef gone in three slurps. Mac took his canteen and filled the small can with water. It took three fill-ups before the mutt had enough. While the dog drank, Mac scratched its ears. Grinning, Mac thought the mutt's tail was going to fall off. It was a young male about ten months old. *Too young to start letting it loose to track.* Taking a set of boot laces from his pocket, he made a collar and a short lead. *Fuckin' a,* he thought. *If the team comes back with a prisoner, it's a three-day in-country R&R. Maybe they'll give us more for a gook dog.* The dog rolled on his back, but Mac couldn't scratch his belly, the sores were so bad. *Cocksucker ought to be shot, treating a dog this way.* Shaking his head, Mac got to his feet and looked for any signs of the gook tracker. He could see nothing moving on the back trail. The dog followed right alongside him and didn't even pull on the leash. With the dog at his side, he had no trouble following the team. He was not ready for the ambush.

Mac walked right into the center of the hidden Rangers. Flash came unglued at the sight of the dog. He tried to yell in a whisper and almost choked to death. "What the fuck you doin' with that dog? Kill it."

Mac just looked at the team leader. "Call it in, Sarge. We captured a gook dog."

Flash lost it then and whipped out his .45. "If you won't kill this fucker, I will," and he pulled the slide back on his pistol and chambered a round.

Mac knelt next to the dog and looked up at Flash. "You ain't gonna shoot no hound dog, Sarge." Flash didn't get the chance to find out if he'd shoot the dog or not. The clinking of metal on metal and a murmur of Vietnamese voices froze the Rangers in position.

They moved only their eyes and all eyes were on Flash. It seemed like hours, but in reality it was seconds, before he signaled the team down. The dog never made a sound and glued himself next to Mac. It was Mac who fought to keep from moving. Not only did the dog stink, but the fleas from the dog were biting the Ranger. *Should of let Flash shoot your ass.*

The sounds were not repeated. The team was in good cover at the bottom of a small brush-covered knoll. Using hand signals, Flash ordered the team to face the knoll, moving them forward just to the edge of the trees, looking toward the small hill. The sounds they'd heard weren't heard again. Leaving Bones and Hollywood in the trees to cover them, Flash signaled Mac and Chief to move up the hill. Flash led. Mac was on his left and Chief had the right. When Mac saw the team leader slowly move the selector switch on his rifle, he did the same. The men had to crawl on their bellies to peer through the small scrub growth on top of the knoll. Mac had a hard time trying to crawl. The heavy bolt rifle kept getting in his way and the smelly dog wanted to lick his face. Mac could see all the way to the bottom of the knoll but not very far into the jungle that started there. Chief had crawled up and whispered to Flash. Snapping his fingers, Flash signaled Mac to join them while frowning at Mac and the dog. Whispering in Mac's ear, he said, "We got beaucoup gooks at the bottom, over on the right," and he pointed Mac's head in that direction.

Mac's asshole got tight as soon as he saw the gooks. It looked like an anthill had been kicked over. The gooks were busy working away at something, but he couldn't tell what they were doing. About five hundred yards away from the gooks' location, there was a small clearing and if Flash hadn't been using his binoculars he wouldn't have seen the movement. More men—and moving this way.

Holy fuck. Grunts, and coming right for the gooks. Pulling both of his men back behind the crest of the knoll, Flash reported what he'd seen in a whisper. "I'm gonna get on the radio and find out if there's any friendlies in the area. You guys keep watching."

Peeking back over the hill, Chief used the binocs. Mac now understood—the gooks were setting an ambush.

Chief grunted and Mac followed his eyes. The dog's hair was standing straight up and he was growling low in his throat.

Mac turned back and looked through the binocs. He thought he saw some small movement where the grunts were supposed to be, but he couldn't be sure. Handing the binocs back, he watched the gooks. His hair rose just like that on the dog. Using a rope, three gooks were pulling a can up into a tree. The can was hung with fresh-cut greenery and a wire tied alongside a vine led from the can to one of the gooks who was very carefully playing it out. *Holy fuck, look at the size of that claymore.* The gooks made their claymores out of scrap. Powder came from dud bombs, mortars, artillery shells, and in some cases black powder or dynamite. They filled the rest of the can with glass, nuts and bolts, rocks, and anything else they could think of. Mac nudged Chief and pointed at the claymore. Flash grabbed both men by their legs. As he crawled back up, Mac felt like he'd come a foot off the ground, the sergeant had scared him so bad. Flash whispered, "Higher higher says we got no friendlies in our AO."

"Those are grunts down there," Chief whispered.

Mac pointed at the claymore hanging in the tree. The gook was hooking the wire to an old car battery. "What are we gonna do, Sarge?"

Flash brought Hollywood up with his grenade launcher, then he whispered his plan to each of them. Mac would fire the bolt gun at the claymore in hopes of setting it off, Hollywood would fire as many high explosive grenades as he could at the machine gun bunker which was open on the Ranger's end, and Chief and he would fire on semi-automatic at targets of opportunity. "Mac, if the dog causes any problems, shoot it, or let the fucker go. You got that?" Mac nodded his head. "Next," Flash whispered the message to the Rangers on the knoll, "we're gonna have to run like a motherfucker. Those grunts are gonna call in arty and tac air and we don't wanna get caught, so get ready to move your ass."

Mac was shaking. *Hope this works,* he thought, as he jacked one of the hot rounds into the rifle's chamber. Crawling up to the crest of the hill, Mac took a good look at the claymore hanging in the tree and estimated the range at three hundred yards. The slight breeze wouldn't affect the shot at all. As he snuggled into the rifle, he could picture the old Marine who had killed the crocodile. It was almost as if he was talking into Mac's ear. Tighter into your shoulder...that's it...safety off... cheek on the stock...get a good sight picture...that's it...now caress Shirley's trigger...that's it...take a deep breath...let some out easy...slow...squeeze...Kaboom!

The front sight blade jumped and came back to rest. Dead center of the claymore. Just when he thought he missed, the claymore exploded. The black cloud and orange-red flash of the explosion caught everybody by surprise. The gook who had been directly under the claymore - sweeping all sign away—was no more. Two feet still in their sandals were all that was left. The rest of his body had been vaporized by the blast. Mac hardly felt the dog lying on his leg. He jacked another round in the chamber and looked for a target. Hollywood fired his grenade launcher just after the explosion.

Rrrump! and his 40mm hit dead center in the machine gun pit. He put another round in right behind it.

Chief and Flash were deadly with their 16s. Quickly, Mac looked for a target at the same time the gook with the car battery stood up to see what was going on. Mac's second shot hit in the center of the gook's chest. The man flipped backward, kicked his legs, and never moved again. The gooks were firing everything they had into the ambush zone. The Rangers only had stray rounds coming their way. They had caught the NVA with their pants down.

Mac didn't get a chance to shoot again. Flash had him by the back of his ruck, pulling him back down the small hill. Sweat was running in his eyes and wiping them clear he could see that the team was running as fast as they could, back into the woods. Mac thought of the artillery that would be coming in and he and the dog were soon running all out to catch up with the rest of the team. Mac entered the edge of the woods and Flash surprised him, covering their back trail. As Mac ran by, he slapped him on the shoulder. "Good shot. Let's get the fuck outa here. I've got the back trail. Move!"

Mac grinned and kept moving as fast as he could. The team was half-a-klick away before the first artillery rounds started bursting behind them. Flash was talking on the radio as the team ran. The sergeant didn't want the air people firing up the team. It was certain that, as soon as the artillery lifted, the gunships would come rolling in and fire up anything moving on the ground. Some of the thicker growth slowed the team to a walk, but they weren't worried about noise now. The clumps of wait-a-minute vines cut their exposed skin. As the Rangers broke out of the vines, they ran like hell as soon as the forest allowed. Chief was well in the lead and he was covering ground like a racehorse. He never saw the high-speed trail until he was on it, lying flat on his back.

He hit the trail at full stride and the gook running the trail at a good clip got run over by the speeding Ranger. He didn't know what hit him. Chief had hit the gook broadside and stunned him. Chief flew one way and the gook went the other. The NVA soldier had no weapon, not even a rucksack. Hollywood burst out of the undergrowth and whacked the NVA soldier across the head with the barrel of his grenade launcher. Helping Chief to his feet they hardly got a chance to look at their prisoner before the rest of the team was there. "Kill 'im," Bones said. Hollywood was already taping the man's hands behind his back and Chief yanked the little gook to his feet. The man was still stunned.

His eyes were rolling around in his head like a pinball machine on tilt.

Flash passed around a full canteen. The prisoner didn't get a drink, but Mac splashed a little water in his hand and let the dog slurp it up. Flash told Mac, "Gimme your long rifle."

Mac took Shirley from around his neck and handed it over. The team moved away. Flash was going to kill the NVA soldier. Instead, he surprised the team when he stuck the long rifle between the man's arms and his back.

"OK, let's move. Mac, get one side. Hollywood, you get the other. Come on, let's go," and the team headed away from the trail.

As the NVA soldier came to his senses, he was able to keep up. Every time he sagged against the rifle, the pain in his pulled shoulder blades made him move his feet to keep up. Mac looked at Hollywood. "Little fucker's heavier than he looks." Hollywood grunted in agreement. Flash was on the radio and relaying the news that they'd captured a gook and they needed their taxi ASAP. He could tell that fired up the rear. Every chopper in the area wanted to pick up the team.

Fuck 'em, Flash thought. *Higher higher telling us there were no friendlies in the area and now they're sayin' they made a mistake and had a unit in contact. Maybe the asshole in charge would come out for a look and get killed.* Flash could hope, anyway.

The Rangers secured the small LZ and Flash told the team, "Ten minutes for the chopper." Mac finally took a good look at the prisoner. The cut from the whack on the head had stopped bleeding and the gook squatted, watching the Americans. Mac lit two cigarettes and stuck one in the prisoner's mouth. Puffing away, the gook looked at Mac and nodded "thanks." Mac was cutting holes in his sweat towel and just grinned and winked at the prisoner. *Little fucker,* he thought. *Maybe five-four or five-five.* The prisoner wore khaki shorts, a green short-sleeved shirt, and sandals. Hollywood searched the man and found a pack of matches, a plastic wallet with a couple of pictures, and a handkerchief. That was it. Except for the belt with the red star on the buckle, the soldier looked pretty ordinary. Finished with the sweat towel, Mac took a drink from his canteen, poured some into the empty spiced beef can and let the smelly dog drink. When the dog had enough, Mac held the canteen up to the bound man's mouth. The NVA soldier spit out the cigarette butt and finished the canteen. Mac put the empty canteen back in its holder and continued to work on the dog with his sweat towel. The holes he cut for the dog's front legs fit. He pulled the towel up and tied a double knot over the dog's back. The mutt never moved, just wagged his tail. Figuring that the dog would try to run when the bird came in to pick up the team, Mac now had a sling for him.

Flash popped a green smoke grenade out into the center of the small landing zone. The inbound pilot identified the smoke. "I got loudmouth lime."

Flash radioed back, "That's a Roger."

The Huey was already flaring to a hover and setting down dead center in the clearing. Hollywood didn't mess around. He picked up the gook and threw the struggling man into the helicopter. Flash was counting the team members when he saw the door gunner laughing over his machine gun. Mac was struggling toward the chopper and the dog in his arms was fighting to get loose. The mutt was so scared he pissed all down the front of Mac's fatigues. Flash was laughing too, but he grabbed Mac by the rucksack, just as Chief ran from his side of the bouncing chopper and grabbed the only handhold he could. The .06 rifle was hanging from Mac's neck. When Chief yanked on the rifle and Flash shoved from the other side, Mac went airborne into the chopper, but he held onto the dog. Flash was still on the skids when the chopper lifted off. The team sergeant had just barely sat his ass on the vibrating floor when the door gunner shoved a radio headset into the Ranger's hands. The helmets with headsets were the only way the crew could communicate. Lieutenant Lance "Bull" Horton had dropped the team off at the start of the mission. Now he wanted Flash to throw the smelly dog out of his chopper. Flash looked over at his team member. Mac had his legs hanging out the door, his piss-stained pants popping in the wind. The dog was calm now and he lay with his head resting on his paws, right beside Mac, watching the ground fly by. The flaps covering the dog's ears flapped from the wind in rhythm with Mac's pants. With his arm locked through the prisoner's, Hollywood was laughing his head off. Even the gook was smiling at the ridiculous sight. Flash keyed the mike on the headset and spoke to the pilot. "I can't throw the dog out; he's attached to my Ranger. But if you say the word, I'll throw the Ranger out and the dog will follow." The whole crew busted up.

It was a fast trip back to Firebase Mace. When the chopper landed, the gook must have thought he was in the movies. Everybody with a camera was taking his picture.

17

Martinez was the point man leading not only the third platoon but the rest of Bravo Company through the jungle. Yesterday, second platoon had led, and each day the point rotated. The company had not had any kind of contact and the grunts were pissing and moaning from the heat. The CO, Captain Doyle, had told Marty to find the small stream that showed on the map. Everyone was getting low on water. With the scattered openings in the forest, they could get a resupply bird in without having to cut an LZ. Marty liked the early afternoon. Sir Charles always seemed to take a siesta and without having found any trails in the area the pointman was moving rather easily.

The single shot charged the grunt company like they were all in the same electric chair. Marty was already prone on the ground when the claymore blew. The gook in the spider hole stood up to see what was going on and he never even saw the point man. The 12-gauge blast took half his chest away. The gook ambush had been blown prematurely. Third platoon sergeant Fast Eddy had the platoon move to the left flank. Shit flew everywhere. The gooks were firing everything they had into the ambush kill zone, but the grunts had not gotten there yet. By blowing the 'bush early, the grunts massacred the NVA. Third platoon maneuvered and came at the ambush from the left. Facing the wrong direction, gooks were getting blown away. Captain Doyle

had the artillery coming down like rain and the gooks—
dragging as many wounded as they could—ran right into
the shit storm of high explosive shells.

Twenty-seven bodies were counted with eighteen
weapons and four of the eighteen were crew-served. The
grunts in Bravo Company were on cloud nine. Two
Americans had been slightly wounded from flying wood
splinters and the medics treated them right there. Bravo
Company swept the area and gathered up all the weapons
and whatever else they could find. As he talked on the
radio, Captain Doyle paid no attention to the soldiers loot-
ing the dead NVA. Bravo Company was pumped. It wasn't
often they got a turkey shoot like they'd had this afternoon.
The captain was grinning into the radio; he felt good. After
this firefight his new men realized that Charlie wasn't any
better than they were. He couldn't put it together: Why had
the gooks blown the ambush so prematurely? The captain
told higher he'd have to call back with a list of all the shit
they'd captured. The company really went wild when he
passed the word that after they policed up all the captured
weapons and materiel, they only had to hump one more
klick and choppers would be inbound to pick them up.
Firebase Blackhorse tonight. Cold beer and showers. The
blood-soaked ambush zone resounded to cheers and whistles.

Fast Eddy Felter came over to talk to the captain. He
held up his arm, showing that he was wearing a brand new
self-winding Seiko watch. "I can't even get one of these at
the PX."

The blast of music made both men turn. Marty had a
brand new radio-cassette player, still in the plastic, booming
away.

"Eddy, get me a list of everything that these guys find
that came from the PX," the captain said. "Let the guys

keep it. Just a list of stuff from the PX. The weapons and other shit, we'll put on a separate list. This shit's gotta be comin' from somewhere," and the captain turned back to the radio.

Fast Eddy grabbed his point man and humped up the small hill. Just behind the rise, there were craters where the artillery rounds had hit. Both soldiers started to find the evidence right away. Empty brass M-16 casings, empty casings from an M-79 grenade launcher. Marty held up one shiny brass casing. "Eddy...," and he handed the casing to Eddy. "...I told you. That's a .30-.06. I don't know who those guys are but they saved our ass. Look here. That's a jungle boot print."

Eddy continued turning the brass casing over in his hand as he walked a little way down the hill. "Hey, Marty, they had a dog with them too. Look at the paw prints." As they talked quietly, both men knew that whoever had been up on this hill had saved them.

Rejoining the company, Fast Eddy went to the CO. Every grunt in the company wanted to show the captain what they'd gotten from the ambush site. Pulling the officer aside, Fast Eddy told the captain what he and Marty had found on top of the hill. Eddy gave the empty .06 casing to his CO.

"Whoever these motherfuckers are, we owe them a lot of beer. They saved the whole fuckin' company." Captain Doyle handed the brass case back. "That's a no-shitter. For once we got very fuckin' lucky. Sarge, get these fuckers ready to move. It's startin' to stink bad around here," and the captain grinned. "Don't let these motherfuckers half-step on the way outa here."

Eddy looked at the officer. "I'll make sure we get all the shit carried out with us." The platoon sergeant set every-body to getting their shit gathered up. At the beginning of the fight, everybody had dropped their rucksacks, so the men were straggling back in after finding where they'd left them. Eddy grinned. His platoon had first dibs at the souvenirs and his guys were stuffing their rucks with canteens and anything else that would fit, and if it didn't fit they tied the stuff to their rucks. Heavy black and blue flies were everywhere and the smell of the dead was getting worse in the heat. As they humped away from the killing zone, the men were glad to be back in the fresh air. First platoon brought up the rear. The platoon sergeant pulled one grunt off to the side and, as soon as the radio man and the lieutenant went humping by, the old sergeant turned and looked at his man.

"Cool, huh, Sarge?" The man had a gook ear strung on a boot lace around his neck.

Beneath the rim of his helmet, the sergeant's eyes blazed. "Off with that shit! Now!"

The grunt was cool, but he knew not to fuck with his platoon daddy. The ear with the boot lace strung through it lay in the trail. Both men had to hump to catch up to the rest of the company.

18

The Rangers were the center of attention at the firebase. After all the picture-taking, Mac and Bones sat with their prisoner, waiting for the Intel people to fly in and pick up the captured NVA soldier. Bones was sitting on his ruck and looking at the prisoner. "You suppose he hates niggers?" he asked Mac.

Mac looked at Bones in surprise. "Naw. Little motherfucker is too scared to hate anybody." Mac looked around. The excitement had died down and most of the picture takers had headed back into the firebase. Mac used his bayonet and cut the prisoner's hand loose.

"What the fuck you doin', man? That motherfucker's gonna kill us he gets a chance." Bones kept running his mouth. Mac gave the gook a smoke and let him drink out of his canteen. The Vietnamese words poured out.

"What the fuck's he sayin' Bones?"

"How the fuck am I supposed to know? I don't understand that shit."

Neither Ranger had a weapon in his hand and when the prisoner used his hand to plug his nose and point at the dog, all three soldiers laughed. From a distance, the three soldiers sitting in the hot afternoon sun looked like friends. Mac and Bones went to work. Mac opened a C-ration can of pork slices. Both the dog and the captured gook had the same look on their faces.

"Try that. Number one chop chop," and Mac handed the NVA a pork slice. The rest of the can went to the dog. "See, I told you, motherfucker. That's fuckin' dog food," and Bones laughed. "You ain't seen shit yet, motherfucker. Watch this shit," and Mac pulled out more C-rations and opened all the cans with his P-38 can opener. Using a cracker can, Mac mixed up peanut butter and jam. He scooped some of the mix out of the can with a cracker and gave it to the gook. "Here ya go, Billy. He looks just like a guy I knew named Billy. Whatta ya think, Bones?"

"Look's like a gook to me, bro," but he watched in fascination as the soldier tried the peanut butter and jam. Billy surprised both Rangers.

"Numba one," and his eyes begged for more.

The rest of the Ranger team came over carrying cold beer and handed some cans to Bones and Mac. "The CO is bringin' the Intel people in," Flash said. "Be here in about an hour. You sure that motherfucker ain't gonna try an' escape?" he asked.

Flash wasn't at all surprised when Bones told him, "Man, this motherfucker is hooked on peanut butter and jam."

Billy was working on a can of C-ration ham and lima beans that Bones had given him. The Rangers watched, fascinated. Nobody ate ham and motherfuckers unless they were starving. Done, Billy gave the empty can to the dog. "Hey, Billy, stand up," and Mac motioned for the NVA soldier to get to his feet. Anybody watching what happened next wouldn't have believed it.

As clear as a bell, Billy smiled at Flash and said, "How are you doin', ya fuckin' cocksucker?"

Chief and Flash went rolling on the ground. Chief had tears rolling down his cheeks. The two Rangers tried helping each other to get up. Their laughter had Bones and Mac high-fiving each other. "Hey, Sarge, the gook wants to work with us. Whadda ya think?" Mac asked.

Flash helped the Indian get to his feet. "What the fuck else you clowns teach this guy?"

"Sheeeit, Sarge. Motherfucker's gonna be a brother when we get done teachin' him," and Bones chuckled.

The sound of the inbound chopper sobered the Rangers. Seeing their expressions change, Billy quit smiling. The first guy off the bird was the Ranger CO, followed by his first sergeant, an ARVN officer and an American lieutenant brought up the rear. The captain was over six-feet and he stopped in front of Mac. "You the mercenary that's causin' all the problems down at MAC-V?" Grinning, he stuck out his hand. "I'm Captain Ira Parker and this ugly motherfucker is your First Sergeant Pace."

Mac shook hands and introduced himself. Nobody saluted in the field, but this was the first time he'd ever had an officer introduce himself like that. "Welcome to the Rangers. With all the shit goin' on, I can't get to all the teams like I should," and the captain turned and greeted Flash and the rest of the team like old friends.

Top Pace stopped in front of Mac. "What'samatter, my Army ain't feedin' you enough?" and the first sergeant shook Mac's hand. "Been hearin' good things about you. Keep up the good work. What the fuck stinks so bad around here?"

"Ahhhhh, it's the dog, Top. But he'll clean up real good." Mac stood there, red-faced.

"Holy fuck," the first sergeant exploded. "Who's the man with a real rifle? Shit, I haven't seen one of these in years," and he reached down and picked up the .06.

"It's mine, Top," Mac answered.

"He can shoot the motherfucker too, Top," Flash chuckled.

Captain Parker was looking at the prisoner. "Good work.

Some motherfuckers will do anything for a three-day R&R, eh Top?"

"AHHHHHH, sir, this gook...we named him Billy... he wants to work with us," Bones said.

The captain looked at Bones. "Bones, this little motherfucker's hard core NVA. Doesn't even speak English."

Bones pointed at the prisoner. "Billy!"

The NVA soldier looked at the captain. "That's right. I'm a baaaad motherfucker." He was doing good until he smiled.

All the men looked at the gook. The captain turned away and lost it. Even Top was chuckling. "What have you motherfuckers been teachin' this guy?" Top wanted to know.

"Shit, Top, we're teachin' him Ranger talk," Mac replied.

"That's right, Top. Teachin' that gook how to talk American," said Bones. "He's learnin' real quick, too."

The riot that followed happened too fast for anyone to stop. The ARVN lieutenant said something to the prisoner in Vietnamese and then he slapped the prisoner. The ARVN officer—with his shiny helmet liner and wraparound sunglasses—was flat on his back fighting for his life. Mac had punched him right in the mouth and the dog had his teeth sunk into his leg. The ARVN was screaming and trying to fight. If it hadn't been for Flash pulling Mac off and Chief yanking the dog off, the Vietnamese officer would never have been able to get up. The officer was hollering in Vietnamese and his starched fatigues were ripped and torn. His wraparound shades were smashed to shit. Flash held Mac and it was all he could do to restrain his Ranger. "Shit, calm down, Mac. For fuck's sake, man. The gooks all act like that. No big deal, man." Flash kept his body between Mac and his weapons.

"Tell the gook that Billy's gonna work for us, Sarge. Come on, Sarge, do somethin'," Mac said between pants.

Bones hopped right in. "Yeah, Sarge. Billy be the first NVA Ranger."

"All right, all right." Flash gave the captain a questioning look, then both men went over and started talking to the intelligence officer. Bones and Mac were well aware that the Americans had the KCS program for gooks who wanted to work for them. Kit Carson Scouts worked out well, especially if the surrendered NVA or VC had been a grunt. The scouts knew how to find their former buddies out in the field. The first lieutenant had learned Vietnamese after intelligence school and he went over and talked to Billy.

The ARVN officer was trying to brush himself off. Hollywood gave the officer a pack of Salem cigarettes. "Mac," Hollywood said, "shake the motherfucker's hand. He's on our side—at least during the daylight."

Mac stuck his hand out. "XIN LOI." It had been one of the first words he had learned when he arrived in country. He was told it meant "Sorry about that," and covered a multitude of sins.

Captain Parker and Top were talking to the team leader. "Shit," Parker asked, "is that little motherfucker always like that?"

Flash looked at both men. "Yup. You never know what's gonna set 'im off," and he went on to tell them how Mac had shot the kid's surfboard in Hawaii. "There ain't no quit in that kid, sir," and Flash looked at the captain.

Top jumped right in. "We need more of them, and the sergeant major's getting us more slots at the school so hopefully Flash here will make the kid into a team leader."

The captain asked his team leader if that were true.

"Yes, sir. Couple more missions and he'll be ready. Just want to give him some more time is all."

The intelligence officer came over after talking to the captured NVA soldier and handed Flash a couple of forms.

"Fill these out, Sarge. That gook says he'll work with you guys."

"Oh yeah? When did he make up his mind?" Flash wanted to know.

The el tee looked at the beat up ARVN and said softly, "After your man there decked the ARVN," and he chuckled.

Flash quickly filled out the paperwork and the Intel officer put a set of handcuffs on Billy's skinny wrists. This time his hands were in front of him. Mac stuffed a pack of smokes in the prisoner's pocket. Bones dropped in a pack of gum and matches. The el tee told the Rangers Billy would be back in two or three weeks, after they debriefed him at a POW camp. Noticing Mac's worried look, the el tee chuckled and said, "Don't worry. That ARVN won't even be around your gook." The captain and first sergeant stayed and the el tee and the ARVN escorted Billy toward the chopper.

"Hang in there, Billy," Mac hollered.

Almost at the chopper, Billy hollered back, "Motherfuckin' Rangers," and waved his cuffed hands.

The men standing on the ground were all laughing and the Rangers started picking up their gear to head into the firebase to be debriefed.

Mac got thrown out of the debriefing, but the first sergeant did it nicely. "Get your smelly ass out of here and that fuckin' dog, too, and don't come back till you're both cleaned up. You got that?"

Mac left all his gear right there and went hunting for a shower. He was nowhere to be found when the debrief was over, but Hollywood finally found him in the shower. Mac had used his dirty fatigues to plug the shower drain. Water was running out the door. When Hollywood walked in Mac and the dog were wrestling in about five inches of water.

Mac had used a whole bottle of shampoo on the dog. "Check it out," Mac laughed. The dog was about six different colors. Black and white spots, brown underbelly, and various blends of grays and browns. The dog tried to bee-line out the door, but Hollywood was too quick and bounced him back in the water.

"Later," he said, and he was careful going out the door.

Mac planned on finding a medic next to see if he could scrounge some ointment for the dog's sores. He figured he'd put some on the flea bites he had all over himself as well. All the fighting and carrying on in the shower had half-way cleaned his tiger stripes, so he just put them on wet.

When Mac rejoined the rest of the team, no one could believe it was the same dog. Flash was still in with the CO when Top came out with cold beers for everybody. "Now that's better. Smells a lot better, too," and he winked at Mac, handing him a beer. "That dog Airborne, Mac?"

"Shit, I don't know, Top. But that's a good name for him," and he reached down and patted the dog's head. Flash came out with a beer of his own and led the team into the barracks they were using. Top came in with box lunches for everybody and while they were eating Top explained that the company was short sixteen people— and that there was no way the teams could cover any more missions than they were already. They had three teams that were nothing more than names on the board and as soon as they could get quality people they would.

The Rangers talked over their last mission. Top wrote on a pad about checking out the grunt units, noting that when the teams were out on a mission all friendly units were to be kept well away from the Rangers. It was too easy for friendlies to be killing friendlies.

Airborne, already at home on Mac's bunk, made the team

wonder if the gooks would be using more of the tracker dogs. The captain came in with the team's mail. He'd received a CARE package from home and he shared it with everyone. He said, "If the gook proves trustworthy he'll make a good scout, but if he doesn't work out you guys dump him right in the field," and he looked right at Bones and Mac. "You two clowns understand that?" and he pointedly continued to look at both men. "Yes, sir," they both answered. "We got it."

Mac got up to go outside and let go of some beer. At a sign from Top Pace, Flash grabbed a couple of beers and headed out as well. Done with his piss, Mac was heading back into the barracks with Airborne at his side. The voice out of the darkness didn't surprise him—Mac knew what was coming. "Com'ere, Mac. Got a cold one." Mac found Staff Sergeant Gordon sitting on top of a sandbagged bunker. While Mac hopped up and sat beside his team leader, Airborne wiggled his way between the men. Mac took a drink of beer and lit a cigarette.

Mac started the conversation. "What's up, Sarge?"

Flash didn't waste any time getting to the point. "You disobeyed my order out there. You didn't get rid of this mutt when I told you to. You could've compromised the whole team." Taking a drink of beer, Flash waited and when Mac didn't say anything Flash went on. "I'da killed this mutt out there ya know."

Mac finally spoke. "Naw. You would've killed me before you shot the dog."

Ignoring what Mac had said, Flash was scratching Airborne's ears. "How in the fuck did you know that this dog wasn't gonna lead the gooks to us? You wanna tell me that?"

Mac threw away his smoke. He watched the sparks fly when the butt hit the ground. "Well, Sarge, I grew up around hounds and I could tell from his bay that he was young and wasn't sure about what he was doin'," and Mac paused for a drink. All of a sudden he tilted his head back and started to bay. Airborne jumped and joined right in. Mac stopped his baying and laughed. "Did you hear that right at the end there? That little yip... that means he ain't settled into his bay yet. So anyway, I waited like you told me and I got a glimpse of the mutt. There was no gook. The dog was loose. The gook must've turned him loose. Fuckin' gook didn't know how to train a hound, that's for sure. Anyway, when I knew the dog was loose, I thought I'd try and see if he was really after us. I used a can of spiced beef and sprinkled some across our back trail. Then I picked out a spot to use the gas crystals if the beef didn't work. How I knew that it worked was...as soon as Airborne here got a taste of the chow he stopped baying. An older trained hound would've ignored the food and stayed right on our trail."

There was a short silence, then Flash spoke. "Why in the fuck ya want this mutt anyway?"

"Shit, Sarge, killin' is the easiest thing to do over here, and the people that don't do the killin' want us to do it, just like turnin' on the fuckin' radio. The fuckin' dog didn't do nothin' but be born here. That's no reason to kill it, but I would've rather killed it than see any of the team hurt." Mac took another drink of beer and asked the question he didn't want to ask: "Am I off the team, Sarge?"

Flash waited awhile before answering. "If you're right, Mac, there's more shit to kill over here and every time I go on another mission, I run into more and more gooks. What I'm worried about is that you're going to get somebody killed, fuckin' around with the wildlife. What's fuckin' next? A cobra?"

"I fuckin' hate snakes, Sarge."

Flash chuckled. "You got the potential to lead your own team. You're good in the bush, but I've told you before, ya gotta control that hair-trigger temper." The sergeant lit a cigarette. "It ain't killin' gooks that makes a Ranger. It's gettin' the mission done and not gettin' any of your team hurt." Flash slid off the sandbags.

"Wait a minute, Sarge. Am I on the team or not?" and Mac stood in front of his team leader.

"Next fuckin' mission you're gonna learn point from Chief. He's the best in the business." Laughing, Flash added, "I thought you missed that claymore today."

Mac was glad he was still on the team. "It's that hot ammo. So fuckin' fast hardly moved the can and I thought I missed, too. You find out who those grunts were?"

"Naw," Flash said, "but the CO will find out...and they owe us a lotta beer."

"Hey, Mac, you think that green beanie can get us any more of these fatigues?"

"Shit yeah, Sarge, but he needs some weapons in trade."

Mac felt better now that he knew he wasn't off the team. Going back into the barracks, the two men were almost run over by the CO and his first sergeant. "See you guys in the morning."

"Goodnight, sir...Top," Mac said.

Flash had stopped to talk to the captain.

"Well Flash?" The captain had waited until Mac was back in the barracks.

"He's stayin', sir. I can't afford to get rid of him. He's too good in the bush and I'll keep an eye on his temper." The three men went over and leaned against the sandbagged bunker.

Top said, "Pay up, Captain." The captain handed over a silver flask and Top took a drink. "Yes, sir. Just love drinkin' your brandy." Top handed the flask to Flash. "Try this. I won the bet. That skinny little fuck's too good out there for you to fire."

"Wow, what the fuck is that shit? Liquid napalm?" Flash could hardly gasp.

The captain grabbed his flask. "You low life enlisted men just don't understand the finer things in life," and he took a drink from the flask. The officer had learned early to let the team leader run the team his way and sure enough there were a lot fewer problems. "Flash, I heard a rumor that Mac changed all the tags in the hospital and all the patients were put in for the Medal of Honor. Would he do that?"

Flash had recovered from the small drink of brandy. "Yeah, that motherfucker would do that, but he won't admit it. And he's gonna make a good team leader. After our talk awhile ago, I found out he's not kill crazy. Bones wanted to kill the gook and Mac wanted to make friends. If the guy had a weapon he'd a dropped him sure, so leadin' a team he won't be out there tryin' for a body count."

"He really get the sergeant major fucked up?" Top wanted to know.

"That's a no shitter. He'd never had any of the tiger piss beer before," and Flash went on and told them how Mac had turned in the Rolex watch he'd found after the air strike. "He didn't even know the value of it. The general gave Mac a squad leader Army issue Timex, so Mac repaid the favor. As a matter of fact, the general's the one that talked Mac into volunteering to be a Ranger."

The laughter flowed and the conversation got slow and easy. Flash did a perfect imitation of the gook: "How ya doin' ya fuckin' cocksucker?" The three men had to hold onto one another, they were laughing so hard. That did it for them. Bidding each other good night, the team was already asleep when Flash walked into the barracks. Hanging his shirt on a nail, Flash lay down on his bunk thinking about what Mac had said about the killing. Just as he had the thought that *the little fucker's right,* Airborne padded over and gave Flash a big, wet slurp across the chops. Flash wiped his face and gave the dog a pat.

19

Tex flew into Fire Support Base Mace early in the morning. Now he had no trouble going wherever he wanted. Swan Blossom poured ice water all over him to get him out of bed. *Fuckin'gook bitch.* The NVA general wanted a story about the mechanized unit that wouldn't fight. Coming in from the air with Swan Blossom at his side, Tex could see the armored personnel carriers and Sheridan tanks parked off to one side of the helipad. Tex had said the night before that he'd do the story but he changed his mind sometime during the night. *Fuck, I'm not sleeping worth a shit. Fuckin' gooks have me by the balls. Fuck, I can't even party with my friends.* Jeannie— who he wanted to fuck so bad—walked out after she called him an asshole. He had already gotten two letters from his editor telling him his stories were shit. Still vibrating from the drugs, Tex wobbled away from the chopper hoping that he wouldn't have to walk but there was no jeep waiting. It was going to be a long day. The heat was hitting him and he thought that if he stood still he'd fall over.

Already smoking grass, Tex tried to mellow out as he walked toward the armored unit. He read the faded bumper number on the first APC he came to: DTRP 17th Cav. The APCs had their ramps down and the crews were drinking cold beer and sodas while they loaded ammo and crates. This wasn't a unit that refused to fight. Tex had been around enough to know that. "Any Texans around here?"

Tex asked the first man standing by the ramp.

The shirtless man looked right by Tex at Swan Blossom. "Ohhhh, baby san," and the GI headed for the girl. She paid no attention and stuck to Tex like glue. Tex thought, *If these guys only knew she was a commie, they'd fuck her brains out and leave her dead in a ditch somewhere.* A crowd gathered quickly around the reporter. The beautiful girl damn sure had that effect. She pretended she didn't speak English and Tex hoped she got an ear full. When Tex finally got the pieces put together it was a hell of a story. The gooks were dug in along Highway 13, waiting to ambush a fuel convoy. A loach pilot flying escort for the convoy had seen two of the dinks before they could get into their foxhole. The Cav unit was already on the march and would have passed through the ambush. The loach pilot radioed the CO of Delta Troop. The Cav unit didn't fuck around. They swung off the highway and came busting at the ambush from the flank. The APCs had the Sheridan tanks between them and just before the ambush zone the pilot fired a rocket dead center toward the gooks' location. That was the signal for the cav to open up. It was another turkey shoot. Two of the APCs had been hit by rocket propelled grenades, but the RPGs had bounced off.

Swan Blossom was mobbed by the horny GIs and they all had souvenirs that they wanted to show the lady. One tank commander even dragged her over and showed her the NVA flag he'd captured and hung on his radio antenna. The gook cameraman Tex had with him was taking pictures of everything. The Cav troopers were only too happy to pose for him, proudly displaying their trophies.

Finally able to get away, Tex had pages of good stuff to write about. He couldn't help but rub it in on their way back to the chopper. "Hey, bitch, how's it feel to know that your general's full of shit. If he'd come out of that hole in the

ground these guys would be happy to make toast of his
ass," and Tex laughed. Swan Blossom never said a word.
She was scared to death to be around so many Americans.
Tex didn't even register the small group of men sitting
alongside the landing pad. The Rangers saw the girl before
they even noticed the man.

"Hey, Tex," and Mac hauled his ass over to intercept the
reporter. Tex stopped at the call. He didn't recognize Mac
in his tiger-striped fatigues, and Swan Blossom had already
walked out ahead about ten steps before she realized that
Tex wasn't there. Mac solved Tex's problem, or at least
Airborne did. First the dog tried to bite the cameraman, but
the loaded-down cameraman was too fast for him. The
cameraman made it into the chopper, so Airborne turned
his attention on Swan Blossom. If she hadn't kicked off her
shoes and run like hell, the growling dog would have had
her. Tex was surprised—he hadn't been this alone since the
NVA had beat the shit out of him down in that tunnel complex. Turning to Mac, the men grabbed each other and half-
heartedly wrestled. How ya beens and good ta seeyas were
flying around.

"Hey, Tex, where did ya get that pretty gook? You fuckin'
her, you lucky motherfucker?" Mac was asking questions a
mile a minute. Tex kept his back to the helicopter and Swan
Blossom was watching him like a hawk, but she wasn't getting back out of the bird as long as the dog was carrying on.
Taking a deep breath, Tex put both arms out, placing a
hand on each of Mac's shoulders.

"I'm in big time trouble, Mac. These fuckin' gooks are
tryin' to kill me."

Mac looked around. The only gooks he saw were the
ones on the chopper. "What the fuck ya talkin' about, Tex?"
Mac could see that the reporter was scared.

Tex whipped out his notebook. "Pretend you're talkin' to

me. Walk this way."

Mac and Tex walked away from the helicopter. Every time Swan Blossom tried to get out of the bird, Airborne went for her pretty legs.

Mac said nothing and let Tex talk himself out.

"Buddy, you in deep doo doo and I know just the man to help ya'," and Mac took him over to introduce him to Flash. "Ahhhh, Sarge, can you come here for a minute? Need some help here, Sarge." As the team leader came up, Mac said, "This guy's in deep shit, Sarge, and he needs your help." Mac introduced Tex and the Ranger leader.

"You the motherfucker that wrote the mercenary story?" Flash wanted to know.

"Shit, that fuckin' story was supposed to be about a mutiny, not about a mercenary," And Tex laughed.

Flash liked the reporter, so he said it. "What's the matter?"

Tex told him the whole story, even about the general in the tunnel complex. "That girl on the chopper...No, don't look at her...she works for the general and has been my shadow ever since." Tex was standing there sweating bullets.

"Fuck, she's the prettiest commie I ever seen Tex," and Mac laughed.

Quickly, Flash asked, "Can you get to BMB tomorrow and bring the girl? We can keep her out of the way better there and we'll have a plan for ya. How's that?"

Tex didn't waste any time. "OK, I'll be there. Here's my number in Saigon and I'll bring the jeep. If you guys don't hear from me, the gooks did me in. Come check it out, OK Mac?" Tex stood there waiting for an answer.

"Yeah, sure, Tex. Right, Sarge?" Mac looked at Flash and Flash nodded.

Tex hauled ass for the chopper and gave Airborne a pat

on the way by. The blades were already turning before the reporter got halfway there. "What do you think, Mac? Is he tellin' the truth?" Flash wanted to know.

"He damn sure has changed since we first met, Sarge. He's pretty scared, so yeah, I think he's tellin' the truth."

As Mac began walking toward the team, Flash said, "Don't say nothin' to the rest of the guys yet. We'll check this out some more."

Tex felt like a load of cement had been taken off his shoulders. Maybe the Rangers couldn't do anything for him, but it sure felt good telling somebody about it. When the chopper dropped them off, the reporter enjoyed the short ride to the villa. As soon as the door closed, Swan Blossom became a regular cunt. Tex told her exactly what Flash had told him to say. "We're going to a briefing tomorrow. Those Rangers I was talking to think they've found another NVA headquarters."

Swan Blossom got over her mad real quick. This was what the general would want to know. She kept questioning Tex about what else he'd learned and she was amazed that the skinny, long-nosed American with the dog was the same man in the picture Tex showed her. "That's the story that made me famous," Tex bragged. Swan Blossom wanted to find out why the Americans would even talk to the reporter.

In her room she wrote out a report on what she'd learned. Written on thin rice paper, the report was rolled and inserted into a hollow piece of bamboo. Next, she went down the driveway in front of the house and as she flirted with the ARVN gate guard, he paid no attention when she handed a begging boy a coin. On her way back up to the house all she could think of was how stupid men were. *They all think with their penis.*

Late that afternoon, Tex finished his report about the Cav unit kicking ass. He knew his editor would like this

story. It was not only about the Cav—it had every Texan in
the unit acting like they were at the Alamo. He thought that
with the addition of soldiers wearing peace signs and love
beads, which he'd written a whole paragraph about, it
would keep the NVA general off his ass. Laying the completed story aside, Tex realized he hadn't smoked any grass
or even had a beer all day. *Man, I'm starved.* He couldn't
remember his last full meal. Swan Blossom startled him.
She'd been watching him write the story and when she tried
to pick it up Tex grabbed it. "Fuck you. Not till I get something to eat."

Tex ate until he could hold no more. Swan Blossom
made a face every time Tex tried to get her to drink iced tea.
She finally told him that drinking tea with ice was as bad as
chilled American beer. Even though her English was excellent she wanted to learn American slang and kept putting
down the story to ask what certain phrases meant. Tex
found out that night she was a great person to talk to and
could switch languages in mid-sentence. He tried drawing
her out about her personal life but she'd never give him a
straight answer and would change the subject. Finally, Tex
gave up and went to bed. It wasn't until morning that he
realized he'd slept without a gun under his pillow. He was
the first one up in the morning and all he could think of
was that his nightmare with the NVA general was almost
over.

20

Lieutenant Bull Horton picked up the team for the short ride back to BMB. On the intercom headphones with Flash, Bull told the team leader he was very glad they'd cleaned up the dog. Mac was riding with his feet hanging out the door and Airborne lay right alongside him. The dog had struggled but hadn't fought and pissed all over Mac like he did on his first ride. Flash was wondering what they'd find out at the brigade's main base about the gook general. The Rangers' three-quarter-ton truck was waiting next to the chopper pad when they landed. The team threw their gear in the back and climbed in. Flash rode up front with the driver. After pulling up at the headquarters building, the Rangers left everything except their weapons in the back of the truck. Bones had already clued Mac in about the debrief.

The Intel folks always had a table set up with all kinds of food for the Rangers. Sure enough, the Rangers went right to the table set up in the map room and started making themselves sandwiches and trying food from all the different trays. Once everyone was fed, the Rangers found chairs and the captain started the debrief. Many of the questions about vegetation, the colors of rock formations and such didn't make much sense. After the overall briefing, each Ranger rotated through a series of clerks and each clerk had a form with a series of questions. As they moved between stations the Rangers pigged out. Airborne ate so much Mac had to take the dog outside for a dump. Just when everyone had been debriefed, the Intel captain hollered "Attention" and the room came to their feet. General Davis came into the room, followed by the sergeant major.

"At ease, men," and the general shook every mans' hand. Getting to Mac, he asked if his watch was still working.

"Ahhh, yes sir."

"OK, everybody grab a seat. This is gonna be short and sweet. I understand you men earned a three-day R&R and you just wanna stay around here. My God, don't you just love that esprit de corps, Sergeant Major?" That brought all kinds of comments and groans from the team. "Hold it up, men." The general laughed then went on to tell them that the POW was from the 222nd regiment and that they'd been planning the ambush for three days. "You saved Bravo Company two-thirds from walking right into the ambush." Bravo Company had kicked ass thanks to the Rangers and only two GIs were slightly wounded.

When the general was finished speaking the sergeant major got up, strolled to the front of the room and waited until the general sat down among the Rangers. "That was a fine job you men did and the brigade thanks you. But," and he held up his hand and, looking at the note in it, asked, "who fuckin' taught the gook to say," and he walked in front of Bones, "'I'm a bad motherfucker honky?'" Even the general cracked up. When the laughter died down the sergeant major walked over and stood in front of Mac. "And who's the bad baaaaaad motherfucker that punched an ARVN officer in the mouth, broke his sunglasses and sicced his dog on that fine officer?" Mac tried to slide down in his chair. "For your punishment..." and he pulled Mac's bush hat off, "...every swingin' Ranger will get a haircut

TODAY."

Even the general clapped and laughed as the debrief ended. The general stopped beside Mac and Bones and asked how they'd gotten the dog. The general had seen Flash Gordon corner the sergeant major and the men had gone out together. General Davis began talking to Chief and Hollywood and did what he always wanted to do: Be with his troops. As the Rangers left the building and stood waiting for Flash, they all stopped to look at six brand new second lieutenants. As both groups stared at one another, a clerk came out to escort the lieutenants in for their welcoming to the 199th. "Poor bastards," Mac commented to Bones. "They don't know what they're in for."

Flash came outside, lit a cigarette and told the team, "We're going back in. The sergeant major needs to talk to us."

The team crowded into the sergeant major's office. The sergeant major had a full case of tiger piss beer right next to his desk and Chief grabbed a bottle. This was the first time the whole team together heard the story that Tex had told to Flash and Mac. When the sergeant major asked Mac to give his opinion, Mac said he thought Tex would be there the next day to finish the story, but he'd have to be gotten away from the gook lady.

The sergeant major handed around bottles of cold beer from his refrigerator. "I need the empties so drink it here." Everyone grinned, then for the next few minutes the soldiers talked over different ways to help the reporter and nail a gook general. The sergeant major said he'd see Flash later that evening. "Go," he told the team, "get the fuck out of here." As they filed out the sergeant major made sure he got his empty beer bottles back. He pointed at the dog. "I don't know what the fuck kinda dog that is, but we're not the humane society here," and he laughed when he saw Mac's embarrassed look.

At the barracks the team had just enough time to get cleaned up and into plain fatigues before chow. All during the meal the team discussed how to find a gook general. Sometime during the meal the talk switched to getting their three-day R&R. Mac wanted to know all about Vung Tau. Flash, Hollywood, and Chief had been to the resort on the South China Sea.

"Oh, man, the pussy is cheap and they bring ya cold beer right on the beach." Chief had surprised the whole team. It was the longest statement anyone had heard the Apache speak, and his words got the whole team pumped as they walked back from the mess hall, the team really got into what kind of party they were going to have.

The sergeant major was waiting for Sergeant Gordon, so after Flash left, the team turned to joshing and drinking. Mac was cleaning the old .06 and Chief handed him an old cardboard mortar tube. "If ya break that rifle down in parts, put them in there, and tie the whole thing to your ruck," the chuckling Indian went on, "ya won't strangle yourself that way." Mac still had a burn mark around his neck from when Chief yanked him by the rifle into the chopper. After cleaning his weapons Mac pulled out the letter the sergeant major had given him. It was from the Frenchman, thanking him for returning his watch.

Mostly in French, Mac read right along. French, being the second language in Canada, Mac had learned it in school. Bones was hanging over his shoulder. "What's it say?"

"Check this out." He held up a family picture the Frenchman had sent in the letter. His daughter looked about nineteen and she wore the shortest miniskirt the Rangers had ever seen. Bones had the letter in his hand. "Now what the fuck does this say?"

Mac grabbed the letter and looked at it. "Says right here,"

and he paused. "He hates fuckin' niggers," and he flopped flat on his bunk, laughing.

Bones hit Mac with an empty beer can. "Motherfucker," and he started to laugh. At all the commotion, Airborne finally came out of the doghouse with Rags close behind. The dogs hadn't left each other since the team walked in. They'd even shared the bones the team brought them from the mess hall.

By the time Flash walked in, the party was over. The team was sacked out and the only greeting he got was Chief, snoring like a sawmill.

Mac was the first one up and he was shaving when Flash walked in. "Mornin', Sarge."

As he stepped into the shower, Flash said, "We got a plan, so it will be a good morning."

When Mac went into the barracks he turned on the radio full blast. "GOOooooood morniiiiiiin, Vietnam!" Everybody hated that fuckin' guy, whoever he was, who said that every morning on the AFVN channel. All kinds of stuff was thrown at Mac until he turned it off.

Coming back from the mess hall, Flash explained the plan. There would be a fake briefing at headquarters and at some point Flash and the sergeant major would take Tex into the general's office. The girl and any other gooks would have to wait in the briefing room. The Rangers were to have side arms only. Mac and Bones were already planning on getting alone with the girl. Mac went into the open arms room and grabbed a couple of bottles of LSA weapons oil. The clerk's voice out of the shadows startled him. Walking over to the clerk's desk, he was surprised when the clerk called him "Sarge."

"Fuck that shit. Just call me Mac," and he stuck out his hand. As they shook hands, the clerk said, "You guys have all the fun."

Mac kept grinning and said, "Shit, come on out with us sometime. You can have some fun too."

The clerk looked at Mac and pointed to his glasses. "I can't go with these. That's why they call me Coke Bottle, but my real name's Reggie Tucker. Did you really shoot that gook and that claymore with that old rifle?"

"Shit, yeah." Seeing the guy's expression, Mac asked, "You wanna shoot it?"

Coke Bottle answered right away. "Fuckin' a, but I heard it kicks like a mule."

"No sweat, GI. Next time we go down to the range, I'll teach you how." Mac signed the forms the clerk handed him. "That's your new life insurance form with your folks' address. Gotta have it on file," and the clerk inserted the forms into a file with Mac's name and stock number on it.

Mac and the rest of the team were sitting around and bullshitting, waiting for Tex and ready to help the reporter. When the designated time passed for the reporter to be there, Mac thought of what Tex had said about the gooks killing him.

Tex was late getting to the brigade main base because Swan Blossom had taken forever to get ready. Her straight black hair was pulled back in a pony tail and her Au Dai was made of the purest white silk. Slit from the waist down, it hung perfectly. The tight turquoise-blue slacks fit like a glove, her low shoes matched flawlessly— and she was scared to death. Going onto an American combat base and being surrounded by the long noses had her constantly feeling like she was going to lose control of her bladder. All Tex could think about on the drive to the base was how beautiful the girl looked and how could he get into her pants.

The Ranger team surrounded Swan Blossom when Tex stopped his jeep in front of the company. Mac was the one who said, "Holy shit, I'd take her back to the world with me." Tex followed the Rangers in their truck down to head-quarters. Once she was the center of attention, Swan Blossom lost all her nervousness. The only one who was worried was Tex. He hoped Swan Blossom didn't catch on that a private briefing for a reporter just wasn't done. Combat soldiers didn't trust the press and often sent reporters in the wrong direction. The sergeant major greet-ed everyone coming into the headquarters and led them into the map room.

Flash was impressed with the dog and pony show; snacks were even laid out for their guests. The cameraman had his camera taken away and the S-1 put on a great show with maps and slides shown on a screen next to the wall map. Swan Blossom hardly noticed when Tex left the room. She and the cameraman—who also spoke excellent English— were trying to memorize the map. She really liked using the ladies room, and the full-length mirror on the wall allowed her to keep looking just the way she wanted. The captain giving the briefing was drooling as much as the Rangers.

In the general's office, Walt Davis listened to the reporter and asked the questions that were needed to check his story. When Tex told him the general's name, it was checked right there against the list of known NVA officers. There it was: Duc Vinn Hoa. Prepared in advance, stacks of photos were given to Tex to look over, trying to refresh his memory about the location of the underground bunker complex with the general. The closest Tex could recall was where he had come to. He had been on Highway 1, west of Saigon. A cement highway marker next to the ditch he laid in read "19." Tex described the western view as the sun set the evening he was kidnapped, and how long he'd walked to get to the bunker complex, and the dry rice paddies he walked through. "Sir," he told the general, "I don't wanna be anywhere around when this operation goes down. I really need to get rid of the girl and her sidekick out there." Tex sat back after saying that.

Flash had listened carefully and he was the one who refined Mac's idea. "Take the bitch back to the States for two weeks. Tell her the newspaper wants to meet her and then dump her at Macys," and Flash laughed.

Tex snapped his fingers. "That would work. By the time we got back from the States, her buddy the general would be long gone."

Sergeant Major Mateau said, "There's not too many women that could turn down shopping in the mall. She'll probably turn in her commie card for a credit card and never come back." That broke up the meeting and the general was convinced that for once the Americans had a chance to strike first.

As the men stood, General Davis added, "This is secret shit and it's not our Area of Ops, so we'll handle it from our end. Flash, you put together what the team needs. Tex, you take the commie out of country. The sergeant major will coordinate it all. Thank you, men, for a fine job," and the general sat down with his notes.

After the briefing and pulling Swan Blossom away from the Rangers, Tex had to pull over after leaving the base and answer Swan Blossom's questions. The Texan could finally see daylight at the end of the tunnel. Taking the girl back to the States for two weeks wouldn't be a problem. The newspaper could pull all the strings and make arrangements.

The five Rangers were in the arms room looking at pictures of the area the tunnel complex was supposedly in. The black and white photos taken by plane didn't make a lot of sense. Matching them to a map went OK but none of the Rangers had ever worked in that area, so finding and matching reference points was next to impossible. Mac told

Flash, "We need Master Sergeant Taylor. That's the area he told me he spent three tours workin'."

Flash looked up from a picture he was examining. "You think he'd give us a hand?" At Mac's nod, Flash said, "Let me make a call. If the sergeant major says OK, then we'll grab our shit and go see him."

When Flash returned with positive news from the phone call, Mac and Flash grabbed weapons and Flash took all the maps and photos and put them into a large canvas bag. "Hang on to these while I drive."

As they got into the truck, Mac asked Flash, "You have any weapons to trade for tiger stripe fatigues?"

"Shit, yeah," and Flash pulled over to the connex container, a corrugated metal packing crate, about six feet long. Unlocking the connex, Flash explained, "We keep all our souvenirs in here," and he handed out five AK-47s, two SKS rifles, and a case of ammo. "That should do it."

Driving down to Long Khan, Mac and Flash kept going over the plan to nail the general. Flash wanted to go on in-country R&R, but both men hoped the rest of the team would go along with postponing it until after this mission. The two Rangers got to the training base just in time. The old master sergeant was driving out the gate with the last truckload of repair items that he was taking to Hawaii. When the Rangers blocked his truck, Taylor took one look and hopped out. "If it ain't the surfboard shootin' fucker." Grinning, the sergeant shook Mac's hand. "Who's your friend?" and Taylor reached into the truck and shook Flash's hand. "You're hangin' around with bad company," and Flash laughed. The three men stood in the heat as Mac and Flash told the big sergeant what the problem was. Removing his green beret, Taylor scratched his head. "Tell you what. Come with me and give me a hand to get this shit loaded. Talk to me on the way over. The fatigues I'll get on the next plane over. Park inside the gate there and put the guns and ammo in the back with the rest of the stuff."

On the way to the airstrip, Flash told the sergeant about the area that the general was supposed to be in, and that they needed help to pick out the area. When the Ranger sergeant finished, Taylor quickly said, "I've been over and over in that area and we've never seen shit." He pulled the deuce-and-a-half up next to the cargo plane.

Sergeant Jimmy Matamura was working hard, trying to get materiel loaded on the plane. "Hey, brah." Mac was already out of the truck and laughing at Jimmy. Master Sergeant Taylor and Flash stayed in the cab of the truck, talking and looking at maps and photos. Mac pitched in and Jimmy was glad for the help in the heat. The two friends got caught up on the news. This was Jimmy's last trip on the plane. He was coming over for a full tour at one of the Special Forces camps. Mac told him about their last mission and the highlight of capturing a gook dog. The two had almost finished unloading the truck before the sergeants in the front got out.

"Lazy motherfuckers, ain't they?" Mac said to Jimmy.

"Lifers are all the same, brah," and Jimmy had everyone laughing.

When the plane was finally loaded and the loadmaster had checked to make sure everything was tied down the way he wanted it, he signed the manifest and the plane was made ready to leave.

Taylor told Jimmy he was staying and he'd catch up with Jimmy back in Hawaii. Jimmy had figured that something was up and he wanted to stay too. Taylor handed Jimmy a list and told him to have the stuff ready when he got there.

The three men were already driving away before the airplane got cranked. Once back at the Special Forces compound, Taylor took them into the small room he used as an office. Handing beers around he told Mac the rifles and shooting rests he made had killed sixteen gooks that had been hanging around the different camps out in the bush.

"You mean there's more of those rifles?" Flash asked. Then he told Taylor how Mac had shot the claymore and set it off. Sitting in the cramped office the men told stories until their beer was gone. Taylor burped and said, "Let's get down to business here," and he unloaded the bag of maps and photos onto his desk. "From what I see here, Tex had to have been dumped right around this area," and the sergeant made a circle on one of the maps. "There's only two places that this complex can be. Here and here. Both are real similar and they're close together." He picked up a pile of photos, handed stacks of pictures to each Ranger and kept the rest himself. He reached into his desk drawer and handed each man a magnifying glass. "We're looking for any kinda white or black line that could be a faint trail."

With the three of them working it didn't take long. Sergeant Taylor took the small remaining pile of photos and went out into the bright sunlight. When he came back inside he had a smaller batch in his right hand. He threw the rest on the discard pile. "These five here," and he laid them on his desk. "This is the best one. Even shows two little people dinkin' around," and—with the magnifying glasses—he showed Mac and Flash how to see the people in the picture. "This has got to be the trail they used." A very faint white line could be seen heading to a wood line.

The big sergeant handed around beers and leaned back in his chair. "You're going to have a fuck of a time getting in there. It's flat and the dried up paddies have thorn bushes growing all over the top of them. Now, I'll make a deal with you guys," but he was looking at Flash when he spoke. "You let me go in with you and I'll guide you to the right location. Otherwise, without me, you'll stumble all around out there and won't find shit. You say that the general only comes out to meditate for fifteen minutes every morning at dawn. Well, you're only gonna get one shot."

Flash thought a moment, then said, "How in the fuck are we gonna even get close? That's flat open country." Taking a sip of his beer he continued, "Glad to have ya with us, Sarge."

The old warhorse grinned. "OK, I'll meet you up at BMB tomorrow and I'll bring some better photos. You guys see if you can get better maps."

Mac had to run out of the office after he made a comment about Taylor being too old. The sergeant tried to put his boot in Mac's ass.

21

General Duc Vinn Hoa smiled at the news that Swan Blossom had sent. His plan was working. Drawing the Americans away from his forces' real location had been his plan from the start. Swan Blossom was not supposed to do anything but make sure Tex added anti-war sentiments to the stories that he sent back to the States. That she'd seen the maps along with the cameraman made the general very happy. That the reporter wanted to take Swan Blossom to the United States made the general even happier. Swan Blossom had never known that the general was her uncle, or that the general's sister had married a Frenchman. As far as the general knew that was the only black mark against his family. That both of Swan Blossom's parents were dead only made the shame a little more bearable. The general loved the girl dearly and he hoped Swan Blossom would find another life and not come back to this war-torn land. The pretty girl had sent the general a written report as soon as she got back to Saigon. She hoped that the general would not assign her to accompany Tex back to the United States.

Swan Blossom was finally doing the work she'd been trained to do and for once her Amerasian looks were not held against her. Tex had called his buddy who worked at the American embassy. Now that Tex had come up in the world, his stories had made him semi-famous and he got right through to his buddy. "A visa for Swan Blossom? Sure, no sweat, buddy. I'll send it right over and I'll stamp it for thirty days," and he said not to forget to invite him to the next party that Tex had at his villa. Tex had grabbed his notes and was surprised to find Swan Blossom already in his office, reading back issues of *Playboy*.

"What the fuck you doing reading that shit?" Tex asked the girl. "You're always complaining that's all Americans ever read."

"I must find out how American girls dress, no?" and Swan Blossom continued to turn the pages. "You think I should get a haircut like this?" and she held up the center-fold of a girl with a shag haircut. Tex realized that the commie girl was a woman first. He squatted down beside her and said, "Your hair is beautiful, and don't worry about clothes, you can buy all you want in the States." Patting her leg, he added, "You'll be just fine, if they let you go."

Tex hit the old typewriter hard and, with the story of the bunker complex complete, he leaned back and thought, *Now that's the first part. All I need is a dead general for the second part.* Wandering through the villa he realized that he was alone. All he could think of was that when he got back he was going to have a lot of great parties. Thinking of parties he wondered, *If I invited Mac's team of Rangers, would they tear the place up?* The phone rang and for once he answered sober. The connection was poor. The *Dallas Star* had gotten the telex and was already scheduling interviews for Tex and Swan Blossom.

Tex thought he heard his editor say "first class on the airline tickets." He realized that he was looking forward to a stay at a Holiday Inn. Clean sheets and room service. Tex was eating Oreo cookies washed down with a cold beer when Swan Blossom got back with her heavily burdened cameraman. Tex asked if she had her passport. Swan Blossom gave it to him. Wordlessly flipping it open, Tex checked her name: Swan Blossom Carre. *That's French sure enough,* he thought. That the South Vietnamese passport was a product of the forgery department that worked for the general never occurred to Tex.

Grabbing her passport back, Swan Blossom asked, "When do we leave?"

"If everything goes right, we'll be out on a flight tomorrow afternoon. Tell dickhead here to look after my house," and, looking at the cameraman, Tex added, "None of your gook buddies partying in my house."

Tex was in his bedroom when he heard Swan Blossom go into the bathroom. Hearing water running, Tex thought, *Hell, yeah. I'll get her while she's in the bathtub.* Hearing the water shut off Tex tiptoed quietly down the hall and *Shit!* She'd locked the door. The house had old style doors and he was on his knees peeking through the keyhole. *My God, she's beautiful,* he thought. Swan Blossom was in the tub and Tex could only catch glimpses of her pink-tipped breasts, but it was enough to give him a raging hard-on. It reminded him of the days when he used to peek at his sister in the same way. Tex took his dick out and was stroking away, watching Swan Blossom in the tub. The tap on his shoulder caused him to crash against the door. The cameraman just stood there. Red-faced, his hard-on lost, Tex slunk to his room.

22

Flash and Mac hauled ass back to the main base. They didn't want to miss chow. The trip to visit Master Sergeant Taylor had taken longer than they planned. Pulling up in front of the Ranger Company, Mac commented, "Made it just in time for chow." Hopping out of the truck he was hit by both dogs; Rags and Airborne made quite a team. He laughed and tussled with them all the way into the barracks. The first thing the rest of the team wanted to know was: Is the mission on? "Ask him," and Mac pointed at Flash just coming into the hooch. Mac hung his M-16 and ammo on a nail and headed for the latrine to clean up.

He missed the beginning of what happened next. The way Bones told Mac was, "These strange grunts came in quietly and started piling cases of beer in the aisle and then the next thing you know Flash is flat on his ass rolling around on the floor and that was when you walked in. All Mac could see was a dust cloud with two sets of legs sticking out. Both dogs were barking up a storm and it took a minute for Mac to realize who these guys were.

"Holy fuck! Smitty! Marty! Pretty boy!" Mac hollered, finally recognizing his old platoon friends.

Fast Eddy stood up, helping Flash to his feet. "You're a sorry fuck. Let an old grunt sneak up on you like that." Both platoon sergeants were laughing their heads off. The introductions were made as beer was handed out. Fast

Eddy took a full can of beer and drank it dry in one swallow, then said, "Thanks guys. We fuckin' owe ya. That was Bravo Company out there."

Flash got the ball rolling. "If we'd have known it was your sorry ass out there, we would've run the other way."

"Whoa. Fuckin' whoa," and Fast Eddy held his hand out. "Bravo Company sent us down here to get you fucks. We got T- bones on the grill, cold beer, and a strip show for tonight. You're the only clerks and jerks we're inviting." The Rangers were already grabbing their bush hats, and beers in hand they went out to get in back of the deuce-and-a-half that Eddy had waiting. Eddy was just starting to pull away when Coke Bottle walked out of the orderly room.

"Hold it up, Eddy. We forgot one." Mac called to the Ranger clerk, "Come on, ya fuck." He and Pretty Boy grabbed the clerk's arms and hauled him in over the tailgate.

"What's goin' on?" Coke Bottle asked Mac.

"You are goin' to an ass-kickin' grunt party. Gonna have a strip show after steaks." MAC told Coke Bottle how Bravo Company was in for their three-day stand down and they got one night of free beer, a steak dinner, and a strip show and band.

Fast Eddy was blowing the truck's horn for all it was worth. As they pulled into the Bravo Company area the party was already in full swing. The mess hall was cooking steaks over a huge charcoal grill any way a man wanted it. After going through the rest of the line for potato salad and whatever else the guy wanted, the jeep trailer at the end of the chow line was full of ice cold beer and soda. Mac's feet hardly hit the ground and Fast Eddy had him in a hammer lock, knuckle rubbing his head and telling Mac what a good job he'd done.

Not letting go, Fast Eddy dragged Mac over to Top Murphy. "Hey, Top, this is the non-swimming mercenary from Bravo Company. A fuckin' deserter to the Rangers." Finally able to stand erect, Mac stuck out his mitt. Top pumped his hand and stuck a cold beer in the Ranger's hand.

"Glad ta meet ya. We thank you for helpin' us out there," and Top Murphy grinned. "Kinda skinny for a mercenary ain't he?" Everybody gathered around started to laugh. Top Murphy already knew Flash, but he shook each Ranger's hand and thanking them, led the Rangers to the chow line. Captain Doyle served each man a steak and he told Mac he'd talk to him after chow. By the time Mac had chow and both leg pockets filled with bones for the dogs, he was pretty well oiled. Captain Doyle finally caught the Ranger trying to war dance with the other drunks. Pulling Mac from the line, the CO shook his hand and thanked him for helping out his old company, and if there was anything he—the captain— could do, just let him know.

Mac wasn't shy. "Now where's that fuckin' el tee at, sir?"

Captain Doyle laughed. "He's in prison. Now go enjoy the strip show."

The officers and senior NCOs had a section reserved in the dusty parking lot full of folding chairs. They were busy during much of the strip show. They tried to catch up on all the news, break up fights among the troops, and watch the band and the stripper. Flash Gordon had the grunts in stitches describing the shit his Rangers did. Top Murphy fell out of his chair when Flash told all the senior NCOs how Mac had put hemorrhoid ointment on his head cut. When the band quit at nine o'clock, since they had to be off the base, the party started to break up. "OK, OK, one more," and Flash told the group how Mac and his buddy Bones had taught the gook to talk English using peanut butter and jam on a C-ration cracker. Flash waited. He knew somebody would bite but he didn't think it would be the captain. *Must be drunker than I thought.*

"Well, what did the gook say?" the captain
  asked.

Flash was pretty wobbly himself. "That fuckin' gook said
clear as a bell: 'Howya doin', ya fuckin' cocksucker?' and he
volunteered for the Rangers."

Mac and half a platoon of friends came over and stood
shakily, looking on. Their platoon sergeants and officers
were hanging on to one another and laughing their heads
off. The sight of Mac standing there set them off. When
Flash asked, "Howya doin', ya fuckin' cocksucker?" that got
everybody started again. The Rangers finally got their arms
around each other in order to make it back to their barracks. Coke Bottle called the cadence for the drunken
Rangers. Falling into the barracks, the team agreed it had
been one helluva good party.

At 0730 Master Sergeant Taylor pulled his jeep into the
Ranger Company area. *Shit, what's goin' on,* he thought.
Nobody around. He checked the empty orderly room. Passed
out sleeping behind the desk, the clerk could barely grunt
when Taylor shook him awake. He smelled the problem
before he even walked into the barracks. *Smells like a fuckin'
poolroom,* and he grinned, picking up a trash can. KLANK!
BANG! BANG! KLANG! "Wakey, wakey, girls!" KLANG!
KLANG! Taylor walked up and down the smelly aisle banging on the trash can. "Come on girls, there's a war on,"
laughing at the team as they tried to get up off their fart-
sacks.

His afro looking like a Brillo pad, Bones popped up.
"Shut up that fuckin' banging."

That was the wrong think to say for the old sergeant just
banged harder. "Come on girls, rise and shine."

Mac had a flashback to basic training at Ft. Dix.

"Oh, man, my head hurts."

Both dogs were sharing his bunk and he thought he saw
about twenty dogs before his eyes focused. He puked once
on the way to the shower. Coming back in, dripping wet,
he'd forgotten his towel.

Sergeant Taylor handed him half of a cold Coke. "Here,
drink that. Fix you right up."

Mac was too sick to argue and he did what he was told.
Sure enough, after a couple of swallows his stomach settled
down and he thought he'd live. While the rest of the team
headed for the showers, Mac started picking up beer cans
and filling the trash can that Taylor had dropped on the
floor. As he picked up trash, Mac started telling Taylor all
about the party and the girl with the shaved pussy who had
stripped the night before. Taylor had sacked out on an
empty bunk and he was trying to ignore Mac's chatter. The
sergeant thought of backing out of the mission. He didn't
want to be stumbling around out in Indian country with a
bunch of hung-over Rangers. It wasn't the way he wanted
to die.

Staff Sergeant Gordon must have been reading Taylor's
mail. As Gordon returned from his shower, he sat on the
end of the bunk where Taylor was resting. Wiping his wet
hair with a towel he said, "They'll be all right. It's on for
tomorrow, if we can find a way out there." Sliding his beret
off his eyes Taylor looked at Flash, then at Mac who was
already cleaning his weapons.

Shit, Taylor thought, *I forget what it's like to be young and
bounce back so quick.*

Coke Bottle came into the barracks with a huge pot of
black coffee. Sipping their coffee, Taylor started to talk
when Bones Washington—fresh from his shower— walked
up and got in Taylor's face. "Who the fuck you think you
are, comin' in here makin' all that lifer racket?"

Bones's face went gray when Taylor stood up. "You are

talkin' to a master sergeant and I will rip your little black lips off and glue them on your asshole. You got that, boy?" and Taylor stuck his black face nose to nose with Bones's. "Answer me, boy."

Bones had a change of heart right in front of everybody. "Yes, Sergeant. I got you."

Mac started to laugh and Taylor had him by the shirt front and on his feet. "You don't be laughin' at your dick-head buddy there. You start gettin' your shit in one bag. You understand me?" Mac was pushed backward and ended up on his ass next to Bones.

"Gottya, Sarge. No problem."

Taylor handed Bones a paper cup of coffee and, nodding at Flash, he added, "You fucks pay attention to your sergeant there."

For the next two hours the team sat in front of the blackboard and the mission was gone over and over. Chief added "We're gonna need a machine gun. Mac and Taylor are gonna be too far away from us to cover with rifles."

Flash laughed. "Good choice for a team," and looking at Taylor he added, "Glad you volunteered. Oki dokie, let's get weapons zeroed. Chief, you're humpin' the 60. Make sure you check it good. If you don't need to zero your rifle, we'll go see the sergeant major," and Flash gave Taylor a questioning look.

"Naw, my shit's good to go," Taylor answered.

Mac went into the orderly room and pried Coke Bottle away from his desk. "Come on, we're gonna do some shootin' and we need you to drive the truck." Mac grabbed some of the cheap military .30-.06 ammo out of the arms room where he'd left it.

Tucker surprised the team. Once he learned to hang onto the heavy rifle—even with his Coke-bottle-thick-glasses - he hit everything he aimed at.

The M-60 machine gun was fired by the team and even using old ammo never had a stoppage. They were cleaning their rifles and waiting for the 60 to cool when Taylor and Flash showed up. Both sergeants fired and Taylor showed off his skill with the CAR-15 he was carrying. The CAR-15 was a shorter cut-down version of the M-16. What the team liked most was that Taylor had two thirty-round clips for it.

The team stopped and picked up their clean tiger stripe fatigues. Mama san had sewn up all the tears at no extra charge. Waiting to go to chow, Flash explained that they would be riding out in a convoy and would drop off the truck as close to the area as they could get. The bitching started right away.

"We can't get a chopper anywhere around there. We'd be spotted right away," Taylor said.

In the mess hall, Flash came over with glasses of milk for everyone. "Start now and we'll drink more at supper."

Taylor said what everybody did: "I hate this shit." Everyone chuckled but drank it anyway.

After lunch every one of the team had a short nap, then Taylor got the Rangers back to the blackboard. He pointed to photos that showed how they could get to the target. The deuce-and-a-half the Rangers would ride in on would be the last truck in the convoy. The steel connex box would be set in the back of the truck with the door opened and facing the cab. Taylor would ride shotgun with the driver and pick out the closest spot to unass the truck. "Probably right here, or here," and he pointed out spots on the photos and on the map. "We'll have to lay up until dark and then hump in from there." Next, he drew on the board. "The tops of the paddy dikes have hedgerows growing on them. If you see an easy opening through it, don't take it. It's where Sir Charles likes to place his booby traps. These hedgerows are mostly thorn bushes. They will rip the shit out of you if you hit them head on. Crawl on your belly and you can get right underneath, then crawl over the dike and out the other side. We learned that from watching the gooks do it, so remember, crawl like a snake and you can get through. Mac and I will set up on this paddy dike here, and you guys will be set up on the next dike covering us." That said, Taylor sat down and Flash took over.

"I'll preplot artillery when we set in. When you guys make your shot, I'll have artillery inbound. As you guys fall back we'll cover you. Alpha a-go-go from the 25th Infantry will be airmobiling in as the artillery lifts. Now this is the hairy part. We have got to stay together. We don't wanna get fired up by these grunts comin' in. Stick together and we'll get our own chopper and get the fuck out and leave the clean up for the bush bunnies. OK, everybody to the barber shop for haircuts," and handing a list to Mac he said, "Pick up your shit at the PX."

Mac was first in the barber chair. The gooks who cut their hair charged forty cents and after explaining what he wanted, Mac got out of the chair, looked in the mirror, and was pleased. He gave poppa san a dollar. As he left the barber shop, he felt like a brand new recruit. As he rubbed the top of his head, Bones asked, "What the fuck is that?"

"That's a fuckin' Mohawk haircut, motherfucker. Bad, huh?"

Hollywood wasn't laughing. "Fuckin' cool, my man," and he went next. He got a Mohawk, too. Chief looked the best.

The three looked at Bones. "Oh no, man. My 'fro is stayin'. I ain't lookin' like you motherfuckers." With his teammates crowded around the barber chair just staring at him, Bones relented. "How do I look? How do I look?"

Hollywood said it the best. "You look cool, man. Now you're an asshole with the rest of us." The Rangers were in the PX and they felt ten-feet-tall when the grunts commented on their cool haircuts.

"Who are those guys?" was heard.

"Fuckin lurps, man. Sneak and peek motherfuckers."

The team didn't wear their bush hats all the way back to the company. As soon as Coke Bottle saw their haircuts, the clerk was on his way to the barbershop.

Taylor and Flash were in the headquarters map room which was crowded. The Ranger XO was there with the Intel captain. The sergeant major had clerks bringing in more plastic-covered maps. There was a casual mention that Swan Blossom had told Tex she was the key to the whole operation. She had told Tex that the NVA general came out of the bunker every morning at dawn for fifteen minutes of meditation, and that was the only time he came out. They argued about how many days they would spend out there. They could only have Alpha a-go-go on standby for three days. The 25th had the air assets, but the big concern was that the longer the op went the more the word would get out. If the general shifted his headquarters over to Cambodia, then he would be untouchable.

Flash looked at the list Taylor was writing. It pretty much matched his own. Rations for five days, everybody humping extra ammo for the 60, eight quarts of water per man and that might not be enough. They would need to hump two PRC-25 radios and extra batteries. The two sergeants compared lists.

Later, in the sergeant major's office, Bill offered cold bottles of Tiger 33 beer. Both Taylor and Flash declined. Kicked back in his chair, the sergeant major tried to talk Taylor out of going on the mission. "You're too fuckin' old, J.L. This is a kid's game, man. You're gonna retire same time as me, so give it up, man."

"Fuck you. I've been fuckin' around markin' time, so I

need some time in the field...but I'll leave it up to Flash."

Taylor said, "That's not your decision."

Staff Sergeant Gordon was no dummy. "Fuckin' a, we need ya, and glad to have ya. I'd take the sergeant major too, but he really is too old," and Flash laughed at the sergeant major's expression.

"OK, you fuckin' clowns. Break it down for me. And Taylor, since you know the little fucker the best—will he have any problem making the shot?" and Bill waited for Taylor to answer.

23

Pan Am flight 109 was full. Half of the passengers were military and the rest were civilian. Tex was glad to be in first class and really glad that he wasn't on a MAC flight. The military chartered planes jam-packed everybody in like sardines. Also, he wouldn't run into Jeannie since she worked the military flights. Thinking of Jeannie, he wondered what the stewardess would have thought if she could see Swan Blossom hanging on his arm tighter than the seat belts they had wrapped around them. He looked at her. *Black miniskirt and red silk blouse. Man, she's a fuckin' knockout,* Tex thought. Once the flight landed in Los Angeles, the *Dallas Star* had booked the couple a direct flight to Dallas. A rental car would be waiting at the airport and there was a suite reserved at the Holiday Inn, just two blocks from the paper. All Tex had to do now was sign his name. The paper paid for it all. *Man, this is the good life.*

Locked in the airplane, Swan Blossom had a hard time not showing her nervousness. She did relax once they were airborne and tried to study her English phrase book. Another reporter sitting two seats up had asked Tex where he got the good looking gook. That pissed her off. No matter where she went—even in Vietnam—she was always the different one.

She was not prepared for how long the flight took, but at the refueling layover in Hawaii she got to shop in the airport stores. Tex had extra bags of things she'd bought stored under his seat. Looking around as she headed down the aisle to the bathroom, she realized that most of the military had left and civilians had taken their place. Returning to her seat, she had a window to look out. Tex caught her looking and said, "Not for awhile yet."

Los Angeles took her breath away. As they approached the airfield, she could see no end to the city. She kept looking around for Hollywood. Tex had told her it was here and that they made movies.

Tex handled the arrangements for their bags to be sent to their next flight. Swan Blossom had been nervous about going through customs, but Tex had taken charge of that too. He'd unbuttoned one more button on her silk blouse and sure enough the customs agent was so busy bullshitting with Tex about the war and looking down her blouse that he never looked at her passport; just rubber stamped it. "Doesn't matter where you go in the world, baby. Sex sells," Tex said, and Swan Blossom would have liked to hit him for grabbing her ass as he pushed her into the terminal. She was amazed at the large crowds. The number of Asians working in the airport had her dumbfounded. This was not what she had been taught in school and the closest thing to an antiwar demonstrator that she saw was the group of Hare Kishnas selling flowers. Tex left her in the boarding area and came back with a brown and yellow bag. "Try this," and he laid out French fries, a strawberry milkshake, and a hamburger—all from McDonalds. She was done before Tex. She said it was the most wonderful meal she'd ever eaten. Laughing, Tex said she'd be able to find the hamburger stands everywhere they went.

"There's only one problem with eating at McDonalds," Tex told her.

"What? They're so good," she said.

Tex leaned over and whispered in her ear. "They make pretty lady beaucoup horny."

Caught, she giggled, playfully slapped his arm and talked just like a Saigon bar girl. "GI beaucoup horny. Want fuck all time." This time it was Tex who blushed and he was saved by the flight being called to board.

The drive from the Dallas airport in the new Chevy had Swan Blossom even more confused. The city lights in the early evening, the fast-moving traffic on the freeways, and she saw a McDonalds everywhere she looked. Tex sped the Chevy through traffic and told her, "Ya ain't seen nothin' yet." She didn't know what a mall was yet, but he told her she'd get to see a lot of them.

The Holiday Inn was much more than she expected and their suite had everything. She ran out on the balcony and looked down on the brightly lit swimming pool. Tex had to stop her from leaning over too far. "Wait until you really see first class." She was running between their adjoining rooms, jumping on the beds. "Can we do the McDonalds again?" Before he could answer she was in the bathroom with the door locked. Tex tried peeking through the keyhole but there wasn't one.

Using his own bathroom, Tex thought, *It isn't gonna take her long to get acclimated to all the new-found-freedom,* and in his heart he was glad for her.

It had come to her stronger than ever that she was all alone here and needed Tex more than ever. She was the one who opened Tex's bedroom door and carefully undressed him. She had never made love to such a hairy man before. His chest hair tickled her breasts and caused her to laugh while they made love—and she had never enjoyed it so much. Lying in each others' arms afterwards, Tex thought it was funny too that she was ticklish. He turned the light on and feasted his eyes on her. She sat up and crossed her legs and stared right back. Looking at Tex's rising hard-on, she smiled and said, "GI got beaucoup big dick," and reached over and started stroking him. The night went by too fast and they were fifteen minutes late getting to the *Star* the next morning. The editor wanted to know if that was a hickey on the reporter's neck. "Naw," Tex answered. "Gunshot wound. Through and through."

Swan Blossom was taken to personnel and given a press pass and photo ID. When the director asked if four-hundred a week was OK to start, she didn't know what to say, so she let him keep looking down her blouse. At her silence, the director continued staring right at her tits and finally said, "OK, OK. Four-fifty. That's as high as I can go." She let him keep looking while she bent over his desk and signed the forms. On the way back to the briefing room, all she could think about was four-fifty. That was more than the average Vietnamese made in a year.

24

The sergeant major had briefed General Davis on the Rangers' status. At odds with himself, and worried about J.L. going on the mission, he drove down to the Ranger Company and walked into a quiet barracks. The team had finished their final briefing and were packing rucksacks and giving their weapons a final going over. Even the dogs were just lying there, panting in the heat.

Taylor broke the silence. "Change your mind about coming with us?" The team chuckled over that.

Rather than answer the question, the sergeant major said, "You guys out of the whole brigade have hands down got the ugliest fuckin' dog."

"Careful, Sarn't Major. I say the secret word—Airborne'll rip your heart out," and Mac laughed while he continued stuffing lurp rations in his rucksack.

Bones looked at Airborne and the stumpy legs of the basset hound. "What's the secret word?"

Mac looked up from his ruck. "Can't tell ya, bro. It's a secret."

That cut some of the tension and the sergeant major grabbed a cold beer out of the mermite can and sat down. Flashing back to a time when he had done the same thing these guys were doing, only a different war, he thought, *Warriors still get ready for battle the same way.*

Flash asked the sergeant major, "Back to American beer?

I heard that tiger piss kicked your ass."

Bill burped and looked at the team leader. "Shit, got a couple of cases of that good stuff down in my office. And yeah, you're right about that. It did kick my ass." That started the comments rolling around.

With a bundle under his arm, Mac said, "I'll be right back," and headed out the door. As Mac walked into the dimly lit orderly room, the XO was just leaving. Mac said "Hello" to the officer and got nothing in return. Tucker had his own closet-sized room and with Rags and Airborne following, Mac walked in to find the clerk reading. As he handed the bundle to the startled clerk he asked Coke Bottle, "What's up with the XO, man? That guy on a bummer all the time, or what?"

Tucker unwrapped the bundle. "Shit. For me, man?" He held up the extra set of tiger stripes Mac had brought.

"Fuckin' a, man. Go good with your haircut," and Mac laughed as he ran his hand over his roach of blonde hair.

Hopping off the bunk, Tucker tried on the fatigues. "Man, you don't know this, but the el tee was out with a team and they ran smack into an ambush. Almost like the gooks knew they were comin'." Buttoning the shirt he continued, "Two guys were killed and three fucked up bad before they could get out. Anyway, the el tee walked away without a scratch and he hardly says nothin' to a team now. Afraid he'll put the jinx on them. The shirt's a little baggy, but I'll have mama san taper it for me. Thanks, man."

"I gotta get back to the team, but will you look after the dogs for me?" Mac asked.

"Fuck yeah, bro. No sweat. I'll pick up your pictures when they come in, too."

"Save me some of those books, Tucker," and waving, Mac took himself and the dogs back to the barracks.

As he was walking in, the sergeant major asked, "You pay

money for those haircuts?"

Without breaking stride, Mac pointed at Taylor. "We got the idea from him."

When Taylor's green beret was off, he had a bald spot surrounded by a fringe of hair. Rubbing his head, Taylor was the first to start laughing.

Everybody started on the sergeant major, wanting to know when they could get their three-day R&R. "As soon as you guys finish this mission, and," holding up his right arm, "if you get the general, I will personally get you a ride down to Vung Tau on the general's chopper and Taylor and me will buy you all the tiger piss you can drink."

The sergeant major left while everyone was pumped about the in-country R&R. Taylor walked him out to his jeep. Standing there smoking, the old friends didn't say much. Finally the sergeant major got behind the wheel and wished him "Good luck and good hunting" before he drove away.

Flash was the only one still up when he walked into the barracks so he grabbed a towel and a shaving kit and headed for the latrine. All three glasses of milk hit about three steps short of the head. He already had his pants down. *Man, that shit worked quick.* Taylor came running in, flashlight in hand. Both sergeants were thinking the same thing and Flash said it aloud: "Fuckin' Ex-Lax milk is hard on us older guys."

The team was ready early the next morning—cocked and locked—but no truck. When the truck showed up an hour late, it was a five-ton instead of the deuce-and-a-half. The deuce had broken down. The five-ton was roomier so Flash and Taylor rode up front. The connex box in the back was like an oven. Someone had taken the door off but even with the truck rolling the Rangers rotated sitting near it so they could catch even a hot breeze. They were hidden from the view of anyone looking at the truck, but even Chief felt closed in and didn't like it one bit. Going through Saigon, Mac and Bones tried to peek out and look at the ladies. One look from Flash had them both sitting back down, pronto. When the five-ton caught up with the slow-moving convoy, Flash turned and pointed at their faces. It was tough trying to camo up. They were sweating so much it was hard to apply and it didn't stay long. One of the trucks broke down and they had to stop. Just the few minutes of waiting made the connex worse than any oven. The camo paint ran off their faces as fast as the water running out of them. They had passed their ambush area and the guys in the back never even knew it.

Flash yelled through the hole, "Comin' up. Get ready to unass." The truck slowed to a crawl. Taylor and Flash were out first. Flash grabbed rucksacks and helped the four men get out of the slow-moving truck. Taylor moved to the rear and, walking backward, provided security. Once everybody had their rucks on, Flash swung up on the back and checked the connex to make sure the team had everything. Slamming his hand against the door, he waved the driver off. The truck was grabbing gears but the Rangers were already headed into the small patch of jungle that grew next to the road. The area Taylor led them into wasn't triple canopy, just a wild patch of woods. The team was moving rapidly deeper into the green. Mac felt good—back in the woods, away from the stinking truck and the hotbox they'd had to ride in. The vines and four-foot-high ferns were easy to get through.

Taylor held the team up and with a circular motion of his hand the team went into a wheel formation. They lay in a circle, facing out, their feet touching and forming the center. Flash used the radio Mac was humping to call in their first sit-rep. Shutting the radio off, he camouflaged Mac's sweat-streaked face again. The whole team had to camo up again. When the team had their war paint on, Flash used the radio that Bones humped, doing preplots for artillery. Mac lay facing the area they were supposed to check out. Taylor lay beside him, using his binoculars. Mac wanted a better look and as he waited for Taylor to hand over the binocs he noticed that the log in front of him began to move. *Oh fuck...the booze I drank...making me see things.* He rubbed his eyes and looked at Taylor. The master sergeant was frozen to the ground. He was watching the moving log. The team had scared up a boa constrictor and the snake was leaving. Black, brown, and yellow colors slowly slid by. Terrified, Mac swore he could hear the huge snake crawling. Turning his head to the right, Mac looked at Flash. The team leader was still holding the plastic-wrapped radio handset, not saying a word, and his eyes were glued to the snake. If they fired the snake up, that was it for the mission. They'd have to be extracted. The three team members on the back side of the wheel never saw the snake and were already dropping out of their rucks. The civilian bus coming along the road broke the spell. The Vietnamese Greyhound was loaded with people, chickens, pigs in crates, and kids riding along on top. The noise of the bus and the chatter of the people made it sound like they were all going on a holiday. From where the team lay they looked out over fairly dry paddies and had a good view of the highway. Mac kept his eyes on the target area. The heat waves coming off the paddies made the patch of jungle he was watching dance, but he didn't see any people. Taylor and Flash watched the bus. It was headed toward Saigon and right in the middle of the paddies it stopped. Two old mama sans got off. Flash motioned to Mac. Slowly, Mac moved, and he traded places with the Indian. The whole team had to view the target area.

Taylor slid next to Flash and whispered, "We might be in the wrong area." Flash went stiff and moved his head slightly. The black-clad mama sans had balanced bamboo poles over their shoulders. Baskets at both ends of the poles were loaded with fresh fruit and vegetables. As soon as the bus was out of sight, the two old ladies— carefully balancing their loads—headed right for the target area. Someone passed a canteen around. Mac drank and the hot, plastic-tasting water never tasted better. Mac watched the area to his front. Starting right in front of the ruck he was laying on, he let his eyes sweep the zone. Using a ten meter strip he searched the area.

With nothing out of place, he paid attention to the sounds. The critters they had disturbed coming in had begun to resume their squawks and buzzing. Once again, crickets started making their racket.

Unless the team was compromised, they would stay here and not move until dark.

Mac watched a scorpion bust through a spider web. The brown spider came out to see what he'd caught in his web. *He's pissed,* Mac thought. *Fuckin' scorpion ruined his web.* The brown spider repaired the web and Mac watched the sun beams as they caught on the new web. The underside of the ferns all seemed to have spider webs built beneath them. Looking at the profusion of webs, Mac knew from their undisturbed state that nobody had been through here recently. Mac loved the green. Every color and shade of green was here. No wonder the gooks blend in so well. A tap on his shoulder and he moved his position in the wheel. A convoy of trucks went by. *Fuckin' highway's a busy place.* Mac was back in his original place when Flash handed him the binocs and pointed out the two mama sans trucking along the paddy dike.

Mac watched the two old ladies. Both of their balance

poles were carrying empty baskets. They were heading for the road. The hot sun went behind a cloud. It got so dark in the green Mac thought, *The fuckin' gooks would need a flash-light to find us.* With Taylor on one side and Flash on the other, both men took turns whispering in his ear. "Those old gooks dropped off supplies out there, so the place is there." Taylor also said he was relieved that the gooks were right where he thought they'd be.

Flash whispered, "We'll leave here and hump right along the paddy dikes and drop you guys off, then go to our posi-tions. We'll be home by morning," and he grinned.

The sun came back out and Mac used the binocs. The two old ladies were almost out of sight, humping down the road. He focused on the target area and nudged Taylor. "Is that some kinda bench or the top of a bunker?" and Mac handed him the binocs.

Taylor looked where Mac had looked. After refocusing the glasses, he spotted the bench. "It's a shrine," and he passed the binocs to Flash. The shrines were all over Vietnam and showed up in the most unexpected places. The plan was well developed. Now that they were here on the ground they were reminded that the maps and photos could only show so much.

Flash gave the chow sign. Half the team dug out rations and the other half kept watch. Mac tapped Taylor and stuck out his hand. Without looking, Taylor handed Mac a lurp ration. Using two small, fairly flat stones, Mac used his spoon to scoop a small hole in the ground, then set the stones around the edge of the hole. Next, he filled his can-teen cup with water and, lighting a chunk of C-4 explosive, he set the cup of water on the homemade stove. While the water heated, he opened the plastic bags. Taylor had spaghetti and shrapnel. Mac's was beef and rice. The water was steaming as the explosive burned out. Careful of the hot cup, he poured the steaming water half in one bag and the rest into the other. He refilled the canteen cup, lit another piece of C-4 and had another cup of water heating. He folded the tops of the plastic sacks, shook the contents and, setting them back on the ground, he dug into his ruck for more things he needed. He added Tabasco sauce and salt to the bag of spaghetti and meatballs and handed it to Taylor. His second cup of water was ready, so he poured half the water into another ration then made coffee with the hot water that was left. He added Tabasco sauce to both rations and dumped in packets of salt. Mac added a lot of salt to everything he ate so he didn't have to take salt tablets. From start to finish the meal took about ten minutes. He added his trash to the bag that Flash sent around. It would be buried or hidden. He tucked the extra meal he'd made into his pants. The heat from his body would keep it moist. The team had finished their meal and were smoking their gook cigarettes when the rain hit.

Mac grabbed Shirley in his arms and wrapped a piece of canvas over the bolt, then he took a condom out of its wrapper and rolled it down over the muzzle. The visibility dropped and, even as close to the road as they were, they could only hear a truck or bus go by. The paddies were sucking up the water and the gray mud was already starting to stink. Taylor and Flash were talking out loud as the sound of the rain drowned out everything. Taylor had said, "Ain't no way we can get through the paddies if this rain keeps up."

Flash agreed, but he didn't want to have to take the team down the road in the dark. "No tellin' what we could run into."

Mac felt like his nuts were drowning, so he moved them up higher. The rain went from a downpour to a drizzle and stayed that way. Mac had set his canteen cup out in the rain.

He washed it out with rainwater, then let the rain fill it up again and filled his canteen adding a water purification pill. His canteen cup filled again, he lit another chunk of C-4. The explosive burned at about 2000 degrees and nothing he knew of put it out. Using his rock stove he added chunks of C-4 until the water boiled, then he added six shakes of Maxwell House instant. He always bought a small jar of coffee for the field since he drank more coffee than he got in his rations. Stirring the brew, he added a pack of cocoa and two packs of creamer. Closing his eyes, he took a sip of the bush coffee. *Just fuckin' right.* Taylor shoved a lit smoke in his hand and took the hot canteen cup. The team passed the cup around taking small sips until it was nearly gone. Mac got the best part. He swished the dregs around and gulped it down. Flash leaned over and quietly said, "That's some wicked shit."

It went from daylight to dark that quickly, like throwing a light switch. The men closed the top buttons on their shirts and pulled their bush hats down. It didn't help much. The mosquitoes ate anywhere they could. If the men didn't wipe their noses constantly, the mosquitoes plugged them. They swarmed everywhere and as their ears plugged up they lost the sound. Tobacco went around and the juice from a chew went on the bites they wanted to scratch. The soaked team was glad to finally get up on their feet and help each other into their rucksacks. They moved to the edge of the small wood they were in by holding onto the ruck in front of them. Flash and Taylor had figured that the only way they could move would be on the highway and only in two-man teams. The teams would march in a staggered line; Mac and Taylor first, Chief and Hollywood on the other side of the road, and Flash and Bones would bring up the rear. The drizzle continued and Mac was scared to death. Even with Taylor in the lead, all he could do with the heavy radio and all his other shit was plod along behind the black shadow three feet in front of him. Taylor stopped and Mac ran right into the back of him. The big man was frozen in place. He turned and whispered in Mac's ear. "Snakes."

The snakes were leaving the paddy and the rising water. Mac pulled Taylor down beside him in a squat. "Just have to wait. They're gettin' the fuck out of Dodge." Each team member had pieces of luminescent tape, one on the back of their bush hats and the other piece on their rucksacks. Chief touched both men on the back and Taylor whispered what was going on. Chief turned and left to pass the word. Exposed on the road by the snake migration they waited. Mac hated the mosquitoes that found them. As the snakes thinned down to an occasional small black shadow, the two men stood, adjusted their gear, and got ready to move. The snakes had held them up long enough so they didn't run into the gooks that had come from the other direction. They were using kerosene lanterns. The smell of the kerosene wafting down the road alerted Taylor. Mac halted and went to a crouch. He smelled the burning kerosene, but in the drizzle he couldn't see anything. The soft glow of the lanterns—so close—took them by surprise. The gooks turned and walked along the paddy dike that the team would have to take. The gook soldiers were talking quietly and had one lantern at the front of the group and one bringing up the rear.

Mac's hair was crawling all over his scalp. There was no place to hide. They couldn't move. As the last glow of the lantern disappeared in the rain, the rest of the team came up. No one wanted to go up the dike after the gooks, but they couldn't go into the paddies either. The noise they would make sloshing in the rice paddies would be heard for sure. A quick huddle: Go or not.

Flash made the final decision: follow the gooks. Taylor

led the way and Mac was right on his ass. The team made no noise at all, creeping along the top of the slippery dike. The Rangers moved as fast as they could. Taylor had his CAR-15 on full auto. Chief was rear security with the 60 machine gun. The team didn't want to be a sandwich, caught by any surprises coming up behind them.

Snap, snap. Flash was snapping his fingers.

25

Taylor held it up. The four covering Rangers were at their cross-dike, where they were supposed to hide up. Mac and Taylor had to hump another seventy-five meters and slide down into the paddy and hump into their hiding spot. Both men humped off. Mac's asshole felt like it was clamped onto his back teeth. *Man, we are exposed out here.* Taylor picked the thickest part of the bushes for them to get down into the paddy. Taylor showed Mac how to slide, grabbing his legs and guiding him under the hedgerow. *Shit. Slicker than snot.* Mac popped out on the other side. They stuck close to the edge of the hedgerow and moved to the corner of the two dikes. Once they found the corner, Taylor moved another fifty meters out toward the center of the dike. At a quiet hiss, Mac followed Taylor into the hide. Lying flat on their bellies, Taylor went first, up and underneath the tangled hedgerow. Mac couldn't believe it, but there it was. The inside of the hedgerow had a clear space.

Taylor grabbed the radio handset and gave a quick sitrep. Flash Rogered they were hidden up on the dike behind them. Taylor was on the wrong side and the thorns stuck them both as they changed positions. Now Mac was on Taylor's left and it was a dark and dripping place where they were trying to get comfortable. All they could do was sit. There was barely room to stand, none to lie down. Mac used his left hand and brushed the ground where he was going to park his ass. He wrapped his sweat towel around his hand and, at eye level as near as he could tell in the dark, he started making an opening through the hedgerow so come daylight he could see to make his shot.

The bushes had heavy-duty thorns sticking out everywhere. Carefully, he stood, with Shirley against the bushes and her stock just touched his knee. The rain dripped down through the branches but it didn't stop the mosquitoes. Mac had taken off the ruck with the radio in it and pushed it between himself and Taylor. Taylor used his for a back rest. Mac's ass was already sitting in a puddle of water. He wondered if he should put a rubber on his dick. The guys had told him that the leeches could crawl right in the head of his dick and plug it right up. The whine and sting of mosquitoes, and not being able to use insect repellant, was making his face swollen. He dug into his left cargo pocket and pulled out his head net. Made of nylon bug screen it had a hoop that held it away from his face. He could see out of it and it had a drawstring to pull tight around his neck. He put the bug shield on and his boonie hat back over the top.

He heard Taylor slapping bugs so he reached back in his pocket and pulled out an extra head net and stuck his arm out in the darkness until it ran into the sergeant. The sergeant whispered, "Thanks." Both of them heard more gooks splash by. From the sounds of the bitching, the NVA weren't happy being out in this shit either. Both men were shaking from sitting and being wet. One at a time they dug out their poncho liners and wrapped them over their backs and shoulders. Even when wet, the light nylon liners held body heat in. The Rangers never carried ponchos in the field; the rubberized raincoat with its built-in hood made too much noise when the rain hit it. Mac dug out his bottle of Tabasco and sucked some right out of the bottle. *Better than a hot cup of coffee.*

"Gimme some," Taylor said in a whisper. Using both hands, Mac carefully handed him the bottle. Mac put his mind in neutral and pictured what would appear when daylight came. He hoped he was lined up on the bench in front of the shrine and that was where the general would show up. Mac would make the shot, the artillery would come in, and the rest of the team would cover Taylor and Mac on their way out. Sitting cross-legged, both men's legs started to cramp and they were forced to move.

Mac said, "Fuckit," and let the thorns dig into his back while he moved his legs. The small noises they made were covered by the rain, yet even as he dozed Mac could still hear Taylor breathing deeply as he slept. He could tell that dawn was not far off. There was a breeze. It seemed there was always a small breeze just before the sky began to lighten. He put his hand on the dark shadow.

"OK, OK, I'm awake," Taylor whispered.

The drizzle had not let up in the least. Mac moved his ass in the puddle he was sitting in. Both of them started touching parts of their gear, getting ready for day. Daylight never happened. The fog came right into the hedgerow. One minute Mac was looking at black, the next at dripping gray. He managed to get to his knees and take a piss. Staying that way, he could hear muffled sounds off toward the target. The visibility was about three feet. The radio clicked and Mac picked up the plastic-bagged handset.

Flash asked softly, "Can you see?"

"Negatory," and Mac listened a second. "Roger that," and he put the handset down. He leaned over to Taylor and whispered, "Pack it up and let's get out of here."

Taylor leaned his face in. "Nooo, man. This is our only chance. We're never goina get another one."

Nose to nose, Mac asked softly, "What's the big deal, man? We can go kill something else."

"Look, Mac, I've been sitting on my ass for too long. I didn't come out here to give it up. We can't find a better place to hide." Looking Mac dead in the eye, the master sergeant added, "I don't want to go away empty-handed. This will be our only chance at a general."

"Fuck it. That means we gotta sit here until tomorrow. What if it's still fuckin' foggy? What then?" Mac asked.

Head net to head net, Taylor said, "Promise me one shot. That's all. One fuckin' shot."

Mac kept his eyes on Taylor. He could see that the Green Beret thought it was important. "OK, fuck. OK, I'll do it," Mac whispered and reached for the handset.

Flash had punched a hole through the hedgerow they were using to look toward the dike where Mac and Taylor were hiding. He leaned over to Chief. "You owe me five bucks."

Chief had bet that Mac and Taylor would pull out. All Mac had said on the radio was "Continuing the mission."

Flash couldn't even see the dike through the fog. That was the hairy part about having your team split. As the light got better, he hoped he'd be able to see enough to provide cover if they got into trouble.

In the improved light Mac got busy. He used a small pair of needle-nosed pliers and began to cut away branches and thorns. The wet branches cut easily and he worked while Taylor peered into the fog. The drizzle kept up and helped to smother any small sounds he made. Soon he was able to halfway stand and now he could lean back with only the odd thorn stabbing him in the back. Taylor did the same and soon he could stretch out his legs. Mac felt like he had a dishpan ass from sitting in water all night. On his knees, he oiled his rifle and quietly took the old round out of the chamber and slipped a new hot round up the spout. He covered the bolt with his piece of canvas and leaned the rifle against the hedgerow. He tried to look through the hole but he couldn't see anything—just gray, cotton fog.

Using salt, the two cleared each others' bodies of leeches. Taylor even had them in the crack of his ass. Mac figured the only reason he didn't have any on his ass was because he'd been sitting in the puddle. They had just settled back down when the first singsong set of voices went by. About noon the drizzle finally stopped and the sun came out. Even that didn't stop the hedgerow from dripping. Mac realized he was about three feet off on his eyehole. Amused, he thought, *I'da shot the moon,* and he used his pliers to make a better window. Peering from his vision slot, he estimated the range at between three-hundred-fifty and four hundred yards to the bench in front of the small shrine. He couldn't see any sign of a tunnel. The two gooks sitting beside the machine gun to the left of the shrine made it apparent that something was there.

Taylor made a window of his own and found one more set of gooks who were better hidden. This was where the mama sans had dropped off the baskets of fruit and vegetables. Mac whispered, "Can you see the tunnel?"

Taylor looked at Mac, shook his head, and pulled Mac back from his window. "I saw two machine guns and they're piling up food so they must only come out at night." Taylor added, "They're fuckin' here, man."

Mac looked at the old sergeant. "Do you wanna attack?" Sitting back, he dug out a ration.

"Don't be fuckin' with me, Mac," and Taylor dug into his ruck and retrieved a can of peaches.

"Hey, Sarge," Mac whispered, "how come Bones is always accusing people of hating niggers?"

Taylor stiffened. *Oh, shit,* he thought, *stuck in here with a fuckin' guy that hates blacks.*

Taylor looked at Mac and took his time answering. He reached down and unhooked the flap on his .45's holster. Mac was hunched over, heating water to add to his ration. "What the fuck you askin' shit like that for?"

Mac added the lukewarm water to his ration bag and leaned back. "Well, he's my friend and he thinks that white people hate him just 'cause he's black."

Taylor thought, then answered, "Lotsa black kids growing up in a ghetto blame all their shit on white folks when they don't even know any."

Mac added hot sauce to his lurp ration. "Guess that makes a little sense," he whispered, and shrugged his skinny shoulders.

Taylor had finished his can of peaches. Sliding his hand down to his .45, he quietly asked, "What about you, Mac? You hate niggers, too?"

Mac turned with his ration and looked at Taylor. "I don't fuckin' know any niggers. Do you?"

Sitting shoulder to shoulder Taylor could tell that Mac was serious and he grinned. "You worried about dyin', Mac?"

Eating his ration, Mac paused. "Dyin's easy. It's killin' that motherfucker over there that's hard," and he nodded toward the gooks and their machine guns. Taylor lifted one cheek and farted. "You're one rotten motherfucker. Whooeeie!" Mac waved his ration around. "Man, you stink!"

Calmly, Taylor looked at Mac and said, "That's for all the niggers," and the black man started to giggle.

Mac dropped his half-eaten ration in the mud and, leaning against the sergeant, held his sides—tears rolling down his cheeks. Every time they looked at one another they started giggling. Settling down, Mac picked his ration off the muddy floor, pulled a leech from his meal and went back to eating.

26

It had been sleeping, but then the deer crashed through the underbrush. With a slight breeze in his face, Wallace Wallace had scared the buck from its resting place.

The skills Wallace had learned killing Japs in the Pacific were still with him. Grinning, he slid right up on that buck. He hadn't roamed these woods since before the war. Hunting men had taken all the thrill out of hunting four-legged animals. The family thought he was at work. *Fuck 'em,* he thought, moving slowly after the buck. *A man can only stand being cooped up for so long.*

Sitting on the bank of a small creek he finalized his plan. He needed a trip or a vacation, so he planned on getting away. The memories of the war and thinking about that rifle had made Wallace realize that the important things in his life were going right on by. Moving with purpose, he headed home. Coming to the top of a small ridge, he thought, *Fuck, I've wandered about five miles from the farm.* It felt good to be out in the woods again.

Yesterday, Wallace had caught Winona blowing his Mexican mechanic in the parts room. Wallace hardly had the energy to call his buddy the sheriff and ask him to make sure the Mexican never came back to Crockett Mills.

Even though he was all dirty and not wearing a suit—which he usually wore at the dinner table—nobody asked where he'd been. Winona made the comment that the shop help was not showing up to work like they should. Shirley bitched about not finding anything to buy on her shopping spree.

Sighing, Wallace thought, *Same old shit.* He finally said, "I'm goin' to a Marine Corps reunion out in San Diego. Anybody want to go?"

"Shit no, Dad," Winston commented. "You guys will just get all drunk and hang around together." Wallace had taken his family to one of the reunions years ago and left the family in the motel while he partied with his old friends.

Shirley had her face set. "Not again. You're too old for that shit."

Wallace threw his napkin on the table. "I'm goin'. You guys can handle it," and he stalked out of the dining room.

The next morning he was headed up Interstate 55 before the family even got up. The sign read St. Louis. *Fuck 'em. They'll never think of looking for me up there.* Wallace found long term parking and, with only a small suitcase, he found a men's room. He adjusted his money belt, pissed, splashed water on his face, took a glance in the mirror, left the men's room and walked up to the first ticket counter he saw. He paid cash for his one-way ticket.

Fuckit. I'll come back when I feel like it. He found a seat in the waiting area and amused himself by watching a girl about Winona's age trying to pull her miniskirt down. She finally gave up and, crossing her legs, gave Wallace a fine beaver shot. *Man, girls weren't like this when I was that age. Fuck it,* Wallace said to himself, walked out of the waiting area, found a bar, and after two double shots of Wild Turkey he felt better. Returning to the waiting area he sat, let the whiskey glow, and wished the miniskirted girl a pleasant good morning.

At their boarding call he was surprised to find he was seated next to the pretty girl. Drinks were served in first class and he had quite a glow on when the plane landed in San Francisco. He had to change planes and he dozed off in the boarding area. After his nap he felt like shit. If they hadn't called the plane right then, he would have turned around and flown home. This time the seat next to him was empty. He ate hungrily and the stewardess even gave him an extra meal. It got dark flying over the ocean and he thought back to being on the ocean in a troop ship, packed like sardines. *Guadalcanal. Only one fuckin' map in the whole battalion. I wonder if the Marines have improved any.*

He finally noticed the small blonde who kept looking at him. About Shirley's age, he reckoned. Nice tits and great legs. She was sitting right across the aisle and when Wallace caught her eye she smiled. Wallace nodded when she said hello and buried his head in the gun magazine he was reading. He awoke with a start. The captain had lit the No Smoking and Fasten Your Seat Belt signs. The stewardess came along to make sure the signs were obeyed. He had awakened with a hard-on. He had fastened his seat belt and had the magazine covering his lap. *Oh, yeah. Shit, that hasn't happened in years.* Making love with Shirley was a once-a-month chore. *Shit, when we were first married we were like rabbits.*

He got off the plane and after retrieving his suitcase he caught a cab for his hotel. *Man, I love this place.* He checked into his room, cleaned up, and he was hungry again. *Fuck yeah, I want a steak,* so he took the elevator to the lobby. The queer bellhop daintily pointed to the restaurant.

He had no trouble getting a table and was waiting for his second beer when the little blonde from the plane asked if she could join him. Wallace stood and stammered, "Sure."

She stuck out the cutest little hand. "Hi. I'm Patty Roberts."

Wallace took her hand and said, "I'm Wallace."

She kept looking at him. "Just Wallace?"

He explained his name and she thought that was cute—having the same first and last name. "Welcome to Hawaii," and she raised her glass of wine.

Wallace paid for both meals and Patty took him to a nightclub just a half a block from the Sheraton. Wallace learned to dance and walking back to the hotel they were arm-in-arm. Their rooms were on the same floor, but Wallace never got to his room. They didn't hit the bed until the second time they made love. Wallace thought the first time was great even though it was on the rug. He started to fall asleep in her bed. Snuggled next to him, Patty whispered, "Can I suck your cock?" Wallace learned how to eat pussy and when they woke up the two of them went at it again.

Back in his room, Wallace showered and lay on the unmade bed the maid had turned down the evening before. He ate the small chocolates and thought of the wonderful night he'd just spent. He fell asleep dreaming about the date he was looking forward to with Patty that night.

The maid coming into the room to clean woke him. *Shit, mid-morning. Haven't slept in like that in twenty years.* He finished dressing, left his room for the elevator and, as he was passing Patty's room, he thought, *Fuck, even my dick is grinnin' this morning.* He went out and climbed into the first taxi he saw in front of the hotel.

"Where ya wanna go, brah?" the Hawaiian asked, pulling away.

Wallace leaned over the front seat and showed the cab driver the address on the envelope. "You know this place?"

"Shit yeah, brah. Get ya there real quick," and the Hawaiian took a good look at Wallace. *Skinny white dude. Hair so short he looked almost bald.* Back to paying attention to the road, he thought, *Green Beret or CI fuckin' A.* Wallace gave the man a five-dollar tip. *No, that boy ain't CIA. Soldier. That's the only guys give tips like that.*

"Thanks, brah. You need a ride back, here's my card."

Wallace took the card and turned to look at the sign: Recoil Gun Shop, and in smaller letters: Shotgun Charlie, Prop.

Wallace jangled the bells over the door as he entered the shop and again when he closed the door. Charlie looked up from behind the counter and slid the .357 back in its hiding place.

Fuckin' tourist, Charlie thought. "Yeah, can I help ya?"

Wallace looked the gun shop over and   breathed deeply of gun oil and solvent. He recognized Charlie right off. He was older, less hair, but the face hadn't changed all that much. Walking up to the counter, Wallace asked pleasantly, "I'm lookin' for a queer Marine that gave head on Guadalcanal," and busted up at the look on Charlie's face.

Even on his artificial leg, Charlie was around the counter and had his customer in a bear hug. "Wallace Wallace, you ugly motherfucker. Motherfuckin' podgy bait Marine!" Stepping back, Charlie took a good look at the Marine he'd known on the canal. "You fuckin' got old."

Wallace laughed. "You did too."

Charlie went to the front door and flipped the Closed sign. Dragging his old friend into his office, he dug out a bottle of Wild Turkey, glasses and cold beers and set them on his desk. The two men sipped whiskey, chased it with beer, and shot the shit like it had been only two weeks since they'd last seen each other.

The beer and whiskey had loosened Wallace up and he finally got around to what was on his mind. "Where's my rifle?"

Charlie looked at Wallace. "You came all this way because of that fuckin' rifle?"

Wallace nodded seriously.

"Well, the fuckin' thing's in Vietnam," and looking at the clock he added, "They're gonna kill a gook general with it."

Jimmy had come in from Vietnam the day before and told Charlie about his brother-in-law going out with the Rangers. Charlie couldn't believe what he was hearing. Taylor, wounded on his last tour in that shit hole, had promised the whole family that he was done with the field and hunting the enemy. He told Wallace the whole story—how the rifle had come from Vietnam to be repaired. "Some gook had it. Don't ask me how the gook had it. Mac found your note in the stock." Charlie left and returned with the note that Wallace had written at the end of World War II. When Charlie talked about Mac putting hot ammo through the rifle, Wallace wanted to know how it shot. "Wallace, I'm tellin' ya, that kid's good. Skinny little fuck, just like you. He even shot a pineapple's surfboard because the Hawaiian fucked with him."

"No shit. Hot-tempered little fucker, is he?" and Wallace took another sip of whiskey.

"You don't know the half of it." Charlie told as much of Mac's story as he knew, then added, "He had a girlfriend here. Taylor told me she was married but they spent every minute they could together." He paused and drank some beer. "Taylor told me that little motherfucker sure could shoot."

"You think he'll sell that rifle?"

Charlie thought a minute and said, "Naw. Motherfucker will give it to you, but not sell it." Both men were surprised when the whiskey was all gone and so was the afternoon. "What are you gonna do tonight? Come on over and meet the wife."

Wallace grinned and shook his head. "I got me a date," and seeing Charlie's look he added, "No shit."

"I thought you might have brought your wife with you," and Charlie stopped right there. Both men agreed to meet again the next day and Charlie would try to have Jimmy come by the shop and meet Wallace. Wallace had Charlie call the number of the cab company and ask for the driver who had dropped him off. All the way to the hotel Wallace thought about Patty and whether she would really be waiting for him.

He had just closed the door to his room when his question got answered. Patty knocked on the door and helped him shower. They tried a different place for dinner and afterward went for a walk on the beach. Giggling like kids, they agreed they didn't have the courage to skinny dip and make love in the ocean.

Patty had just gone through a messy divorce and had promised herself two weeks in Hawaii. She also had two kids and planned on going back to teaching. She hadn't worked in fifteen years and was looking forward to it. Wallace told her about why he was in Hawaii and how much he wanted his rifle—named Shirley—back. "I'll even go to that fuckin' place called Vietnam to get it," he told her. Later, in bed, he told her about his life since the war. Both of their lifetime experiences made them appreciate each other that much more.

27

Mac was asleep in the greenhouse. The humidity in between the hedgerows had both men dripping water. The puffs of breeze across the paddies didn't even get a leaf to move. Taylor looked at the sleeping Ranger, curled in a fetal position. There wasn't room enough in the hide to stretch out. The kid slept with one hand wrapped around his .38. *Fuckin' kid eats this shit up,* the master sergeant thought. Mac twitched from the flies that were crawling in his ear and that fast he was awake. Taylor handed him a lit gook cigarette. With the civilians back and forth on the dike, it was safe enough to grab a smoke, at least during the day. The only way the gooks could get into their dripping greenhouse was either the same way Taylor and Mac got in or use a chain saw. Puffing his smoke, Mac quietly asked, "You wanna take a nap?"

Taylor shook his head and started digging in his ruck for another ration. He was looking for more spaghetti. *Didn't have this good shit when I was a pup,* he thought, finding what he was looking for. Mac got on his knees, took a piss, and got out his canteen cup to make coffee.

By dark both men hated each other. Tired, wet, dirty, and full of flies, the close confines of the hide had them on each others' nerves. Closer than a husband and wife, there wasn't even room to breathe their own air. At dusk the mosquitoes came back. Just trying to pull their headnets on—looking like beekeepers—had both of them bumping arms and cursing softly at one another. Both men tried to keep as far away from the other as the enclosed space allowed. Taylor thought that if he heard one click or even what sounded like Mac was pulling his pistol, he was going to open fire before that motherfucker got the drop on him.

The rain came down in sheets and it saved their sanity. Taylor and Mac were already wet but an hour after the rain started, the men were huddled together, both ponchos wrapped around them to stay warm. "What a fuckin' place," Mac said. "Burn up, then we fuckin' freeze."

Taylor passed his canteen full of cold coffee to Mac. "It's the sittin' that's makin' us so fuckin' cold."

"If this keeps up we won't get a shot in the mornin' either," Mac whispered shakily. Mac felt like every bone in his suitcase was rattling. By the time Mac had dozed off, then come to, the rain had let up. The mosquitoes outside his head net sounded like jet planes. Every bit of exposed skin was fair game. Even where his fatigues touched snug against his skin became a lunch counter. Somehow they both shook their way through the night. There hadn't even been any gooks walking along the dike to keep them awake. Mac had sat with his poncho liner wrapped around him, his eyes glued to the opening through the hedgerow. The fog came off the paddies and even though he could hear the gooks, he couldn't see to shoot.

Flash waited too long to pull Mac and Taylor out. With the fog fully lifted, he couldn't get them across the open paddy in daylight. Alpha a-go-go called and they were assigned a new mission starting the next day at noon. The whole thing had gone bust.

Mac was pissed that Flash made them wait and continue the mission. He was even more pissed that his cool new haircut—the shaved sides of his Mohawk— were itching and driving him crazy. What Flash had said about sloshing across the paddy in daylight made sense, but he didn't like it. He only had half a bottle of hot sauce left. He began making a beef and rice meal. He added a can of C-ration beef with spice sauce. *Fuckit.* He boiled the water and added it to the plastic bag, then boiled another cup of water and made cocoa and coffee. The two men tried to ignore one another. Mac was contemplating his rotten wet boots when Taylor—looking through his opening—gave a quiet hiss.

Mac peered through his own hole, hoping the gooks were attacking them. The gooks had come out of the tunnel. At least two men and two women were humping supplies down, but neither Taylor nor Mac could see the tunnel opening itself. In five minutes they were gone. The two machine gun teams were still in place, but the rest of the gooks had disappeared. The sun came out and stayed out. All the birds and critters that lived in the hedgerow went about their business. They had accepted the humans living with them. Flash called just before dark and gave them the bad news. Team Asp had been ambushed on insert and had lost one man. He also gave them the choice of pulling out as soon as it was dark. Taylor was burying the trash and checking his packed-up rucksack. Mac asked, "Where the fuck are you goin'?"

Taylor whispered, "Let's give it up. We're going to have more fog."

Sitting cross-legged, oiling his rifle, Mac whispered, "It's gonna be clear as a bell tonight and we'll be able to see our shot in the mornin'."

The man's confidence had Taylor call Flash on the radio and tell him to set things up—they'd make the shot in the morning.

Flash was not at all convinced. Flash whispered to Chief,

"What about fog in the mornin'?"

Chief looked up from eating. "Gonna be clear."

Flash was aware that the Indian knew what he was talking about and he called Taylor and told him to Charlie Mike. Taylor wanted to reach over and choke Mac. The old sergeant hadn't stood up in three days and he was about at the end of his rope. Mac found the sergeant's hand in the dark and pressed a Hershey bar into it. The bar was flattened, but it really hit the spot.

The clear weather brought an endless parade, coming and going from the well-hidden bunker complex. Mac leaned over and whispered to Taylor, "You think we're gonna win this war?"

Taylor's first tour had been back in '62. Now, there were more NVA soldiers and they were better equipped than way back then. He thought for awhile and finally leaned in and whispered, "Fuck, no."

Mac had been feeling the same way, but the destruction caused by the B-52 strike had made him believe that if they pinpointed the gooks for the planes it would slow the enemy down. Wrapped in his poncho liner, he stayed warmer than the night before. Taylor slept first and Mac kept licking raw coffee crystals from his hand to stay awake. He chewed tobacco but he had to clean his mouth out after he swallowed some of the tobacco juice. He curled up and went fast asleep.

Taylor woke up on his own and tapped Mac on the shoulder an hour before dawn. The cold coffee he drank out of Taylor's canteen made him gasp. *Whew, that shit is nasty.* Mac rolled and stuffed his poncho liner into his ruck. Everything else had been packed up the night before. The frogs in the paddies were still making a racket and just before Mac saw the first pink line through the window of the hedgerow they quit. *That's better than any alarm clock.* He buckled his pistol belt and checked grenades and ammo pouches.

Taylor spoke softly into the radio. Flash answered instantly. Taylor slid both of their rucks under the hedgerow in preparation for their hasty exit. After taking another piss, Mac wished he had a cigarette. Instead, he took his oily rag out of his pocket and wiped Shirley down. *The early morning dew wet her pretty good.* Mac could just make out the white painted blade sight when Taylor hissed. Mac peered out of his bush window. There were two men standing by the bench in front of the shrine. It was still too dark to be able to see any details. On one knee, Mac wrapped Shirley's sling around his left arm and loosely laid his rifle into the opening. As soon as Mac made the shot, Flash would have artillery dropping in.

Hope that shit doesn't fall short, Taylor thought. Mac used his whole right hand to move the rifle's safety. Next, he laid his cheek lightly on the stock. Not quite right, he made a few minor adjustments. *There, right there.* It felt just right. On one knee, he prepared to shoot. Only then did he pay attention to the target.

Dawn lightened the sky. The first man was sitting on the bench and the other man was standing alongside. Both men had their back to him. Mac heard nothing. He was totally in his own bubble. No wind. He focused the front sight blade through the peep sight and lined it up. Aiming for the neck, he took a slow deep breath and slowly let some of it out. His finger started to take up the slack on the trigger.

Fuck. What's takin' this motherfucker so long? Taylor mentally yelled at Mac. *Shoot! Fuck, shoot!*

Bloom!

The flash from the muzzle lit up the hedgerow greenhouse. *Heart shot.* Mac had seen the target fly into the shrine.

Click, and he had another round up the spout. The standing man had turned and was trying to pull something out of the ground. Mac took a quick sight picture and slowly squeezed the trigger. Bloom, down went the target.

Only then did Mac realize that the two machine gunners were searching for him. Taylor had him by the leg and boot, pulling him under the hedgerow.

"Move! move!"

Takatatatatata...

Shit was flying everywhere.

...flizzzz...tok...tok...toktok...

Rounds were buzzing by and hitting into the paddy. Both men were dragging their rucks, the radio in Mac's.

They stuck close to the paddy dike as they low-crawled to meet the rest of the team. Taylor grabbed Mac and pulled him closer to the dike just as a rocket-propelled grenade exploded in the paddy. Only then did Mac hear Chief working out with the M-60. The red tracers firing at the gooks were being answered by the gooks with green and white ones. The artillery started coming in. When the first rounds fell in front of the hedgerow where they'd been hiding, Mac and Taylor really started kicking it in the ass.

Flash was already waiting at the junction of the two dikes, cheering them on. Flash grabbed Mac's arm with both hands and yanked him out of the paddy. Taylor landed next to him. Mac was sucking air for all he was worth, but he got to his knees and slipped into his rucksack.

Hollywood popped up and fired the grenade launcher. The gook running toward them on top of the paddy got blown in half. A round from the 155 artillery fell short and landed dead center where Mac and Taylor had been hiding. There was no dike or hedgerow left; just a crater. The high explosive was having an effect. There was only one machine gun still firing. As Mac turned to join in the firefight, he heard the inbound choppers. Flash was screaming at Chief. Bones was feeding the machine gun and Chief had the 60 pouring the bullets out. Hollywood took off running for the spot he'd dropped the gook and came racing back carrying an AK-47.

Taylor led the team back toward the highway. They only got halfway there before the sky was filled with choppers. Flash held the team up and popped yellow smoke. As soon as the lead chopper Rogered the yellow,

Flash had the team moving again. The artillery had lifted as soon as the choppers carrying Alpha A go-go started their approach. Some of the grunt-carrying choppers bypassed the LZ and flew on. Lieutenant Bull Horton flared the Huey in and landed right on the highway. Flash gave the captain commanding a quick brief, bowed toward the gooks' location and, as always, he was the last man on the chopper. Bull Horton flew his chopper right over the tunnel complex on the way out. The grunts were advancing through the muddy paddies. The choppers that had flown by had deposited their grunts on the other side of the wood. The only dead gooks visible were the two Mac had shot and half of the one Hollywood had exploded.

Bull Horton felt his chopper tilt to one side. He was talking to Flash on the intercom and the chopper crew was as pumped as the Rangers at nailing a general. Fighting the controls, he turned to see what was causing his bird to tilt. "Holy fuck" could be heard on the intercom. Four of the Rangers were in the door of the chopper and had their bare asses hanging out, mooning the press chopper that had come up alongside. Flash was hanging on to the back of the pilot's seat, laughing his ass off. The pilot talked to the crew chief and as soon as he opened the cooler and handed cold beer around the four clowns in the door pulled their pants up. Taylor was too exhausted or he'd have joined the team in the door. Mac and Bones had their arms around each other and were sucking down their beers. Hollywood leaned out the door and test fired his AK-47. Taylor thought that he'd lost twenty pounds and he grabbed Mac's leg to get his attention. When Mac looked at him, Taylor stuck his closed hand out. Puzzled, Mac stuck his free hand out. Taylor laid an empty .06 casing in Mac's dirty palm. Taylor had caught the casing from Mac's first shot. On ejection it had fallen right into Taylor's hand. Two beers apiece on the flight back to BMB and when Bull landed the chopper the tired Rangers were feeling no pain.

The sergeant major had received the word almost as soon as Mac made the shot. He'd had the clerk monitoring the radios and the clerk had run to the sergeant major's hooch and told him the news. The sergeant major in his jeep, and Coke Bottle with the three-quarter-ton, were waiting to pick up the successful team. The team looked terrible, especially Taylor. Mateau helped Taylor into the jeep. "I told you you're too fuckin' old for this shit J.L."

Grinning, Taylor looked at his friend. "You're right, Bill. But fuck, I wouldn't a missed it for the world."

Captain Greene lead the debrief. The other man that Mac had shot was a colonel, but they didn't have his name yet. The 25th and Alpha a-go-go were claiming the whole operation as their own. The grunts had to call in another company to help secure the area. Twenty-one of the NVA had been killed trying to get out the back doors of the complex. Intel was going in to check all documents and captured equipment. They had also captured six POWs.

Hot bacon and egg sandwiches were passed around. Cake and ice cream followed. The general came in and calmed things down, first by saying he was sorry about the dead Ranger. That put a damper on the team. Even though the team didn't know the cherry, he was still one of them.

The general took Flash, Taylor, and Mateau into his office. As he passed Mac the general patted the skinny Ranger on the shoulder. "Nice shot," and laughing, asked Mac if his watch was still working.

The team finished with S-1 and Captain Greene let them take all the leftover sandwiches. They didn't wait for Flash or Taylor. Coke Bottle gave them a ride back to the company, dropped them off, and went back to headquarters.

Rags and her partner Airborne came flying out of the barracks to greet the team. Even though Mac threw all his gear and dirty clothes on his bunk on the way by, he was still last in the shower. Two other teams were in and had their own bunks piled high with gear. By the time Flash and Taylor came in, all four men were in clean fatigues and cleaning weapons. Mac asked Taylor if he was coming on R&R with the team. Taylor sat down next to Mac. "I'm fuckin' wore out, but it depends on flights back to Hawaii."

Flash added, "You earned some in-country. Don't let us go party on our own."

"I'll think about it," Taylor said as he stripped off his dirty war suit. Flash and the master sergeant headed for the showers. Mac cleaned Shirley and hung her on the wall nail. He never got around to dumping out his ruck before he was asleep, curled between the dogs on his bunk. Coming back into the barracks after their shower, Flash and Taylor grinned. All four of the team were passed out on their bunks. In pants and shirts and still wearing shower flip-flops, the two sergeants went into the orderly room where the executive officer listened to Flash's brief of the mission.

Whiskey-laced coffee in hand, both men went into the arms room and discussed the mission. "I wanted to strangle that little cocksucker," Taylor said.

Flash sipped his coffee. "I wanted to kill those motherfuckers that I was with, too." Flash added, "It's a bitch being cooped up like that."

Taylor was having trouble staying awake. "I wonder how that motherfucker knew it was going to be clear?"

Flash said, "I checked with the Indian and he said the same thing. I'm going to try to keep that little shit on my team. He's too good to promote." He stood and gave Taylor a hand up. "Let's get some sleep."

Mac woke up in mid-afternoon wearing his bright baggies from Hawaii. He went into the orderly room, brought Coke Bottle up to date on the mission, then borrowed from Tucker's small stash of books: Mao's *Little Red Book*. Handing it to him, Tucker said, "Don't let the lifers see you reading it. They think it's a subversive book."

"Hey, when you get caught up on your shit, I'll be in the arms room," and Mac turned and went out. He worked away in the arms room and he got everything to fit. He oiled Shirley for the last time. In oily pieces, the old rifle fit perfectly in the mortar tube that Flash had given to him. He put a short note in with the rifle: "Mr. Wallace. Killed a gook at four hundred yards using 180 grain Winchester hot rounds. It does shoot good. Thank you for the use of your rifle." He wrapped the note around the empty casing, dropped it in the mortar tube and sealed the whole thing with hundred-mile-an-hour-tape.

Coke Bottle had typed a mailing label for him and Mac stuck the self-sticking label to the mortar tube. When Mac, Bones, Chief, and Coke Bottle all went to chow, Mac stuffed himself on salad. He couldn't get enough. "Man, I miss this shit in the field." Telling the guys he'd catch up in a little bit, Mac went back into the arms room and opened the *Little Red Book* to the place he had marked. As Mac read he kept thinking, *This is the same book the gooks are reading*. He had found several of Mao's books at the B-52 strike, but they were written in Vietnamese.

He was startled by the huge bare-chested black man who filled the doorway. Bush hat pulled low over his eyes, a woven set of black boot laces with a bone hanging from it dangled around his neck. The black man walked in, put a weapon in the weapons rack, leaned over and pushed Mac's feet off the table. "Boy, don't be touchin' my shit," he rumbled, then turned slowly and ambled out.

Mac sat there in shock. He put the book down, got up and walked to the weapons rack. *Holy shit. A fairly new M203.* He looked over his shoulder then picked up the weapon. Mac had heard about the weapon, an M-16 with a grenade launcher built right underneath, it was new in the Army and hard to come by. Another quick look and he was checking the rifle over. *Nice,* he thought, and set the weapon back in the rack. He returned to his seat, found a pair of demo pliers and went to work.

He could hardly get into the barracks. There were Rangers everywhere and beer cans were as numerous as the lies that were being told. Threading his way between half-drunken soldiers, Mac found what he was looking for halfway down the barracks. The huge black man was sitting on a foot locker, drinking out of a bottle of Jack Daniels. Coming to a halt in front of the man, Mac stood there. James Brown was screaming from the tape deck. Mac reached over and turned it down.

"What the fuck you want, boy?"

All the Rangers were watching as Mac pulled the pin on the baseball hand grenade and let the spoon pop. Afterward, even Taylor and Flash couldn't agree on it, but the huge black man seemed to turn gray. Someone screamed "Grenade" and both ends of the barracks had a traffic jam of men trying to get out the doors. The huge black man wasn't first but he was very close. He ended up standing next to Taylor and Flash, shaking and waiting for the explosion.

"What's wrong with that motherfuckin' clerk?"

Taylor, as big as the scared man, told him, "That ain't no clerk, BOY," and Taylor and Flash peered into the barracks. Mac was sitting on his bunk, drinking a beer. Both dogs lay beside him. Flash came in, followed by Taylor.

Flash sat down across from Mac. "What the fuck you do that for?"

Looking at the grenade next to Mac, Taylor added, "Is that thing live?"

Mac looked at both of his friends and grinned. "Naw, I pulled the fuse out of it. Motherfucker called me 'boy.'" and he pointed at the black man peering around the corner into the barracks.

Flash lay back across the bunk, laughing. "Hey, Youngblood, come on in here and meet the baddest motherfucker in the hooch."

Youngblood came in but he had his eyes on the grenade. Flash picked the grenade up and tossed it to him. "Staff Sergeant Youngblood, this is Sergeant McDonald. He's the shooter on my team and this time you picked the wrong guy to fuck with."

Both men shook hands. "Man, I thought you was a clerk. Man, my shit was weak, bro. Ya fuckin' had my black ass. Come here. Meet my main motherfuckin' man."

Handshakes went all around and Mac met team Asp, the Ranger team that had lost the cherry. Blood picked his bottle off the floor. There wasn't much left in the bottle but he offered Mac first shot. Mac took a small sip and handed the bottle back. Blood went right to work in front of everybody. "Bro, you wanna work on my team?" That got the party rolling again.

Taylor, Flash, and Rattler's team leader McCleod were

outside talking quietly. "He always like that?" McCleod asked.

Taylor answered first. "I was ready to kill the little prick out there, but he really is a good guy. Just such a hot- tempered motherfucker."

"Well," McCleod said, "Youngblood got what the fuck he deserved. Cocksucker's always fuckin' with somebody."

Flash took a drink of beer. "It's always his team that's losing people and he's always gettin' the latest shit, too."

"Says that he got ten dinks with that new grenade launcher though," McCleod said.

Taylor chuckled. "Well, there's one motherfucker he didn't get."

The three sergeants were still laughing when Mac came out of the barracks. Mac grabbed Taylor's arm and pulled him away from the group. "Aaaaah, Sarge, thanks for takin' care of me out there. Couldn'ta had a better partner."

Taylor looked at the Ranger. "You better learn to control that temper of yours. You're gonna kill somebody." They both realized how dumb that sounded and started to laugh.

"Aaaaah, Sarge, that new grenade launcher Youngblood got. Well I looked at it. It's got a broken firing pin. Never been fired," and Mac turned and went back into the barracks.

As he stood there thinking about what Mac had said, Taylor's thoughts were interrupted when the sergeant major's jeep pulled up. "Come on, you ugly fuck. Get in."

Back at the sergeant major's hooch, both men kicked back. Taylor never stopped eating. Bill had all kinds of goodies laid out. "Fuckin' nice way to live," and Taylor grabbed some shrimp and started dipping them in hot sauce.

"You could live like this, too, if ya quit tryin' to play bush monkey," and the sergeant major leaned back in his easy chair. Bill had a hooch all to himself and, looking around, Taylor could see Bill had made himself comfortable.

"I almost got killed tonight." Taylor told Bill about Mac taking Youngblood down a peg. "No shit, Bill. Calm as you please, he pulled the pin on that grenade and you didn't see nothin' but assholes and elbows goin' out the door. I was first, of course."

"That little shit did that?" Bill poured more whiskey.

Taylor had motor-mouth bad. He couldn't stop talking. "When he started talking about niggers in the hide, I damn near shit. I even unsnapped my .45, so real quiet like I ask him if he knew any niggers. If he says 'yes,' I'm gonna blow him away."

"Well, what'd he say?" Bill asked.

"Real calm, Mac says, 'I don't know any niggers.'" Both men started chuckling.

Taylor ended up sleeping in the sergeant major's hooch that night. Declining a ride, he walked back to the Ranger Company in the morning. He needed to clear his head and let his stomach settle. Team Viper was not in the barracks, so Taylor went into the orderly room and asked Tucker where everybody was. He'd expected the team to be getting ready for their R&R down at Vung Tau. Tucker told him that they had to take Mac to the aid station, that "He was some kinda sick."

Taylor asked where the aid station was and Coke Bottle walked him to the door and pointed to it. Taylor took off, heading for the building with the red cross on the roof.

28

The waves lapped gently at the white sandy beach and the sun reflected brightly off the water. Their arms holding each others' waists, the couple strolled just at the water's edge. Corpus Christi had the best hotels in Texas as far as Tex was concerned. Swan Blossom and Thomas, as she now called him, had walked miles on the beaches of Padre Island. The pretty girl didn't want to go back to Vietnam and didn't want the reporter to go either. She didn't understand that Tex was now a hotshot reporter in Nam, but back here in the States he was just an average Joe. He'd tried to explain it to her but she didn't get it. Her two interviews with the television stations in Dallas had been "super." She was well received and one station manager even offered her a job doing the weather. The Ranger had been right, that the girl could shop. She spent hours trying on clothes and different cosmetics. Once they'd screwed standing up in the ladies dressing room at Macy's. As they walked along now they were talking seriously about returning to Vietnam, wondering what would happen if they lived together under the watchful eyes of the NVA.

They had a boat trip planned for the morrow and Tex—already pink and peeling—planned on wearing more clothes. His sunburn was starting to itch.

Back at their hotel Tex ignored the messages to call the *Star*. Their activities in the shower almost prevented him and Swan Blossom from making it to dinner. They were making love in the shower when Tex slipped and fell, busting his ass, his hard-on gone. Lying flat on his back, Swan Blossom burst out laughing. They both started to laugh again when she helped him up, but the laughter turned to passion and they finished up in bed with her on top.

They decided to take a taxi to a place that served both seafood and steak. The taxi dropped the couple off in front of the restaurant and, walking up to the door, out of habit, Tex looked at the *Dallas Star's* newspaper box next to the door. *Holy shit, they did it,* he thought, reaching for change for the news box. GIs KILL NVA GENERAL was the bold black headline. Swan Blossom read over his shoulder as he pulled the paper out of the box. She even grabbed one of her own. Both of them sat on the bench outside the eatery and read the story. She flipped to the pictures. Halfway through the front half, tears came to her eyes. The general was crumpled against a shrine; his dead back was to the camera. The next picture showed a GI holding up the general's head for a front view. Memories flooded her mind. The stern man who had come to the orphanage had shown her nothing but kindness. He had guided her and now she was a lieutenant in the NVA instead of working in the rice paddies.

Her short time in America had her very confused. These were not the people she had been taught to hate. Most of the people she'd met in Texas had no idea where Vietnam was and, except for the news, paid no attention to the war. With the general dead, she had nothing to go back to. She had no doubt that the north would win, but what then? For her, a half-breed given to a life of working in the paddies, her service to her country shunted aside. No choices. Tex couldn't look at Swan Blossom sitting beside him. Her tears were falling softly onto the newspaper. *Shit, the fuckers really did it. They got the motherfucker.* If she found out that he had anything to do with this, she would hate him forever and more than likely cut his nuts off once they were back in the Nam. The 199th wasn't even mentioned in the story, just the 25th Infantry and supporting units. Supposedly they'd wiped out the headquarters for the Saigon area.

The couple kept both of their papers and went into the restaurant. Swan Blossom ordered wine right away. Tex was surprised because she very rarely had a drink. Most of the time she left her drinks untouched. Tex left her to find a pay phone.

His editor was pissed. "Where in the fuck you been? We want you back in Nam covering this story. Get that fuckin' girl back there too. Call me as soon as you've got reservations. Now move your ass," and he slammed the phone down.

Swan Blossom was already on her second glass of wine. Tex told her straight up, "We have to go back to Vietnam, soonest."

She looked up, shrugged her shoulders, and said very little. She barely tasted the shrimp that Tex ordered for her. Her mind was on what would happen to her once she got back. She would end up with the VC or in an infantry platoon, training to be a sapper. Her body would be trained to crawl through the fences and wire surrounding American firebases and blow things up. She scared Tex worse than the NVA general had when she asked quietly, "If I marry you, can I stay in Texas?"

Thinking fast, Tex answered, "I don't know. Let me check it out." The rest of the meal went by in silence. When she stood, Swan Blossom had to lean on Tex. Her four glasses of wine had fucked her up badly. In their hotel room, the Texan gently helped her get out of her clothes. He even had to help her sit to pee. When she passed out on her stomach in bed, Tex didn't bother to pull the sheet up. He packed some of his things in his suitcase and called the airlines for a direct flight to San Francisco. On hold, the telephone stuck to his ear, Tex couldn't take his eyes off that fine ass lying there. Talking on the phone, Tex leaned back in the chair and, using his bare foot, he spread Swan Blossom's legs apart. After he hung up the phone, having stared at her pussy, he wasn't sure where he had reservations for. Taking a shower, Tex fought a losing battle with his dick. Quickly drying himself, he stood at the end of the bed. Swan Blossom hadn't moved and her pussy winked at him. Tex climbed between the girl's legs and fucked away. She never moved and Tex fell asleep feeling great. *She never even knew I was there,* he smirked.

No hangover Tex ever had in his life matched the pain he felt. Asleep on his back, snoring softly, Tex didn't know what hit him. His hard-on sticking straight up had been the target for Swan Blossom's slap.

Tex sat straight up and grabbed his deflated cock, tears running down his cheeks. He couldn't scream, only gasp and keep his hands between his legs. A few minutes later, Swan Blossom came out of the bathroom drying her long black hair. "Good morning. Do you want to order breakfast?"

Tex couldn't even speak. It was a half an hour before he could stagger to the bathroom and he had to sit to piss. His tight jockeys felt great, holding his swollen dick. Once in his clothes, Tex asked, "What the fuck did you do that for?"

Smiling sweetly and looking up from her magazine, Swan Blossom said, "Do what?" and she crossed her legs and let her robe fall open. Looking at her pussy, Tex knew he had fucked up big time. He fell to his knees, wrapped his arms around the beautiful woman and said, "I'm sorry. I was a shit last night." She kissed him quickly and stood. "Let's eat.

I'm so hungry."

Tex turned in the rental car at the San Antonio airport. They had made up on the drive from Corpus Christi. Swan Blossom still had a sackful of McDonalds. She had cuddled next to him on the drive and even tried stroking his dick, but Tex wouldn't let her touch it. The couple had plenty of time before the flight and Tex wished he'd kept the car longer. "I could have taken you to see the Alamo." Diving into her McDonalds' bag, all she could say was, "Do they have another McDonalds there?"

Thinking about marriage, Tex laughed. "You'd be cheap to keep. We could eat hamburgers seven days a week." Sucking on her milkshake, she grinned and all she said was, "OK."

They had a direct flight which meant they only had to stop once in Salt Lake City. Their flight landed at midnight in San Francisco. Tex felt his blood quicken. The airport was crawling with GIs in uniform. *Fuck yeah, goin' back for the big story.* He left Swan Blossom sitting on their bags while he confirmed reservations on Pan Am. On his return, he was really surprised to see Swan Blossom standing between two men.

"Get lost. Get the fuck out of here," were his first words to the two short-haired suit-covered men.

"Aaah, Mr. Payne, would you and the young lady come with us please? We need to talk to you," and he stuck out his hand. "I'm Mr. Jones and this is Mr. Smith."

Oh, fuck. FBI, Tex thought. *How did they track me here?* Swan Blossom and Tex looked at one another. Her two brand new suitcases were picked up by Mr. Smith. Tex had to carry his own. After a short walk, Mr. Jones opened a locked airport door with a key. Once the door from the terminal was closed, Tex was surprised to see an office. The couple was told to have a seat. Two side by side chairs were in front of the desk.

"OK, who the fuck are you guys?" and Tex sat where indicated. Swan Blossom was already seated. Both men opened wallets and flashed their IDs. *Oh, man, I'm in the shit now. CIA. This is the big leagues now.*

Dickhead One opened a briefcase that was already on the desk and said, "This will only take a few minutes of your time." Opening a file, he spoke perfect Vietnamese to Swan Blossom. She was so startled she came halfway out of her chair. So few long noses spoke her language, this one took her completely by surprise. Tex started to rise to see the file Dickhead had in his hand. Dickhead Two pulled him back into the chair. "Sit the fuck down, Mr. Payne."

Swan Blossom answered softly in Vietnamese. The two spoke for about fifteen minutes and Tex didn't understand one word. The man behind the desk closed the file and stood up, nodding at the other agent. The door locked behind the agents as they left.

Tex turned. Swan Blossom had her arms around him. "What the fuck's goin' on, honey?"

Shaking, she whispered, "They know I'm NVA. They have my whole life in that file," and she started to cry. "The general was my uncle. Even I didn't know that." If she went back to Vietnam and didn't work for them, the CIA was going to release the information that she turned in the general. Shaking and crying, she gasped, "They will have me killed. I won't last one day after that hits the streets. I won't even have a chance to defend myself. What can I do?"

Tex held her tight. "It'll be OK. I'll take care of you." The two agents came back into the office and this time several color pictures were laid in front of Tex. The dead general with his heart blown out stared up at him.

"Now, Mr. Payne, we need your help." He sat behind the desk and nodded at his partner. The agent reached down and helped Swan Blossom to her feet. "Mr. Jones needs to speak to Mr. Payne. Alone," and he escorted her out.

"OK, motherfucker, what's this all about?" Tex barked angrily at the agent. The "dickhead" just smiled and leaned back in his chair. Waving his hand with the file, he started speaking. "We don't want her back in Vietnam, Mr. Payne. We need her here, working for us, interpreting our captured documents and identifying agents that are supposedly working for us. She knows, Mr. Payne. She knows all them little commie cocksuckers and if you don't help persuade her to work for us... well," and Dickhead actually chuckled, "You're fucked. Your pinko ass will never send another fuckin' story back to your paper because you'll be dead as soon as you get to Saigon. Whatta ya say now, Mr. Tex Payne?"

Tex leaned across the desk. Dickhead had his suit jacket open and the gun was clearly visible. "You fuckin' promise that she won't have to go back to Vietnam? 'Cause she's damn sure dead meat if she does."

"She'll be workin' in Langley and the company will take good care of her. Now what do you say?"

Tex had his nuts in the grinder and he finally nodded. "OK." Dickhead banged on the door.

"You have fifteen minutes, Mr. Payne. Make sure you say goodbye."

Swan Blossom came in and threw herself into Tex's arms.

At least she would be safe. He was only now realizing how much he cared for Swan Blossom. Quietly, they whispered and set up a code word and a way to communicate. She memorized Tex's mother's name and home phone number. Tex's mom would pass on any messages and how they could find each other in the future. Time passed so quickly they both jumped when the door opened. That was their goodbye. Tex was amazed when he went to the ticket counter to cancel Swan Blossom's ticket. The ticket had already been cancelled and the girl at the counter had the money for it waiting.

Tex headed for the nearest bar and kept looking for Swan Blossom. *There must be a back way out of here.*

Swan Blossom was still in the office. Forms had to be explained and she had to sign her full name to all of them. The last form was a name change and she could wait until she was at Langley to decide what name she wanted. She also had to take on both men. She was surprised that both men had waited so long. They didn't even ask her—just pushed her face down on the desk and took turns fucking her from behind. They left the terminal through a different door and didn't let her clean up until they were flying away to the east.

29

Mac had awakened at 0400. In agony, he'd barely made the shithouse. He was shitting in one hole and puking in the other. He was shaking so bad he thought he was going to fall off the hole he was cramped up on. He had to shower because he had puke and shit splattered all over his legs. The lukewarm water running over his skin was agony. He managed to make it back to his bunk and with his poncho liner and both dogs under it with him he still couldn't get warm. He was lying there, vibrating like his mother's Singer sewing machine, when Flash got up. Coming back from his shower, the team leader took one look at Mac and knew he was in bad shape. Holding his hand to Mac's forehead he thought, *He's burning up.*

Mac could hardly stand on his own and had to have help getting dressed. All four team members escorted him to the aid station. As early as it was, there were medics on duty and it was already a busy place. An MP had shot himself in the foot playing quick draw with his partner and one of the cooks from the 3rd of the 7th had sliced his finger off in the mess hall.

The medics had Mac lie on a gurney. The doctor took one look at the chart, put his hand on Mac's forehead, signed his name to an evac tag and stuck it to the grunt's shirt. He was walking away when Flash stepped right in front of him and forced him to stop. The tired doctor looked up.

"What's wrong with my man, doc?"

The doctor took a look back at Mac then turned back to the sergeant. "Malaria. And a bad fuckin' case of pneumonia," he said, as he disappeared through a set of swinging doors.

Flash read the tag stuck to Mac's shirt then cornered a medic wearing a combat medic's badge. *This motherfucker's been in the bush. He'll talk to me,* Flash thought.

The medic came over with Flash and read the tag. "He's goin' to 93rd evac. We can't treat this shit here. We got priority on a dust-off. Gotta take these shitbirds out, too," and he started to leave. Remembering something, he turned back to Flash. "Get as much fluid as you can in him. Juice or milk. That kinda shit," and the medic headed off.

Mac had gone out with Bones and was sitting on a bench. The full sun was keeping him warm. "You fuckin' got malaria and some other shit," said Flash, squatting in front of Mac.

Mac's color was a white-red from ground-in dirt, but he still managed to ask, "What about R&R?"

Flash cuffed him lightly on the head. "You little motherfucker. You're gettin' clean sheets and bed rest. Then, when you get back, I'll take you to the best whorehouse I know. Right, Bones?"

"Fuckin' a, Mac. We'll save you some pew-ssay," said Bones. He was worried about his friend.

Flash said, "I'll be right back," and took off. Chief came over and squatted where Flash had just been. He opened his shirt and the Apache warrior took Mac's hand and placed it on the small buckskin bag that hung around his neck. Bones and Hollywood looked on in amazement. The last time a guy tried to touch Chief's medicine bag he fucked him up good.

Flash didn't know whose mess hall he went into and he didn't care. He went right in the exit and, ignoring the shouts, walked into the stock room and grabbed the first two cans of juice he saw. The fat mess daddy tried blocking the door, but one look at Flash and he stepped aside. As soon as Flash got far enough away, the mess sergeant hollered, "I'll have your stripes, motherfucker."

When he got back from his trip Flash whipped out his belt knife and punched holes in a can. "Here ya go, my man. Drink that." Sitting there, shaking in the sun, Mac shook his head "no."

"Grab him Bones. Hold his head."

Hurrying around the corner, Taylor saw the dust cloud. Hollywood was sitting on one arm and Chief had all he could do to hold the other. Mac was flat on his back and Flash squatted on his chest. Mac kept trying to knee Flash in the nuts. Bones damn near had him in a hammerlock. They were working on getting him to drink the other can of pineapple juice. Flash was so pissed at Mac that he wanted to knock him out. The wiry fuck had the whole team sweating up a storm. Taylor pitched right in and held Mac's legs down. By now even the REMFs getting their clap shots were out watching the show.

Flash drained the last of the juice down Mac's throat and stood up, yelling, "It's for your own good, ya hardheaded fuck."

Taylor picked Mac up off the ground. Even in the hot sun he could feel Mac's fever. At Taylor's questioning look, "He's got malaria," Flash said.

Mac hung on to the master sergeant. "Sarge, Sarge, there's a present for ya in the arms room. Would ya see that guy gets it, please?" Taylor was already leading Mac to the open back doors of the waiting ambulance. Mac waved weakly from his bench in the ambulance. He and the other two were going for the short drive to the helipad. The dust-off would fly them the short distance to 93rd Evac Hospital. Watching the ambulance pull away, Flash was still trying to catch his breath. Walking back to the Ranger Company, Flash filled Taylor in on what the medic had told him.

Both men had seen malaria before and it definitely kicked ass. "You sure ya won't come down to Vung Tau with us?" Flash asked.

"Naw, I gotta get back. Momma's waitin' on my tired black ass," and Taylor laughed.

Flash and Taylor went into the arms room and lying on the table was the mortar tube. Taylor leaned over and read the label. "Holy fuck. Mac's sendin' the rifle back," and he picked up the mortar tube with the broken down rifle in it.

Flash grabbed Taylor's free hand. "Thanks, man. We couldn't of done it without you."

Squeezing Flash's hand, Taylor said, "You're one helluva fightin' man your own self."

All three teams lined the path to the sergeant major's jeep that had just pulled up. Taylor shook each man's hand. Even Rags and Airborne barked. As he got in the jeep, he really wanted to stay with the Rangers.

Hollywood came up and thrust the AK-47 into his lap. "It's from team Viper."

Taylor tried to speak, but all he could say was, "Thanks," and, "The next plane over will have a pallet load of tiger stripes."

The sergeant major quickly drove away. "The chopper pad at noon," he yelled at Flash. "Well, J.L., you wanna stay?" the sergeant major asked, driving out the gate.

"Fuck you, Bill. Those young studs made a believer outa me. Check this out. Mac's sending that rifle back to the guy who killed the crocodile," and he pointed to the mortar tube in the back seat.

"What the fuck's wrong with that kid? How sick is he?" Bill asked.

"Malaria for sure, and when I caught up to them this mornin'...shit, it took all of us to hold that motherfucker down." Both men were laughing when Taylor, serious now, said, "Bill I forgot to tell you last night, but Mac checked out Youngblood's grenade launcher. The firing pin's broken."

The sergeant major drove onto the dirt shoulder. "You're shittin' me. He said at the Intel debrief that he killed ten dinks with that thing," and Bill looked at Taylor.

Taylor looked at his friend. "Mac said it had never been fired."

"Holy shit. Ya know what this means?" and he pulled back onto the highway. The conversation was a lot more subdued on the way to Taylor's camp.

A medic had to help Mac walk from the flight line to the entrance of the hospital. Mac was seeing everything in triplicate. The crew chief on the dust-off was pissed. Puked pineapple juice stunk up the whole chopper. Mac was forced onto a gurney and the horse-faced nurse who read the thermometer was pushing him as fast as she and a medic could go. Mac's temperature read 104.

Mac came to at one point and wondered about the tube running into his arm. Just as he started to go out again the horse-faced nurse came in. She pulled the sheet all the way down to the end of the bed and flipped him one-handed onto his stomach. Mac screamed like a baby. The penicillin shot felt like she was using a fifty-five gallon drum for a needle. Swabbing his sore cheek with alcohol wipes, she calmly leaned over and told him to "Shut the fuck up." She didn't even bother to pull the sheet up and when she left Mac had passed out.

That evening Lieutenant Susan Fitzgerald was helping in all the wards. The 93rd was full. Wounded were tended and stuck wherever there was room. One of the patients had died and she went into the ward to get his paperwork started and pulled the sheet up over the body. The patients who were sitting up just stared at her.

The nude patient in the bed next to the door caught her eye. *Oh, man he's torn up bad.* Red sores—some weeping—covered his body. Pulling the sheet up she thought, *Another booby trap.* She stopped and read the soldier's chart on the end of the bed. *Huh. Malaria and pneumonia.* Letting the chart dangle, she pulled the sheet down. *Bug bites. Not shrapnel.* She quickly soaked a towel and rubbed alcohol all over him, from neck to feet, then flipped him and did the same to the front. *Skinny shit. Sure looks familiar. What a fucked up haircut.* She pulled the sheet up and left.

The dead man was quickly removed and a live one took his place. Mac came to in the morning and he didn't even know there was a doctor at the end of his bed. He didn't hear the doctor tell the nurse to soak him, that his fever was going up. The four medics earned their combat pay. They took the skinny guy down to the latrine on a gurney and prepared to slide him into a tub of ice water.

Up to the point his feet slipped into the tub of ice cubes and water Mac had been unconscious. The screams coming from the latrine brought Horseface on the run. With her pitching in, they held the screaming man in the tub. He lapsed into unconsciousness again and all four medics stood by during the hour he was in the tub. After his soak, Mac was pulled from the tub and Horseface took his temperature rectally. It had dropped to 102. "He'll be fine now. Put him back to bed." The four medics had to put on dry clothes before they could continue their shift.

In mid-afternoon, when Mac came to, he felt like he was

starving. He ate the package of Lifesavers out of the Red Cross bag hanging from his dresser. He drank every drop from his pitcher on the nightstand. *Man, that ice water tasted good.* He tried to stand, nearly collapsed, and pulled himself back into bed. *Man, something kicked my ass good,* he thought. The old gook who brought the dinner trays was amazed. Mac had eaten his meal before he was finished serving all the patients. As soon as the gook went out, Mac helped himself to the food served to the unconscious man beside him. He switched his empty tray for the full one. *Man, that was good. I wish they'd bring me some pajamas.* Papa san came back and got the empty trays. He said nothing about the unconscious man's empty tray.

Susan and Dawn were doing charts at the nurses' station. Dawn had told Susan about the patient who gave Horseface a bath and both girls were chuckling about their boss being all wet. Dawn told her friend that Horseface had informed her at shift change that the agents from the Criminal Investigation Division had been back to snoop around. "Those fucks think we have nothing better to do than change the tags on patients and put them in for the Medal of Honor."

Susan looked up from her charts. "Do you remember that little shit's name that was down here?"

Dawn thought for a moment. "Mic.. .Mac.. .something like that. Skinny little shit."

Susan looked through her stack of charts. "We've got twenty from the 199th," she said. "Here we are. McDermott and McDonald. One gunshot and one malaria with pneumonia for backup."

Dawn commented, "Shit, Susan, you're never gonna get him to admit to it anyway."

Looking at Dawn, Susan held both charts in her hand. "That little shit caused us enough problems." Laughing, she went on. "I'd just like to know for myself. You know, I worked on this one," and she held up the chart marked McDonald. "Little shit's sick enough. I didn't recognize him. He's got a real fucked up haircut." Then she added, "I gave him a sponge bath. At first I thought he was full of shrapnel. Turned out to be bug bites." The women looked at one another.

Dawn commented first. "Don't start, Susan. I already know how fucked up this place is."

Susan giggled. "OK, OK. Sick as that shit is, he got a hard-on when I was wiping him down."

"Shit, Sue, tell me something new. These guys were born horny." Both nurses were laughing over Dawn's comment.

"That gives me an idea," and Susan set both charts aside.

"What are you thinking now? You already get us in enough trouble around here as it is," Dawn said.

Writing away, Susan commented, "I wish that fuckin' captain was as well hung as the grunt. Sonofabitch acts like King Kong." Both girls chuckled. "You know, the Army's right.'Grab them by the balls and their hearts and minds will follow,' " and she finished her last chart and stood up.

"Don't do anything stupid," and Dawn added, "You got that look in your eye."

"I'm not gonna let some dumb grunt come in here and get the best of me, that's all," and Susan had both arms on her hips— pissed—thinking about the trouble Mac had caused.

"That's where you are so wrong, girl," and Dawn got up and filled her coffee cup. "That's what everybody thinks, that grunts are ignorant. You know my brother's a captain up north with the Marines. He says the draftees and grunts are guys he could take to Hanoi."

"I know. I know. My brother's got two years in college to go. I hope he stays out of this shit," and as she walked out of the nurses' station she added, 'I'll be right back."

Mac was awake and hoping he could get some pajamas, even a nightgown with his ass hanging out. He couldn't even get outside to grab a smoke. *Oh, Oh.* Mac had dozed off and the pretty nurse was pulling the privacy curtain around his bed. He was fully awake now and watching the nurse as she leaned over and fluffed his pillow. Mac couldn't keep from looking down her uniform. *Wow, she has beautiful tits.*

Susan stepped back and thought, *If the tent pole in the middle of the bed is any indication, he's getting better in a helluva hurry.* "Hi, how are you feeling? That's some haircut you have there," she said softly.

"Aahh." Mac was thinking about looking up her uniform the last time he'd been there—lying on the floor looking up at her panty-clad pussy. "Ma'am, I feel fine. Aahh, if I could have some pajamas..." Mac was lost in the smell of her perfume.

Susan looked at the sick grunt. "Do you remember the last time you were here? Hmmmm?" and she smiled.

Mac looked at her with bloodshot eyes. "I don't remember being here before, ma'am."

She calmly grabbed Mac's hand and said, "I'll find you a robe or something and maybe this will help you to remember," and she slipped a bullet into his hand.

She slipped through the curtain and Mac looked at the M-16 bullet. *So that's where that motherfucker went. It must have fallen out of my pocket when I was sleeping under Pepe's bed.*

The nurse scared the shit out of him, slipping back in to stand beside his bed. She didn't let up on the young man. "Do you remember now? Would you like some help putting that on?" She laid the open-backed gown on his bed.

"Aaahhh, ma'am, I'll put that on myself and thank you, but I'm not sure if I remember exactly when I was here last." Mac had the sheet up to his neck and had turned on his side, trying to hide his hard-on.

Susan pulled up a chair and sat down next to the bed. Keeping her voice low, Susan explained the problem and she let him have it with both barrels. Resting her chin in her left hand she quietly said, "We really don't mind that you slept under your friend's bed, and that you ate everybody's breakfast. What we need to know is," and she leaned in even closer, "who switched on more medication for all twelve patients, and who wrote on their tags and put everybody in for the Medal of Honor?" She then reached over and picked up Mac's hand with the bullet in it. "You know, giving a sick man extra drugs could kill somebody," and she squeezed his hand. "I know you wouldn't want to be responsible for killing somebody, would you?"

"Ahhhhh, no ma'am. Sure wouldn't want to do that." Mac was squirming under the sheet.

"We've also had these Army cops all over the place, trying to blame the nurses for switching those award tags."

Mac wasn't admitting anything, but she almost had him as she slipped her hand under the sheet. Lightly, she ran her hand over his leg. "Come on, Mac, you can tell me, honest," and she gently grabbed his dick.

Mac was sweating more than before. His fever broke. She stroked delicately and Mac said, "I love you," and came all over her hand and arm under the sheet. Red-faced, he stammered, "Ma'am, I'm sorry." That was as far as he got.

Susan smiled and said, "You're going to be here for awhile and I'll be back," and she surprised herself. She kissed the skinny grunt on the cheek before she left.

Mac lay there, stunned and in shock. *Holy shit...she's coming back...fuck...I'll tell her everything...shit...Long Binh jail for my ass...fuckin' over the Army like that. Fuck. ..they got me now...Oh man I love that nurse...she's gotta love me too after doing that.* He laid

back. The wet, cold sheet on his stomach brought him back
to reality. He slid out of bed and wiped himself off before
trying to put on his hospital gown. He wobbled around getting it on and leaned on his nightstand to catch his breath.
He finally opened the drawer. The stuff out of his pockets
was inside. Wallet and smokes, comb, and his other junk.
Grabbing the smokes and his Zippo, he started down to the
end of the bed. *Hot damn.* His ground transportation and
boonie hat were tied on the end.

The outside door was self-latching. Somebody had
jammed a Bible in it to keep it from closing. He lit a cigarette and almost killed himself coughing and wheezing. His
first drag made him throw it away. Weak-kneed, he hoped
the nurse would come back. That brought him back to reality again. He stayed in the shadows and, barefoot in the
dark, he made his way around the hospital. He kept having
to stop to catch his breath. Finally, he found what he was
looking for—the softly lit chopper pad. There it was—the
door where the wounded were brought in. Two galvanized
trash cans were right where he remembered them to be.
When he opened the tight-fitting lids the smell made him
hang on and grit his teeth. He couldn't find what he was
looking for in the first can so he tried the second one. The
same stink came from the second can, but he started
pulling stuff out anyway. The first pair was missing a leg.
The second pair had no crotch and, from the smell, was
shit-stained. Reaching back down into the trash, he pulled
out another bundle and the pants had only a small hole in
one leg. The shirt was useless; half the chest was burned.
Holding his breath, he dived back into the can. Near the
bottom, he found a complete shirt, without blood stains,
and he put that with the pants and repacked the trash cans.

Mac retraced his steps back to the door he had left open.
Finally, he found the door and decided to try another

smoke. This time he didn't inhale and as he smoked he went through the pockets of the clothes he'd found. One grenade pin. One rubber. A toothbrush with half the handle cut off. The shirt had a plastic C-ration spoon in a pocket; nothing else.

Mac wondered how he could hide his escape kit. He stuffed the fatigues in his pillowcase and took the used toothbrush and a small tube of tooth paste out of his Red Cross bag. *Fuck, Motherfuckers never put toothbrush and paste together.* He felt well enough to shower and, using the dead man's toothbrush, brushed his teeth. He fell asleep dreaming of his nurse and how he was going to marry her. He was awakened by the old gook delivering breakfast. He had hardly finished his bacon when the horse-faced nurse came around and gave him another shot in the ass. He didn't scream this time. In the confusion of shift change and breakfast tray removal, he took his stuff and went to the latrine. Dressed, he slipped out through another ward. His pants were too short and too bulky so the breeze made the legs billow like a parachute. His shirt fit pretty well and, except for a small bloodstain on one pocket, he could pass for any grunt in Nam. There was no name tag on the pocket and there was a 25th Infantry patch on the shoulder— and that's who gave him a ride out the gate. A gun bunny driving a deuce-and-a-half dropped Mac at the turnoff he needed. The next ride he got had him headed for the place he sought and the two Aussies in the truck turned out to know all the places he could find what he was looking for.

30

———

Wallace Wallace had taken Patty to meet Charlie Johnson at his gun shop. They'd ended up at Charlie's home and his wife Leona had made the couple feel right at home. They had spent the evening after dinner at a local watering hole and both men had gotten plastered. Patty had taken charge and gotten Wallace back to the hotel. Wallace couldn't remember when he'd had such a good time. The next afternoon he was back at the gun shop with Patty. They were taking Charlie and Leona out to dinner downtown and Leona was late. Wallace was showing Patty a black powder rifle up near the front of the shop. He was explaining how the rifle worked and hardly noticed the huge black man who walked in.

"Hey Wallace, you got mail." At the call, Wallace turned, surprised. Charlie and the black guy were both looking at him. Followed by Patty, Wallace walked back to the counter.

"Wallace, meet Master Sergeant J.L. Taylor."

The big black sergeant reached out a mitt and shook Wallace's hand. "Pleased to meet ya. Hear ya been hangin' around with my worthless brother-in-law," and Taylor chuckled. The mortar tube lay on the counter. "Here, I brought this for ya." At Wallace's puzzled look, Taylor added, "It's from a friend of ours."

Wallace picked up the mortar tube. Grinning, Charlie

handed Wallace a pocket knife. Wallace cut through the tape holding the end cap in place. As soon as he smelled the gun oil, his puzzled look turned to amazement. Her chest, glued to Wallace's arm as she peeked over his shoulder, Patty couldn't believe it. Wallace was misty-eyed and each news-paper-wrapped piece that he slid out of the tube caused his eyes to leak even more.

"Holy shit. Holy shit. Motherfucker sent me this. Holy shit, I don't believe it." Wallace unwrapped each piece of the old .06. He didn't even have to ask: Charlie laid a screw-driver on the counter. Wallace assembled the rifle just like it had never been out of his hands. The bolt slipped into place and he swung the rifle, aimed at the street, and dry-fired.

J.L. picked up the tube and shook it. The empty brass case with the note rolled inside fell out on the counter and tinkled to a stop. Wallace quickly grabbed it and pulled the note out of the casing. He read the note and, tears flowing freely, he passed the note to Patty. "Holy shit. I got my rifle back." Gulping for breath, he turned to Taylor. "Thank you. How much do I send the kid?"

Sucking on a beer, Taylor said, "That kid don't care about money. Here," and he shoved a Polaroid picture into Wallace's hand. Wallace took the picture to the window. Sitting on a bunk, bushy blonde hair, skinny, the rifle across his lap and two dogs watching him, was Mac.

"Skinny fucker, ain't he?" and he passed the picture around.

Taylor handed the picture back. "Keep it. The next day he got a Mohawk haircut, so he looks even funnier now."

Patty looked the picture over again. "I think he's cute."

Charlie held the picture up to the framed photo. "Look who's talkin' about bein' skinny." Wallace was just as skinny as Mac way back when he'd shot the crocodile.

The note, on dirty paper, stained red, and oily, lay on the counter. Taylor walked around the counter and searched through a stack of old newspapers. Finding what he wanted, he laid the paper next to the note. "That's the gook he shot, and he got another one with his second shot."

Patty stood there next to Wallace with her mouth open. These men were talking about killing people like they were just out for a drive. Wallace read some of the article and looked at Taylor. Putting his arm around Patty, he asked, "You think it was four hundred yards?"

Finishing his beer, Taylor paused. "Four hundred easy." The door opened and Leona and Leah came in. Leona and gave Taylor a kiss and a hug then stood back and looked at her husband.

"You look like shit and I've been worried sick. You promised no more, J.L. You promised," and she started to cry.

Taylor reached out to comfort his wife.

Wallace looked at the wall. "Charlie, can you wrap that up and get it to Mac?"

Charlie walked over, took down the rifle, brought it back and laid it on the counter. "This is a Winchester Model 70, Redfield 3X9 scope, bull barrel, .30-.06 caliber. You really don't wanna send that to Nam. Send him a gunbelt instead."

Wallace picked up the rifle. "Nope, send him this and some more hot ammo." He laid the rifle down carefully, pulled out a very large roll of cash, and peeled off ten one hundred dollar bills. "Will that cover it?

Old Charlie picked up the money. "Way too much, but the rifle comes with a hard case."

Wallace had Shirley back in his arms and he felt like the missing piece of his life had returned. Waving at the money, he said, "Keep it. Come on. I'm taking all of you to dinner."

Patty pulled on his arm and laughed. "I think you better leave that here."

Wallace laid Shirley on the newspaper and Charlie grabbed the mortar tube. "We can paint this, Wallace. Mark it 'Telescope' and you can take it right on the plane with you."

"OK, sounds good to me. Come on, girls. We're gonna eat at the finest place we can find." Wallace felt like it was Christmas morning.

Charlie had already called a taxi. He had a feeling nobody would be able to drive after this night out.

31

The Australians Mac had caught a ride with were stationed just down the road from Vung Tau and were headed back when they'd picked him up. The Aussie driver made Mac switch places and sit next to the passenger window. "Bloody well stinkin' to high heaven there, mate."

"Shit yeah, man. These are all the clothes I could find." Mac had to sit even closer to the open window. The odor of his clothes wasn't so bad with the hot breeze blowing. The first place the Aussies pulled up at was deserted.

"No worries, mate," and he was right. At their second stop Mac found what he was looking for.

"There they are. Come on, I'll buy you a beer," and Mac waited while the Aussie corporal parked the truck.

Flash was sitting at a table with the rest of his team. His watch was lying on the table. The team had run out of money and Flash had a Seiko watch that he was going to sell to the first GI that came along. The team had blown their money on booze and pussy and still had a day left on their R&R. Vung Tau sat on the China Sea, but the team wanted to party, not watch the ocean waves roll in. The shout from across the street caused the team to look.

"Holy fuck. That's Mac," Bones said as he stood.

Mac came flying across the street. After seeing Mac almost get hit by an ARVN jeep, the Aussies hung back. Flash slipped his watch back on as Mac hopped up the three steps to join his team. Only after Flash established the fact that Mac had money did the team inquire about his health and what he was doing there. Mac was forced to sit on the street side next to the railing. Even hung over, the Rangers could smell him. With beers all around and the Aussies at the table, Hollywood asked, "Where the fuck ya get those clothes? Off a dead man?"

Throwing all his money on the table, Mac answered, "Yeah, I did." The team cracked up. The laughter and partying attracted more GIs and Aussies who came up on the veranda and joined in. Mama San had her girls working the crowd and the amount of Tiger piss beer she was selling had her smiling. The soldiers were spending their money like there was no tomorrow. The passing foot traffic couldn't help but see that the party was a lot of fun. Looking up from the street, there wasn't a spit-shined boot on the veranda. This was Bush Bunnie Heaven. Mama San's girls set out bowls full of Vietnamese food and she turned up the music.

Two passing Special Forces soldiers joined the party. Both sergeants recognized Mac, stopped and yelled, "Hi." They handed him a half gallon jug of Wild Turkey whiskey, but they got away quickly. Mac smelled pretty ripe. Mac yelled his thanks and set the jug on the table.

He'd only had half a bottle of Tiger piss beer, but he was feeling no pain.

The Australians started the whole thing. Mac had spent three extra dollars and the pretty Vietnamese was blowing him at the table. Danny, the Aussie cowboy, commented that blow jobs were better in Australia. The comments over that flew fast and furious. The sergeant major next to Flash leaned back in his chair and said to the Ranger, "Now you'll hear the real story, mate." The sergeant major was part of the Royal Australian Regiment and he knew the man who had made the comment.

The silence around the table started an Aussie corporal off. "Yeah, down under by the Great Barrier Reef they got snakes that will slowly swim right up underneath you, mate." He took a slug of whiskey and a hit from his beer and continued, "Those snakes, mate, they go right for your dick. Start suckin' your dick right there in the water. Don't even know they're on you till it's too late. When you come, that's it, mate. That's when you get the poison. Everybody they pull out of the water—even dead—they have a smile on their face."

That brought the grunts to their feet. Everyone agreed that was the best lie they'd ever heard. A Green Beret called for quiet. "I'm from Texas and this story is about the baddest man I ever knew."

Everybody started shouting, "No war stories, No war stories."

The Aussie sergeant major nudged Flash. "He'll never top my man, mate."

"Shit, mate, ain't nobody can out-lie a Texan. How about betting a round of drinks?" and Flash looked at the sergeant major.

"You're on, mate."

The Texan started. "This was way out in west Texas. Billy had robbed a bank in Alpine and was getting clean away. Well, he'd borrowed the saddle and him not being used to it, it was really chafing his ass." The green beanie took a slow drink of whiskey and a pull at the beer bottle. "Now as I was sayin', all that ridin' and chafin' gave the man a terrible case of hemorrhoids. OH—they was BAD—hangin' out his ass like grapes. He was feelin' so bad he was thinkin' about ridin' back to find the posse he'd lost. Well, just when he turned around, a Texas blue northerner stuck. In three minutes it went from eighty degrees to ten below. That gave

Billy an idea. He slid down his jeans and gunbelt. Two minutes later and those hemorrhoids were frozen solid. So he
reached back there and broke them right off. Hung that
chain of hemorrhoids on a mesquite tree, pulled his pants
up and rode right off, headed for Florida." The Green
Beret took another drink out of his beer bottle. The laughter and applause that greeted the end of the story had
everybody wanting more.

The Aussie sergeant major bought a round for everyone.
Danny, the Aussie, was back on his feet. Everyone on the
veranda got quiet. "WE Aussies showed YOU Yanks how
to make jerky," and he took a drink from the jug of
whiskey.

"Again, mate?" and the sergeant major nodded at the pile
of money on the table. Flash, in the spirit now, just nodded.

Danny got into it. "The Outback in Australia is so big
and so hot that they built a road out there." He was waving
his arms around. "Right in the center there's another road,
one runs east and west. The other road runs north and
south. Now right where those roads cross is almost dead
center. Well, everybody knows that Australia is full of kan-
garoos. Me and me mates were pushin' these 'roos, kinda
like a roundup. Well, it was bloody hot. We didn't know anything was wrong until one mornin' the herd of 'roos would-
n't move. We started ridin' in amongst the herd when I realized they was all dead. They was all standin' right there.
Dead. Not a one alive. They were cooked right on the spot.
Well, hell it was breakfast time and the cooked 'roos
smelled good so I jumped down and cut me off a steak.
Hell, it had been cooked too long. I was so mad I cut up
two of those 'roos and headed for Sydney. Just so happens
I was on the docks when that big Yank tour boat let everybody off. They smelled that cooked 'roo meat and bought
all I had, and that's how it came to be called jerky. They was

jerkin' it right out of me hands."

The applause, whistles, and stomping of feet made Flash pay up. Danny had more beer in front of him than he could ever drink.

"More!" "More!" The grunts were laughing and having a great party and Danny was taking a bow.

Shakily, Mac got to his feet. "Now I'm gonna tell you why Canada has the only school for liars in the world," and he picked up the whiskey jug and took a small sip. "I was workin' in a log camp just north of Wawa and a little west of Moosonee. Now everybody knows that you only log in the wintertime up there." Mac looked around at the crowd.

Flash had bought a round and he pushed the pile of money and his Seiko watch in front of the Aussie: "Double or nothin'."

The sergeant major twisted both ends of his handlebar mustache. "You're on, Yank."

"Well, my job was a flunky in the cook shack. Hell, the cook stove was a hundred yards long. All the young guys like me had to keep the stove greased. The rest of the camp—the loggers—were all Frenchmen and Swedes. How we kept that stove greased was, we cut square ten-pound blocks of lard and set the blocks outside to freeze. We'd come in in the mornin' and strap on the blocks and keep the top of the stove greased. We also had six foot poles of maple that we used to push ourselves around and make sure the lard got into all the corners. After three days with the same maple stick, it would have curved at the end so you threw it in the fire. Well..." Taking a small drink of beer, Mac went on. "...that was the coldest winter ever. Seventy-two below before the thermometers froze. It was so cold that the coffee in the pots was boiling on the bottom and still froze on top. That was the winter they ran out of bacon so they switched to sausage. Now those loggers were big eaters, so each slice of sausage was about a pound. Well, it was the third day on my stick and I was greasing that stove, slidin' around. Now, they had a whole platoon of cooks 'cause each table sat a hundred and twenty loggers. Well hell, I was halfway down the stove, thinkin' about gettin' a new stick when one of the cooks flipped one of them sausage patties and missed. It hit my stick just as I was slidin' grease to the corner. Well, that's how I invented the slap shot. I hit that sausage patty and it flew halfway down the table. A Swede had just stuck his plate out for more flapjacks and that sausage patty hit dead center of his plate. You know those Swedes are hard to understand and the hot grease from the sausage got him and he said, 'Hockey puck,' but what he meant was, 'Holy fuck,' and that's how I invented the hockey puck."

Mac was mobbed. Danny was the first to grab Mac. "Holy shit, mate, you come to down under I'll make you famous."

Mac had to sit down, he was so weak from the malaria. Flash picked up the money from the table and put his watch back on his wrist. Grinning, he said, "Thanks, mate," and he turned and hollered, "Open bar on the Rangers."

The sergeant major grabbed Flash's arm and pulled his head down so he could be heard. "I'll trade you two tanks and your choice of men. That's the best liar I ever seen. He's a bit smelly, but we can clean him up. What ya say, Yank?"

A New Zealand sergeant and his American partner were in an alley just down the street from the grunt party. Curfew had begun half an hour before, but the MPs didn't have enough men to enforce getting all the GIs back to the R&R center.

Hitching up his gun belt and checking his Billy club, the red-haired sergeant gave his orders. The American drove the truck, did exactly what his partner said, and coasted to a stop in front of the bar. Walking up onto the crowded veranda, Red glanced at the sign. Someone had spray-painted under MAMA LOI'S BAR: Bush Bunny Heaven.

Red zeroed in on the two singing men who were holding each other up; the Aussie sergeant major and Flash were singing Waltzing Matilda.

Grinning, the MP cornered both men and told them the party had to move to the R&R center. Flash hollered, "Rangers, saddle up. Time to move." Chief woke up Mac who had fallen asleep sitting in his chair and who was also the one sober Ranger. Red was the only MP on the veranda. Most of the grunts were armed. They had pistols and knives hidden under their shirts, and the black grunt passed out on the floor—who he helped to his feet—had one or two grenades in his pocket. Moving slowly, laughing and joking, the MP worked the mob of grunts off the porch and out into the street.

The Aussie sergeant major sorted out his troops and Flash got his team poured into the back of the three-quarter-ton MP truck. Shit, Flash realized. Missing one. Bones and the Aussie Danny were in the Aussie formation. Flash grabbed Bones and helped him to the truck. The American MP couldn't believe it. He had expected a riot. He gave a sigh of relief when Red took the passenger seat of the truck.

Sweat rolled off Red. Grunts surrounded the truck and people were heading for more of the empty waiting trucks. Hooting and hollering drunks were helping other drunks. Everbody shouting good nights at friends they'd probably never see again. That's when Red found out the Rangers had been voted the best liars in Vietnam.

The recon Marine started it. He grabbed the tailgate and started rocking the truck. "One more lie, Mac."

Soon the MP's truck was hopping up and down like a pogo stick. The American MP grabbed his M-16 from its rack. Red slammed his arm. "Leave that alone, mate."

Mac had already fallen asleep in the back of the truck. Flash and Chief helped him to his feet. Flash was scared shitless these guys were having too good a time and he wanted a ride home.

"What? What?" Mac was rocking back and forth in the truck.

"They want another lie," Bones yelled. Like a prize fighter, Mac held his arms up. The rocking of the truck slowed to a stop.

Mac looked at the drunks. "OK, OK. Everybody knows that a Canadian logger named this country Vietnam," and he looked around. The grunts were silent. Someone stuck a beer bottle in his hand. Mac took a small sip and continued. "My grandfather was a flunky in the log camp but he told me the story. The cook stove was so big...a hundred yards long...it took a whole platoon of cooks to keep them loggers fed. Now right in the cook shack they had their chain saw just to cut six foot logs to feed the stove. Everybody hated feeding that stove, so Henri from down in Montreal, had the idea to bring in gooks to feed the stove." Mac took another small sip of beer. Even the MPs were listening. "Well, he got his no good brother-in-law to find him some gooks, and he sent about a hundred of the little fuckers...and it worked out just right. Henri found out they were just the right size to catch the logs coming off the saw and hump them right into the stove. Well, everything went good. Nobody could talk to the gooks, but hell, once they knew what to do you didn't need to talk to them. Everything went good until the camp ran out of rice. Shit, those gooks were pissed, so they decided to slow down. Well, the camp went a little crazy. The food was getting colder and colder. So since Henri brought the gooks into the log camp, he had to straighten the mess out. He didn't speak gook and hell, he only had a couple of words of English, but he came up with a plan. Henri went out that night to the edge of the camp and brought back two fifty-five gallon drums of perfect Canadian snow. He said he got the snow at the north end of the camp because it was colder on that end. Well, the next morning the gooks were slowing down even more. The stove was barely red hot. Henri dumped that snow on the stove and told those Frenchmen to fry it up. The gooks saw the snow frying and thought their problems were over. They forgot about Henri. He was pissed having to carry all that snow. So Henri stood over that crew of gooks all day long hollering at them. 'Vite. Vite.' That's French for hurry. Well, he had a gallon can for a cup and he finally got a cup of hot coffee. He'd stand there drinking that hot coffee and scream at those gooks, 'Vite, Man. Vite, Man,' and ever since that day the gooks were happy because now they had a name: Vite Man. Vite man."

The Marine hanging on the tailgate was shouting and laughing. "That's a fuckin' lie."

"Thank you. Thank you." Mac was laughing his ass off. He yelled at the MPs. "Let's go." The laughing grunts parted for the MP truck and the three-quarter-ton with the Rangers headed down the road for the R&R camp.

The red-haired MP climbed over the roof and, laughing, handed Mac a bottle. "That's the best damn lie I ever heard, mate."

Mac looked at the straw-wrapped bottle. "What is that stuff?"

Red looked at the Rangers. "That's Catholic Cape Brandy."

Mac took a small swallow and handed the bottle to Flash.

"Holy fuck." Mac fell to his knees.

"That's right, mate. That's why they call it Catholic Cape Brandy. Knocks you to your knees and you'll pay penance the next day."

That was the only time the MP could remember that there wasn't a fight in Vung Tau.

32

The military police were the first to call. The sergeant major shook his head as he hung up. He didn't think the captain knew what he was talking about. The Rangers he had down in Vung Tau didn't have the money to buy a Vietnamese bar and the only troublemaker he had on that team was still in the hospital. His second call confused him even more. The sergeant major wanted his grunt back. No, he didn't know the man's name, but he was hanging around with his Rangers and had a 25th patch on his shirt, plus he had won a large amount of money, so the sergeant major wanted the money and his grunt returned ASAP. Bill told him to go fuck himself and hung up.

The USO called and the faggot director wanted to know if he could book the Rangers on a tour of officers clubs all over Vietnam. The sergeant major was so confused, he started drinking tiger piss as soon as he finished his coffee. The sergeant major from the First Cav called Bill. He hated the prick since they were in basic together, but he did shed some light on things.

Seems his Rangers had put on quite a show down in Vung Tau and won all kinds of money. Hanging up, the sergeant major thought about his team down there. *What the fuck did those guys do down there?* Hoping his team wasn't in jail, Bill wondered what kind of scheme they could have pulled to end up owning a bar—and it wasn't even the whole team.

Shit, that does it. I'm going down and fly them out anyway. The phone rang again just as he started for his door.

It was Major Grand from the 93rd Evac hospital. McDonald from Mateau's outfit had been declared AWOL from her hospital. Absence without leave was a serious offence at her hospital. She also complained that one of her medics had a black eye from that soldier of his because he wouldn't get in the tub and take a bath like he should. The sergeant major had the phone six inches from his ear.

Fuckin' bitch sounds just like a Nazi. She finally wound down and the sergeant major said, "I'll take care of it." He couldn't help himself. "Major," he added, "have you checked with all your medics? Maybe my man and him are shacked up somewhere." The phone almost melted in his hand.

The last thing Bill heard before hanging up was the major telling him that "My fuckin' medics aren't queer and you'd better watch your fuckin' mouth!"

Whooeeeee, that bitch was wound up. That explained where the trouble came from; Mac had escaped from the hospital. *Wonder where he got the clothes? That old bitch said his uniform was still there.*

The sergeant major got his driver to bring his jeep around. He was going to fly down to pick up the Rangers and find out what the hell was going on. *How the fuck did they buy a bar? Damn,* and he thought about the terrific possibilities that would have for the 199th.

Next in the Uncommon Valor Series

DINKY DAU

THE GRUNT LOOK LASTS FOREVER

1

The sun hammered down without mercy, yet the old man waited in the only shade he had—his beat up Stetson. With long sleeved shirt and vest, everything about the man was faded in the summer heat. The long Fourth of July weekend was over and the busiest place in Phoenix was the door of the building the old man was watching. Mostly Indians turned loose from the drunk tank, pushing their way to freedom. Larry tried to get by his grandfather without being seen but the old man was too quick and, like cutting a sheep from the herd, pulled him out of the crowd where he was hiding. Larry was too sick and broke to even attempt to flee. The judge had taken what was left of his prize money from the rodeo. Two days and they'd cleaned him out. The bars, the women, and the judge hadn't even left him enough to get drunk on. Grandfather didn't let go of him until his ass hit the hot seat of the Chevy pickup. Stinking the way he was, Larry could have been any drunk Indian.

Two coffees in their paper cups sat on the dash, the hot sun coming through the windshield had them damn near boiling. Larry gave the Phoenix jail the finger as his grandfather drove by. He set the coffee back on the dash—it was too hot to drink. He slumped down in the seat and adjusted his black Stetson over his eyes. Fuck, he thought, back to the reservation and those stinkin' cows. He was never going to get on the rodeo circuit this way. He woke up with the sun behind him and he knew they should have been on the reservation by now. His grandfather spoke for the first time: "Shut up."

Larry pulled his hat back down. Oh, man. He's pissed. They were on Interstate 10 headed east. Twenty miles from Lordsburg, New Mexico, the old man turned off. Larry sat up and started to look around. He thought they were still in Arizona but he'd never seen this part before. He breathed a little easier when he saw the truck-stop sign. His grandfather didn't stop and turned onto Highway 80 southbound. Larry turned to his grandfather and before he could ask why they hadn't stopped the old man said: "Shut up."

Just past the six-house town of Rodeo the old man took a dirt road heading east. Larry read the shot-up sign: "Skeleton Canyon 13 miles." The old man was good on the dirt road. The pickup had a dust cloud behind it for half a mile. Grandfather slid his truck to a stop on top of a small hill. Larry could see a patch of green about a quarter of a mile away. The old man pointed at the green spot and Larry hopped out. He had to piss bad. As he was taking his leak the old man fooled him—he drove away and left him right there in the middle of the desert. Larry sat on a rock half the night waiting for his grandfather to come back and get him. When he was so thirsty he couldn't stand it anymore he started walking toward the green spot. His one-week drunk sweated out of him in the first mile. With the sun already starting to come up during the second mile he promised himself he was going to kill the old man. His brand new Tony Lama boots were tearing his feet up. It felt like a hundred scorpions were inside each boot. He finally reached the water hole around noon. He didn't even strip off his clothes. He climbed right into the cattle tank and drank, sitting down. The coldest beer in town never tasted so good. He sat in the tank the rest of the day, so he missed the treasure. Not until the next morning while walking to keep warm did Larry stumble across it. He was amazed. The colors were so bright. One red-and-green woven Navajo blanket with a Winchester rifle lying on it. He kept rubbing his eyes. He walked up to it and knelt next to the blanket. Fuck. That's my grandfather's .30-.30. A box of bullets, a small frying pan, a small bag, and a short length of neatly coiled rope were inside the neatly folded blanket. Now what in the fuck am I supposed to do with this shit? The brown paper bag got his attention. Inside, he found a box of Morton salt and a magnifying glass. Larry jumped to his feet and screamed at the top of his lungs, "I'LL KILL YOU MOTHERFUCKER!!!!"

The hawk that noticed Larry's leaping and yelling wasn't impressed and just floated higher on the air currents. By the time he'd calmed down it was dark and he realized he could have had a fire if he'd used the magnifying glass while the sun was up. The next morning he shot a desert jackrabbit and cooked it over the fire he'd started using the glass. He circled the whole area looking for empty cans to fill with water but there was nothing. Shit, I'll never get to the highway without a way to carry water. Larry stayed at the oasis for a week before moving further up into the canyon.

Larry figured out that Skeleton Canyon was haunted the first night he slept there. He'd found a cave with fire-blackened walls and he moved in, because he'd also found water. The small seep at the back of the cave had swarms of bees coming and going. Working in the gray darkness he'd cleaned the small opening. The bees drove him off once, but the next time he'd come armed with a smoky torch. With the small spring clean the cool water tasted sweet and its trickle never stopped.

He shot two deer and ruined the first one trying to make

jerky. He figured there was a mountain lion living in the canyon because the first rotten carcass had been carried off. He worked in the cool of the mornings and explored the surrounding area the rest of the day. When his Tony Lamas began to fall apart he used pieces of the iron-hard deer hide to make repairs. Trial and error. After he figured out how to soak the deer hide he made repairs on the boots and he learned to avoid the sharp rocky areas that tore his makeshift repairs. For a pillow he used his shirt and two weeks went by before he realized he hadn't been wearing it at all. He cut the tops off his cowboy boots and made moccasins. Rough, but they protected his feet.

He'd never paid any attention to the old ways his people were always talking about. He and his friends thought it was all bullshit. Geronimo was an invention made up to scare the kids.

But his thoughts were changing. Man, if I had a horse and a couple of bitches I could stay here forever. Fuck going back to Cibecue. "Stabacue" the whites called it because drunk Indians were always knifing each other. Taking a bath in the stock tank during one of the few times he'd left the canyon, he noticed he'd lost his beer belly. That was also the day he climbed to the top of the canyon and sat looking south. *I wonder how far Mexico is.* Giggling to himself he thought, *I'll go down there and steal some horses*—and some girls too.

That was also the night the dreams started. The nightmares were so bad they woke him up in a cold sweat. All he could remember was horses everywhere and lots of gunfire. After that he slept wrapped around his grandfather's rifle. By accident he found a way to carry water. He'd killed another deer and tried his hand at making sausage. He knew he had to wash the guts out and when he did he discovered that the deer's stomach held water. He hung his homemade canteen on a tree branch. Full of water, it dried and cured. Shit, yeah.

Doesn't hold all that much and the 'water tastes like dead deer but it -works.

The shadow on the canyon wall across from the cave drew his attention. When the sun moved for fifteen minutes the shadow disappeared. He took the Winchester with him when he climbed up to the disappearing shadow. The cave opening was only about two feet across. Right away he figured he'd found the mountain lion's den. Finding no paw prints at the opening, he turned to leave but something made him change his mind. Halfway into the small cave it struck. Larry's hat stopped the rattlesnake from biting him on the forehead.

Larry was as quick as the snake. As it pulled back to strike again, Larry grabbed it right behind its shovel-shaped head and dragged the fighting snake outside. He kneeled on the diamondback and his folding knife really pissed off the four-foot rattler. Larry cut off half its rattles and threw the snake into a pile of rocks. Larry chuckled. The snake was still rattling away from the rock pile. He checked his beat-up Stetson and found that the snake had dented the front. Hat back on, he crawled into the small cave. Just past where he had encountered the snake he could stand. Barely four feet across, with a sandy floor. Good place to hide. His eyes had adjusted to the dim light by the time he turned to leave. He saw the trash pile. So that's what the snake was guarding. Letting more light in by moving, Larry saw that it wasn't a trash pile at all. Two rifles stood against the wall. He picked up the leather-wrapped bundle next to the rifle. The dry leather felt like iron. He carefully pried the leather open and there were two curved wooden bows, their leather strings rotted away. The metal heads on the half dozen arrows were still tight but the feathers had turned to dust.

On his knees, running his hands over the old things, he felt like he was in a holy place. Whoever had stored these things left no doubt that they were Apache. The rifle butts stood not in the sand but on a worn out pair of moccasins.

The moccasins were the only thing Larry took from the hidden cave. He soaked them in spring water to soften and shape them—Apache old style—into their original shape. The soles were worn out and the toes curled, but the softened tops went almost to his knees. No other Indian tribe that Larry knew about wore the full boot-style footwear. He was in too much of a state of awe to keep them on his feet. Instead, he folded the moccasins and added them to his shirt pillow. Larry thought about the rifle shrine and what it meant. All he could come up with was that whoever the Apaches were who left the weapons planned on coming back. That started his plan.

Up near the other end of the canyon he killed another deer and made more jerky and another canteen. Hair side out, he made foot wraps with the green hide. As long as he didn't have to walk over too many rocks they would do. He was already on top of the canyon when the sun set. He was surprised by how busy the desert was at night. He was just one of the creatures that moved through the dim nocturnal light.

He was down to his last few swallows of water when he smelled the place. He holed up under a paloverde tree and watched all day. That night he walked in, bold as you please, filled his canteens from a horse tank, then spent two hours sitting outside the horse corrals. After a few minutes of fussing, the horses settled down. He let them get used to his smell and was back under his paloverde long before dawn. Next morning he watched the ranch for any sign that the Mexicans had seen his tracks. People came and went all day long. No one he saw raised any kind of alarm. Larry had turned nineteen that summer and he celebrated at the Mexican ranch.

Thinking of a birthday present he made his selection. That night he picked his gifts, he drank all the water he could hold and topped off his deer-stomach canteens. The buckskin stud was first and he watched Larry in the corral. Wild eyes flashing in the moonlight, he let Larry get right up to him before he tried to bite. Larry sidestepped and moved his arm out of the way. Using one of the halters off the corral pegs, he haltered the stud then rubbed his hands up and down his neck, over and over. The stud gentled right down. Next, Larry haltered the stud's two main ladies. During the day he'd watched the herd and he knew which mares the stud was always fooling with. His blanket for a saddle, Larry led the horses out. He was worried that the whole bunch would follow so he stood ready to wave the rest back, but they stayed and he got the three he wanted out of the corral. He was halfway back to Skeleton Canyon before the sun hit with full force. He never had figured out where the border was. He rode the buckskin and led the two mares into the canyon.

He rested the horses for a week and finally decided it was time to head for home. The lightly burdened and rested horses covered ground rapidly. He rode straight north. Water was his main worry but the ranches had tanks and the farmers had irrigation canals that he used. After four days he rode up to his grandfather's house in Cibecue.

His grandfather didn't say anything until Larry put the horses in the corral. "You have learned the old ways well," and his grandfather smiled and led Larry into his house. Like lightning, the whole village knew about Larry's horse stealing down in Mexico. The girls who never paid him any attention before definitely took notice of him now. Larry was sure he'd added enough horses to his grandfather's herd and now he was ready to carry out the rest of his plan.

After two days at home he double-checked the calendar on the wall next to the cook stove then asked his grandfather for a ride into Show Low. With fall roundup about to start his grandfather wanted to know why he wanted to go to town. The old man grinned and approved. He waited for Larry outside the Army recruiter's office. The next day Larry left Show Low for basic training at Fort Benning, Georgia.

Books In The Uncommon Valor Series

BOOK ONE:

Here Piggy

The story of Mac, an ordinary US Army grunt during the height of the Vietnam War — except he's mischievous, bright, inventive, an experienced outdoorsman, and a Canadian.

He's kicked out of his platoon by an inept lieutenant for falling into a raging river and losing his machine gun. Alone, he makes his way through terror-filled jungle, eludes the enemy and staggers out of the boonies to a highway. A second-string reporter finds Mac hitchhiking and stumbles onto the story that creates his reputation as well as havoc and hilarity from the jungle to MAC-V headquarters.

BOOK TWO:

A Salt

Dead Accurate at 800 Yards

We follow Mac, the Canadian volunteer, again in A Salt. He's sent to Hawaii to get his US citizenship after an erroneous story gets back to the States that he was a mercenary grunt hired by the US Army to fight in Nam.

During his ten days there, Mac continues to get into humor-laced trouble, makes new friends, scores with the ladies, shoots a troublemaker's surfboard, and refurbishes WWII rifles to be returned to Nam for snipers.

With a 1903 model .30-.06 rifle (with its own fascinating history), Mac returns to Nam and the Rangers he feels at home with. Mac and the Rangers spend their days and nights trail watching, gathering information, snatching prisoners, saving other grunts, killing an NVA general, and kidnapping a short-legged VC tracker dog. Their hard work pays off and they are given in-country R&R where Mac's humorous side blossoms as a champion liar

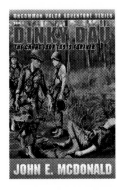

BOOK THREE:
Dinky Dau
The Grunt Look Last Forever
In Dinky Dau, the third novel in this Vietnam trilogy, Mac's exploits continue to trigger our tears and laughter. Sergeant Youngblood's rogue Ranger team goes on a rampage. They ambush, rape, kill, steal, smuggle goods, and hole up at an old Frenchman's villa near the Cambodian border.

On their way home from Reporter Tex Payne's party, nurses Susan and Dawn, Captain Garibaldi, and CIA agent Hart are in a car crash with an Army truck stolen by Blood's team. The mavericks kill the driver, kidnap the captain and nurses, then take them back to their hideout where they brutalize and repeatedly rape the nurses.

With their Ranger teams and tracker-dog Airborne, sustaining characters Mac and Sergeant "Flash" Gordon are sent to the field to track Blood and his men. Later, using his incredible abilities to improvise, economize the truth, and manipulate, Mac arranges for former VC Billy and Airborne to take a most unusual trip. McDonald once again takes us into the lives of the grunt in Nam, giving us a grin one minute and a look at evil the next.

BOOK FOUR:

Minnow Lake
Ranger to the Rescue

During Mac's flight home from Vietnam he's treated to extra booze and attention by two friendly stewardesses. He loses his duffle bag in the Toronto Airport and, instead of a quiet retreat from war he's found by the Royal Canadian Mounted Police. Mac meets Inspector O'Neil, Constable Carolyn Finch, FBI Agent Cavanaugh and becomes a critical player in stopping gun-running terrorists.

Along the way we're taken on a brief and hilarious side trip back to Nam, we meet Mac's first love, his Canadian family, and we get to know more about his growing up years. As always, MacDonald delivers a novel with heart-warming humor and heart-stopping action.

BOOK FIVE:

Rosebud Diane
Let Me Grow Up to be An Airborne Ranger

We find Mac living as a happy recluse. He reluctantly leaves his ranch and rediscovers two beautiful nurses who have had hard times since Vietnam. Together, they track down a pair of runaway girls who have taken refuge in a church camp guarded by handpicked veterans and run by a wacko. Using Ranger tactics, they attempt a rescue that's full of surprises. In Rosebud Diane McDonald serves up another story packed with action, adventure, and many of the characters who made his earlier novels so memorable.

BOOK SIX:
Borrow Pit
Fire in the Sky

In Borrow Pit, a government raid on an Arizona ranch goes tragically wrong. Vietnam Vet Mac saves a wounded female ATF agent and delivers dramatic payback to fumbling bureaucrats. This action-adventure introduces new characters-look for the TV reporter in the front-zippered silver jumpsuit- and brings back some of the author's most beloved characters. From the Southwest to Texas to D.C., we find Mac in dangerous, very personal, and often humorous situations that have become hallmarks of this author's style.

BOOK SEVEN:
Baby San
Only Fight The Battle You Can Win

In Baby San, McDonald returns to the Vietnam War but this story is revealed through the eyes of soldiers on both sides. The author moves effortlessly back and forth from the perspective of the American GI to the lives of a North Vietnamese soldier and a beautiful bar girl who becomes an expert sniper.

GLOSSARY

AK-47 *Clip-fed, gas-operated assault rifle, 7.62 mm, used throughout the world by armed forces and paramilitary organizations*

M-14 *American carbine*

M-60 *primary U.S. machine gun*

M-79 *Blooper, Bloop Gun, M-79 grenade launcher*

M-203 *40mm grenade launcher, while attached to an M16A2 5.56mm rifle. Lightweight, compact, breech loading, pump action, single shot launcher*

AO *Area of Operations*

ARVN *Army of Republic of South Vietnam*

Au Dai (AO' YAI) *garment for formal occasions like weddings or special parties*

beans and dicks *C-rations of beans and hot dogs. Also "beans and motherfuckers" for C-rations of beans and lima beans and "ham and motherfuckers" for ham and lima beans*

bird *helicopter*

BMB *Brigade Main Base*

body count *number of enemy KIA*

boonie hat *soft hat worn by a boonierat (combat infantryman) in the boonies*

CAR-15 *a carbine rifle*

Cau Mau *as in Cau Mau prison*

Charlie *slang, Viet Cong or NVA personnel, from phonetic Victor Charlie*

chien si *Vietnamese for soldier*

Cholon *aka Ho Chi Minh City, Saigon*
CIB *Combat Infantryman's Badge*
clip *ammunition magazine*
CMOH *Congressional Medal of Honor*
CO *Commanding Officer*
connex container *corrugated metal packing crate, approximately six feet in length*
dap *handshake and greeting which may last up to ten minutes, characterized by the use of both hands and often comprised of slaps and snaps of the fingers*
deuce-and-a-half *two-and-a-half ton truck*
dew *marijuana, grass*
DiDi *slang from the Vietnamese word di, meaning "to leave" or "to go"*
Dien Bien Phu *village in NW Vietnam: besieged and captured by Vietminh forces (1954), marking the end of French occupation of Indochina*
door gunner *soldier who mans M-60 mounted inside hatch of Huey gunship*
D-Ring *a buckle*
dust-off *medical evacuation by helicopter*
El Tee *for lieutenant*
FAC *forward air controller; person who coordinates air strikes*
FNG *fuckin' new guy*
frag *fragmentation grenade*
FTA *Fuck the Army*
gook *chiefly military, derogatory slang; native of Asia, esp Japan, Korea, Vietnam; derived from Korean slang for "person" and passed down by Korean war veterans*
Green Berets *U.S. Special Forces*
GI *Government Issue, or a soldier*
grunt, grunts *infantryman. Originally slang for a Marine fighting in Vietnam but later applied to any soldier fighting there; a boonier-at*

G-3 *a division level tactical advisor; a staff officer, does not refer to G-1 or G-2*

Gunney *Marine gunnery sergeant, E-7*

HE *High Explosive*

higher-higher(s) *honcho(s), commander(s)*

hot LZ *landing zone under hostile fire*

Huey *UH-1 Helicopter*

in-country *in Vietnam*

Intel *Intelligence, military*

jarhead *U.S. Marine, unknown origin*

K-Bar *Combat knife*

KCS *Kit Carson scout, former Viet Cong who acted as guides for U.S. military units*

KIA *Killed In Action*

klick *kilometer*

lifeline *straps holding gunner aboard the helicopter while he fires M-60 out the hatch*

loach *a LOH, Log Bird, logistical (resupply) helicopter; also small scout or spotter helicopter*

loo *Brit. toilet*

lurps *for LRRPs, members of Long Range Reconnaissance Patrols. In Nam, lurps slang for MREs (meals ready to eat) because they were first issued to LRRPs missions.*

LZ *landing zone*

MAC-V *Military Assistance Command Vietnam*

magazine *metal container that feeds bullets into weapon*

mag pouch *magazine holder*

mama san *pidgin used by American servicemen for any older Vietnamese woman*

marmite *large insulated food container, also used to keep beer cold*

MI *Military Intelligence*

MIA *Missing In Action*

Minigun *electronically controlled, extremely rapid-firing machine gun. Most often mounted on aircraft to be used against targets on the* *ground*

mike *a minute*

mike-mike *shorthand for millimeter*

Montagnard *tribal people living in hills of central and northern Vietnam. "Montagnards" is French for mountain dwellers throughout the world. American English pronunciation: "mountainyard." During the Vietnam War, American servicemen referred to them affectionately as "Yards." The Montagnard tribes of Vietnam refer to themselves as "Dega Peoples."*

MPC *military payment currency. The scrip U.S. soldiers were paid in*

NCO *noncommissioned officer*

nipa, nipa palm *a large palm, long leaves for thatching*

nipa *an alcoholic beverage made from the sap of the nipa palm*

Numba One *something very good*

Numba Ten *something very bad*

Nuac Nam *Vietnam fish sauce*

NVA *North Vietnamese Army*

OCS *Officer Candidate School*

OD *Olive Drab*

Pfc or PFC *Private First Class*

Point *the most dangerous position on patrol, lookout*

point man *usually the only man carrying weapon on full auto; the very dangerous position of walking ahead of others on patrol, a lookout*

PRC-25 *Pronounced "prick 25," the standard U.S. infantry field radio used in Vietnam*

punji, punji pit *A very sharp bamboo stake concealed at an angle in high grass, in a hole, or in deep mud, often coated with excrement, and planted to wound and infect the feet of enemy soldiers*

push *a radio frequency*

P-38 *a tiny collapsible can opener, also known as a "John Wayne"*

Puzzle Palace *MAC-V headquarters building*

PX *Post Exchange*

rack(sack) *GI backpack*

REMF(s) *rear echelon motherfucker(s)*

Recondo School *training school in-country for LRRPs. The largest was at Na Trang, where the training action was taken against the 17th NVA Division.*

recondo *Reconnaissance Commnando, Doughboy*

R&R *rest and recreation/relaxation*

round *bullet*

RPG *rocket-propelled grenade. A Russian-made portable antitank grenade launcher*

RTO *radio telephone operator*

RVN *Republic of (South) Vietnam*

sapper *soldier who digs, lays mines, satchel charges*

sit-rep *situation report*

SKS *Russian-made carbine*

spiderhole *tunnel entrance*

S-1 - S-1/G-1
Administration and Personnel

S-2 - S-2/G-2 *Intelligence and security*

S-3 - S-3/G-3 *Operations*

S-4/G-4 *Supply and logistics*

S-5/G-5 *Civil affairs and psyops (Generals have G-sections to support them; others have S-sections)*

slackman *the second man back on a patrol, directly behind the point*

slick *a UH-1 helicopter used for transporting troops in tactical air assault operations*

SP4/Spec Four/CPL *Specialist Fourth Class or Corporal*

The World *anywhere but Vietnam*

Thud *F-105 Thunderchief fighter-bomber,*

Ti Ti *Vietnamese for "little"*

Tiger-piss, Tiger 33, "33" *Vietnamese beer*

Unass *leave seat quickly*

Uzi *small arms, sub-machine gun (SMG), Israeli Military*

Industries Ltd

VC *South Vietnamese Communists, Viet Cong, Victor Charlie*

Viet Minh *Viet Nam Doc Lap Dong Minh Hoi, or the Vietnamese Allied Independence League. A political and resistance organization established by Ho Chi Minh before the end of World War II, dominated by the Communist Party*

Vietnamese *the people, language or culture of Vietnam*

wait-a-minute vines *"... 'wait-a-minute" vines, which would grab you and could suspend you in the air." - Tim Lickness, VIET-NAM 1968, ©1996*

WIA *Wounded In Action*

Wilco *will comply*

Wire *perimeter (trip wire sets off booby traps)*

Xin Loi *"Sorry about that," or "Goodbye."*

XO *executive officer, the second in command of a military unit*

Yard *Montagnard*

ABOUT THE AUTHOR

John E. McDonald, Author
A Modern Day Mark Twain

Born in Hamilton, Ontario, Canada, John grew up amongst the quiet back-country lakes and wide assortment of beautiful wildlife. As John grew up he moved throughout Southern and Northwestern Ontario, from Sault Ste. Marie, to Sudbury, to Elliot Lake. His younger years saw him through an education in the Catholic school system and was taught to speak both French and English. Leaving home at 14, over the next few years he worked in sawmills, for the railroad, and even in a suitcase factory.

John enlisted in the Canadian Armed forces from 1965-1967 as a Recon Crewman in the 8th Canadian Hussars (same designation as Cavalry Crewman in the U.S. Army). John enlisted in the U.S. Armed Forces from 1968-1971. His tour in Vietnam was 1969 -70 where he served as an 11th Bravo, Light Weapons Infantryman (grunt). He was one of the many men to contribute his skills during the conflict in Vietnam on the front lines. Following his tour in the Army, John spent the following years going to college in Rochester, New York with a major in Criminal Justice where he received his degree. In 1980 John re-enlisted in the Army and spent four years posted Stateside on various Army bases, followed by two years in Germany, on the border before the wall came down that separated that country.

Since leaving the Army, John has led an interesting life, working as an armored car driver, a horse farrier, and a long haul truck driver. John now lives and shares his home of 80 acres in Apache County, Arizona, with his fiancé, Nancy, and their dogs and horses. He is currently working on book fifteen as well as a play.

John's passion for writing has created some of the best material of our time. As an Author, John has learned to open up his consciousness, giving life to his characters' voices and finding them living great adventures. His gift portrays areas that go beyond those of Military Fiction, exploring the human relationships and bonds between ment and women that go beyond daily living, and taking us along with them on their continuing journeys as they go.

When not writing at his ranch, John gives his time touring various Armed Forces facilities, spending his time with fellow soldiers, wounded and back from Iraq, talking and signing his books for them. Thus far, John has visited Walter Reed Army Hospital and VA hospitals in Phoenix, Prescott and Denver. He is a welcome speaker at various local schools, Vietnam dedication memorials and numerous Veterans' groups. He has also donated 600 books to be sent over seas to the troops in Iraq.

CPSIA information can be obtained at www.ICGtesting.com
Printed in the USA
BVOW070710100412

287163BV00001B/1/A